ANGEL FALLS

SOUL FORGE BOOK THREE

LESLIE CLAIRE WALKER

sfp

ALSO BY LESLIE CLAIRE WALKER

THE AWAKENED MAGIC SAGA

THE SOUL FORGE

(The Complete Series)

Angel Hunts

Angel Rises

Angel Falls

Angel Strikes

Angel Roars

Angel Burns

THE FAERY CHRONICLES

(The Complete Series)

Faery Novice

Faery Prophet

Faery Sovereign

SHORT STORY COLLECTIONS

Ink & Blood

Ink & Stars

Ink & Sword

DEDICATION

*This book is dedicated to Kristine Kathryn Rusch,
without whom it may never have been written.
Thank you for that workshop assignment,
for the opportunity to learn so much from you,
and for your wonderful friendship.*

My name is Night Sanchez. Every choice I make is built upon a secret.

I'm prepared for the day the Order finally gets close enough to take vengeance. I expect them to strike first and ask questions never. Problem is, their latest assassin has an unexpected angle.

She makes me an offer I don't dare refuse. The stakes: my daughter's life.

I'll do anything—risk everything—for Faith. The Order fears the sleeping god inside her. If I prevent the god from waking, the Order wipes the slate clean. They'll let us live in peace.

Of course, there's a catch. The Order's help comes with deadly strings attached. And it blows wide open the secret that created the Order. The secret that created me.

It draws me into a terror I thought I'd left behind forever—and offers a chance at the only redemption that matters…

CHAPTER 1

I CLOSED THE FRONT DOOR of Justice Gym, peering through the glass into the darkness before dawn. A scan of the sidewalk and the street on the other side showed nothing except an early Monday morning drenched in December mist. Tires slicked on wet pavement and engines hummed. Normals on their way to work grabbed breakfast and coffee at Stumptown Diner across the way as if nothing earth-shattering had just happened.

As if the dangerous, powerful woman who'd been my mentor in the Order of the Blood Moon hadn't just shown up out of the blue, asked for my help, and then vanished.

That she'd found me didn't surprise—I'd made a stand in Portland. No more running. Nowhere to hide. That someone who'd spent so much time hunting me and mine with the intention of killing us would ask for my help?

Under my black fleece hoodie, my skin turned to gooseflesh. The soft fall of the mist took on a sinister sound, the morning's peace irrevocably shattered.

I performed a second scan of the street, this time with my magical vision. I shifted my sight, studying the halos of the people on the street, the fields of life force that surrounded every living person. I searched for everything from ill intent to unnatural attention.

Nothing.

There was only the world outside, and the gym inside, with its perfume of rubber and sweat. The elevated waiting area with its brown suede, people-eating sofa crouched on my left. The empty black cubbies against the wall. The short open staircase that led down to the office and workout space.

Not five minutes ago, I'd risked my heart in a way I never had before. I'd told Red Jennings that I loved him. He returned that love in spades. In spite of the chaos all around us, we'd found something precious.

He stood behind me now. He had my back, and I had his.

"She's gone for now," I said. "Along with her backup."

Red's faint Texas drawl grew more pronounced with each word. "I didn't see any backup. Just her."

"Standard operating procedure when walking into the den of the enemy," I said. "There was backup with her, and they left with her."

"That's why you only listened," he said. "You didn't throw down."

I nodded, then glanced over my shoulder to meet Red's gaze. I read worry in the lines around his green eyes, but not a single trace of fear.

His shaggy salt-and-pepper hair was still wet from the shower, the ends curled. He still wore his dark green down jacket against the cold. We hadn't been inside long enough for him to take it off.

"Tell me about her," he said.

"Her name is Lily." I moved past him, descending the steps two at a time onto the gym floor. I made a beeline for the garage doors at the back.

Red dogged my heels.

"She was my Mentor inside the Order," I said. "She recruited me. She picked me up on the street outside my house the night after it burned down and brought me into the fold."

Red had been my next-door neighbor at the time. He'd been sixteen. I'd been twelve. He'd saved my life, and then I'd disappeared into the arms of the Order.

The Order gathered every child with magical ability its recruiters could find. It trained them to use their magic to kill. The Order's objective had always been a mystery, even to its operatives. I hadn't cared. I'd only wanted revenge on the people who'd hurt me and those like them.

It wasn't just that, though. I'd been devoted to the Order because it was the only place I belonged. I'd been a good killer. I'd enjoyed it. The world was a bad place, and the people I'd targeted deserved what they got. I'd believed that with every fiber of my being, once upon a time.

I jogged across the gym floor past barbells, plates, racks and pull-up bars, interlocked black rubber mats on the floor dulling the thud of my step. The garage doors were still locked. A small window beside them provided the only view out. I scanned the rough asphalt parking lot out back and the high weeds that lined the chain-link fence on either side. No sign of foul play or anyone watching. The street looked clear, too. Just parked cars slumbering along the curve of the far curb and the glow of Christmas lights hung on the eaves of the houses and four-plexes.

There was no other way in or out of the gym. Not perfect, but decent for defense. Two exits were better than one if we were forced to leave.

Red caught up, slowing to a stop beside me. "Lily's like you?"

Lily had done her best to turn me into a reflection of herself. Deadly. Heartless. It hadn't turned out the way she'd planned.

"No," I said. "Mentors like Lily are predators. They're also a kind of judge, jury, and executioner. Potential operatives don't make the cut? The mentors do the culling."

I heard myself say those words as if I was talking about opening the fridge to retrieve a late-night snack. It was cold, but that was how things were. Colder still? The murders I'd committed under orders, what taking those lives had done to my victims' people, and what the killing had done to me.

It had shattered my soul.

In the end, I'd left the Order. Therefore, I could not be allowed to live. The Order hunted me mercilessly. Sent operative after operative after me, and then finally the Angel of Death. Yet Lily had made no magical attack at the door. She'd brandished no physical weapons. She hadn't even threatened.

She'd asked for my goddamn help.

She hadn't said what for, only told me to find her when I decided one way or the other. As if I had a choice. And then she'd just walked away as if we weren't mortal enemies.

"So this is it," Red said. "When you made the decision to stick here and not to run anymore, you declared war against the Order. And now they're coming to the fight."

"I wouldn't have put it exactly that way," I said.

Lily had knocked politely and asked her question. I couldn't believe a single thing about her—nothing she said, nothing she did. There would always be an ulterior motive. Not all wars were hot, with magic flung and bullets flying.

"But I'm right," he said.

I nodded.

"I'm out of my depth with these people," he said.

His magic was solid, but not offensive in nature. He saw through to the heart of a person—what made them tick, what was real. He could recognize the good in someone even when they couldn't see it in themselves.

He owned this gym. He had regular customers, but in and among them, he had taken in magical kids, including mine. He'd given them somewhere to go to keep out of trouble. Someplace they felt at home.

He'd taken me in, too. Given me a home. Given me his heart.

"The kids will be here any minute," I said.

"You sure that's a good idea, them being here?" he asked.

"No," I said. "But it's too late to head them off."

He reached for my hand, twining his fingers with mine. "I'm here."

I squeezed his hand. "I know."

It meant the world to me that he'd gone all in on being with me. He'd grown up in a very different world than I had, with his share of hardships to be sure, but not with violence and obedience and brainwashed belief. He'd had a quiet life before I'd walked back into it. Neither of us wanted to lose each other again.

The fact that he stayed, that he committed to taking on my trouble—I knew what it meant to him. I also knew what it could cost him.

"We need to go on lockdown," I said. "Everyone accounted for, where we can keep them safe."

The gym had some magical protection that Red had laid down and that I'd augmented, but not enough. I could ask the kids to leave here and head out of town, but I knew they wouldn't go. They'd proved that by now.

We had a local Watcher—a descendant of fallen angels—on our side. Her house was our best bet.

"Call Addie and let her know what's up," I said.

Red pulled out his phone without a word.

I did the same, dialing my closest friend: Sunday Sloan, who had been my only friend inside the Order, and more than that for many years. She'd followed in my footsteps, leaving the Order to fight by my side after the Angel of Death had come to town. She'd risked her life, and she'd killed, and in the end I'd defeated the Angel in a battle of mind and will. I'd imprisoned him in my mind.

Sunday could've moved on then. Instead, she'd stayed. I trusted her with my life. I trusted her with my everything.

She was not a morning person. She picked up on the fifth ring.

Even jolted from sleep, her voice was musical, like the sound of water flowing over rocks. "Who died?"

"Lily was here," I said. "She wants my help."

I heard the creak of bedsprings and then a sudden echo as Sunday put me on speaker. "The hell?"

"I need you and Miguel," I said. "Can you meet us at the gym?"

She hesitated, leaving me with the slide of drawers opening as she dressed.

Miguel was our newest team member, if our group of former assassins, gym owners, and high school kids could be called a team. Sunday and I had known him when Lily first recruited the three of us into the Order. During a harrowing river survival test, he'd vanished.

We thought he'd drowned, but it turned out he'd been pulled into a shadow organization within the Order that tended the Angel of Death —the chameleons.

Unlike other magical beings, chameleons weren't born. They were created.

Miguel's innate magic had been altered. He'd been remade into one of them. He could look like anyone he wanted to. He could assume another person's magic as well.

He'd been sent to jailbreak the Angel from the prison of my mind. Instead, he'd ended up on our side, and put his life on the line. Even that wasn't enough for Sunday to trust him.

I had only slightly more faith in him than Sunday did—ten percent trust and ninety percent wait-and-see. But it was go time, and he had our Order training plus a damn fine, creepy-as-hell chameleon skill set that we might need.

"Ten minutes." She hung up.

A knock sounded on the front door. That would be the kids.

The jingle of keys confirmed my guess. The door opened, the electronic chime echoing against the concrete walls.

My daughter's voice rang out. "Night? Red?"

I raised my voice to carry. "In the back. Lock the door behind you."

Red and I made our way toward her, and met her at the bottom of the steps while the others who'd come in with her dumped their stuff into the cubbies upstairs.

Faith's brown eyes were still sleepy and threaded with gold. Her silver halo was streaked with gold as well. I could make out the impression of a pillowcase wrinkle on her right cheek. Her long black hair fell in waves to her shoulders. She wore a purple T-shirt under her hooded black coat, along with black leggings and black sneaks. She held her black backpack by one strap, dropping it on the floor with a thud at the sight of my face. She blanched, her light brown skin turning a shade paler.

Then she held still for a moment while Red took a good look at her, making sure that she was who she appeared to be. We'd had "visits" from chameleons other than Miguel. Checking each other like this had now become part of our normal protection protocol.

Red gave her the thumbs-up.

"What happened?" she asked.

"The Order," I said.

"Here to kill us?"

"Eventually," I said.

She cocked her head. "But not right now?"

"No," I said.

She rolled her eyes. "They shouldn't keep trying. It's embarrassing."

I stared at her.

"What?" she said. "It's true."

"Maybe so," I said. "But once upon a time the Order scared the crap out of you. And they should."

"That was before, Night."

Before, in her former life, back when we'd been on the run. Before the Angel. And before we'd discovered that in addition to having the power to talk with gods, Faith carried a god inside of her.

That god was called the Awakened. A misnomer, because the Awakened had slept for thousands of years, its soul—or whatever spirit gods possessed—passing from one magical human to another across time.

According to our Watcher, Addie, the Awakened was a big deal, even if no one knew exactly what it was. The thing we did know: the Awakened had begun to come alive within Faith. The gold in her eyes was new, and belonged to the god.

The Awakened had saved her and Red's lives when the last Order operative to come after us had tried to take them out. It had saved them by vaporizing the operative.

I'd been waiting for Faith to break down over having killed a man, even if that man had tried to kill her. She still carried an innocence inside of her, and a tender heart. But she'd held it together. I didn't know how.

The Order had brought us together. She'd been my last mission—

she and her family. I'd ended her parents, but I hadn't been able to kill a child, so I'd taken her and run. That was why and how I'd left the Order, and why and how she'd become my family.

Hearing her talk about how Order operatives should feel embarrassed by their failures might be appropriate on one level, but it didn't sound like her.

Red cleared his throat. "I need everyone down here now."

The other three kids made their way down the steps, decked out in their gym clothes and, like Faith, a little bleary-eyed. Red scanned them as they descended.

Ben served as the unspoken leader of the group. His long, brown hair and even longer bangs hid half of his face. He had a thin nose, a meticulously groomed soul patch, and a halo that might as well have been a gray stone wall.

Ben was a shield. No magic could penetrate the barrier of his halo. He could shield himself and at least one other person if they stuck close.

Jess was Addie's niece, and Watcher-in-training herself. Her halo looked like a night full of stars. She'd twisted her dark, kinky curls into a loose bun on top of her head. Her favorite gold hoops dangled from her ears. She was all of five feet tall. Easy to underestimate, but she was strong, her moral compass true.

Which was a good thing considering that Watchers, as direct descendants of fallen angels, were born with the power to hold the fabric of the Universe together—or tear it apart. Young Watchers had to be trained to use that magic, and each had different strengths and abilities with it. If Jess was too young and untrained to manifest that yet, it was only a matter of time before she did so on her own. Or before circumstances forced the question.

Last but not least came Corey, with her fire-engine red bob and painted black fingernails. She wore black-and-white skull cameos in her ears, around her neck, and on her fingers. Her polished white halo reminded me of bones—her magic allowed her to speak with the dead, which had been instrumental in saving all our skins.

Corey moved to stand beside Faith. The way she leaned toward

Faith seemed protective. That wasn't entirely new. The group took care of one another, and they'd done more than contemplate how to keep Faith safe from me if need be—if the Angel managed to take me over and I lost control. What felt new was Corey taking point on that rather than Ben, who'd always done so before.

I explained the situation to them as clearly as I could. No one else took it as nonchalantly as Faith had.

Ben folded his arms across his chest. Disbelief tinged his deep voice. "You're not actually going to go looking for your mentor, are you? That'd be like handing yourself over to the Order. Or walking into a trap."

"It's one hundred percent a trap," Jess said.

"Yep," I said. "One that's already set and closed around us. I don't think there's a way out of it."

Corey blinked at me. "What—they have us surrounded?"

"They wouldn't have made themselves known without covering all their bases first."

"What now?" Faith asked.

"The only way out is through," I said.

Red met my gaze. "Play the game better than they do."

I nodded. "Any of you drive over here?"

"Me," Corey said.

Unlike Red's truck, her car would hold five people. "Addie's expecting all of you. Red will drive you over in Corey's car, and you'll stay there until you hear from the rest of us."

She didn't ask why Red had to do the driving. The answer was obvious: in case of trouble.

Ben poured on a little sarcasm. "What do we do if the Order kills you and dumps your body in the Willamette?"

"Whatever Red and Addie tell you," I said.

I glanced at Red. "Take them out the front door and walk to the car. Stay close to each other. Ben, can you shield the car once Red pulls into traffic?"

"Definitely," he said.

That should conceal them from magical vision and any magic the

Order might throw at them. It wouldn't cover electronic surveillance or a good old-fashioned tail. Then again, the Order would've staked out Addie's house, along with my apartment and Red's place.

"Just watch yourselves," I said.

The kids trudged back up the stairs—all except Faith. She met my gaze with her gold-streaked eyes, and suddenly I saw only her, not the god.

"This is different than anything we've done before," she said.

I nodded.

She swallowed hard. "Please promise me that you'll come back."

I'd spent almost all the time I'd known her lying to her. About how I'd come to find her. About who I'd been. About why I'd saved her life. I'd promised myself I'd never lie to her again. It had to be the truth, and only the truth, or else how could she ever trust me again?

It came down to one thing: I was her rock.

She could count on the others. They were her friends. They'd do anything to help her, to protect her—even if it meant finding a safe house and keeping it secret from me so they'd have a place to go to ground if there were ever an altercation between the Angel inside of me and the Awakened inside Faith. Which her friends had actually done. Thinking about it still left me gobsmacked.

They were good friends. The best, in fact, and I was grateful that Faith had them.

She hadn't known them as long as she had me, however. I was the touchstone, the bridge from her innocence to where she stood now.

I called her my daughter, and she accepted it even though I wasn't her birth mother, and "adopted mother" didn't suit either. Even so, I was the closest and only thing she had to a mother. I'd die for her.

"I'll try," I said.

She held my gaze for long minute, then nodded.

"Okay." She wiped her palms on the front of her leggings, then turned and followed her friends.

I took a shaky breath and blew it out slowly.

Unless I'd read things all wrong, the initial level of risk was relatively low. Sunday, Miguel, and I would find out what Lily wanted and we'd go from there. I didn't expect it to be simple. I didn't expect it to be safe.

Red closed the distance between us. "I can see what's happening in your brain. Gears turning."

Faith wasn't the only one who needed me to come back, and come back whole and well. After the conversation Red and I had in his office before Lily had shown up, things between us felt clearer, and at the same time more vulnerable, more tender.

Love was no small thing. It was everything.

"You can't read my mind," I said.

"You're thinking there's too many considerations for us to handle. The kids and me, we're not professionals. What if the Order decides to do something we can't counter? What if they kill us and dump *our* bodies in the Willamette?"

I wanted to tell him that if that came to pass, I'd kill Lily with prejudice and bloody as much of the Order as I could before someone managed to take me down. I'd mean it, too.

He knew all that, and he didn't relish the thought.

I sighed. "Just be careful."

"Careful as I can," he said.

He cupped his hand against the nape of my neck and pulled me close. I slipped my hands inside his coat and wrapped my arms around him. He kissed me on the mouth and then in the center of my forehead, breathing me in.

I did the same, drawing in the scent of grass and earth, tasting the lingering sweetness of his mouth. I held him as tightly as I could, molding my body to his, letting him know that as much as he was here for me, I was here for him.

After a moment, I loosened my grip, and he drew back.

His eyes crinkled at the corners. "See you later."

"As soon as I can," I said.

It was the best adult promise I could give him.

He pulled free and followed the kids up the steps. I watched him go, saying a prayer under my breath for safety.

I did it automatically, as if it were something I did all the time. I hadn't prayed since the night my parents had died. I didn't believe in God with a capital G. I believed in people, whether human or fae—even the damn angels. I believed in the world. All the worlds.

Maybe that was who I prayed to. All of us. The better angels of our natures.

I let the last word of prayer leave my lips and float on the air to follow my people, to watch over them.

As they filed out into the hush before dawn, the two people I needed most right now filed in.

CHAPTER 2

I BREATHED OUT the last of my sentiment. The next breath, I filled with purpose. The air in the gym shifted accordingly, taking on an edge that could slice the skin. The light seemed to dim as my halo darkened. The barbells and plates and pull-up bars seemed to recede, leaving me standing in space.

Sunday's voice echoed as she bounded down the stairs. "Hey."

That one word broke the spell I'd built around myself. The altered space became a gym once more, and I was just me.

Sunday wore black from the knit cap that covered her blond curls down to the steel-toed boots on her feet—mission-ready. Her halo glowed like a rose-gold fire. She studied me with blue eyes that caught every detail.

Her magic worked through her eyes. She could blind anyone with whom she made visual contact.

"Where's Miguel?" I asked.

"Dealing with the door," she said in a tone that implied magic as well as mechanics—and also that she'd left him to deal with it on purpose.

I cocked my thumb over my shoulder. "Office."

I led the way into the sparsely furnished room where the uneaten breakfast sandwiches and coffee that Red had bought sat forlornly on the desktop. I took the far guest chair in front of the desk, planting my ass on its cold blue plastic surface.

"How was she?" Sunday asked, meaning Lily.

"The same," I said. "No-nonsense and to the point."

"She say anything else besides 'I need your help?'"

"No, other than that I'd know where to find her."

Miguel strode in, dressed exactly like Sunday. His long black hair hung in a braid to his waist. He met my gaze with a familiarity that took me back to the time the three of us had still been small. When we'd still had enough innocence to look for a friend inside the person beside us instead of a ready enemy.

He had a chameleon's halo, a purple-and-black bruise of a thing that changed constantly as I watched. He carried a cardboard tray with three go-cups of fresh coffee and more breakfast sandwiches from the diner.

"I called in the order before we left," he said. "We need sustenance as much as we need a plan."

I nodded my thanks and took what he offered me. "We know what this is about."

"The Angel," Miguel said.

The Order's reason for existing—the Angel of Death—had gone missing last month.

The Angel had come after me, not to kill me but to make me his vessel. He couldn't walk in the human realm without a human body, and not everyone had the magical juice to be able to house a being that ancient, vast, and powerful. He'd needed me to complete his destiny.

He'd tried to take me over. He'd tried to break me. His plan had backfired spectacularly, and I'd trapped him within the cage of my mind.

That was my magic—the ability to see the nature of others' magic, and the ability to take over their minds, trapping them in their own nightmares and using those nightmares to kill them if necessary.

It shouldn't have been enough. The Angel should have been able to overpower me without lifting a finger. Neither of us had known at the time why it hadn't turned out that way.

I wasn't one-hundred-percent human. An archangel's blood ran in my veins. I was the Archangel Michael's descendant. No idea how far back his magic had entered my bloodline, but it burned strong in me. That was how I'd trapped the Angel. That was how I'd lived to tell about it.

Stranger still, a week ago, the Angel of Death had an opportunity to escape from the cage in which I'd imprisoned him. I needed his help to save us both from an elder being—an asshole named Shadow, who'd been around since the dawn of time. Shadow was part human, but mostly fallen angel—an unfriendly Watcher—and he'd come within precious seconds of erasing my existence and taking control of the Angel of Death.

The Angel had helped me. Then, instead of taking the opportunity to get the hell out of my mind, he'd calmly walked back into his cage and shut the door.

The flutter of his wings within me scared me more now than it had before. I didn't know what he wanted, and he hadn't answered when I'd tried to ask him.

As if on cue, I felt that flutter now, inside my rib cage. I pressed a hand to my side.

Sunday gave me a pointed look. "He awake in there?"

"Feels like it," I said.

"Good." She sat in the other guest chair, propping one foot on the edge of the desk. "We may need him."

I held up a hand. "He helped me once. That doesn't mean he'll do it again. Or that his goals are our goals."

"I'll take what I can get right now," she said. "We can worry about the rest later. You're talking to each other?"

I shook my head. "He doesn't answer my texts."

"Ha," Sunday said. "Try again."

I looked up at Miguel, who leaned against the doorjamb with one arm folded across his chest and his free hand serving up long draws of coffee.

"She's right," he said.

I didn't want her to be. I didn't want to have to consider what could happen if the Angel came to the forefront and I receded, never to be seen or heard from again. I didn't want to help end the world, and what else could the Angel of Death be about? He was a Horseman of the Apocalypse, for crying out loud. It scared the shit out of me, and I'd fight him down to the last molecule of my being if it came to that.

I didn't share my fears. They knew my thoughts without hearing them spoken aloud.

"Are you prepared to deal with him if he takes over?" I asked.

Sunday rubbed her eyes. Which was as good as "no."

Miguel stepped forward. "I am."

He was the one who'd been remade to serve the Angel directly. He didn't have the juice I did, but he had the knowledge and the ability to follow the Angel into his natural angelic habitat if necessary.

"Get on with it," Sunday said. "Tell him it's an emergency."

That much was true. I sighed.

I closed my eyes, allowing my magic to rise. I reached with my mind for the cage in which the Angel lived, placing an image of myself outside the bars, giving him a moment to recognize that I'd sought him out.

The bars looked unbent and clean, as if they hadn't disintegrated in a magical battle and been rebuilt by will and magic alone. The terrain beneath my feet looked like packed earth and throbbed with the pulsing of my blood. Sparks fired all around, the signal fires of my nervous system.

Shadows moved behind the bars. The Angel coming to meet me.

He moved into view, a construct in this place in the same way my form was, showing me how he preferred to be seen: golden hair, golden eyes without pupils, skin the same medium brown as mine. He stood at an even height with me, which seemed ridiculous—he felt as vast as the heavens. He'd crafted a compact body, wiry with muscle. The strength that emanated from him could flatten a continent with one fell blow.

We'd done this dance a handful of times in the last week. Stared at each other through the bars.

I understood why he'd joined the fight against Shadow. If the Angel hadn't intervened, and the oldest Watcher had torn me apart and thrown the remains to the stars, Shadow would've had access to—and the potential to truly control—the Angel for his own purposes. What the Angel had done in defeating Shadow and saving my life had been nothing but self-preservation.

What I didn't understand was why the Angel had walked back into his cage. Why he'd stayed. What was in it for him? How did it help his cause?

I'd asked him those questions each time we'd met here. He never answered, only looked at me with those fathomless eyes, then turned on his heel and returned to his solitude.

I don't want to be here, I said. *I don't know whether I should be talking to you at all. But we have a situation.*

He said nothing, but I hadn't expected him to. He only continued to look at me.

The Order is here—they've sent my mentor, Lily, to ask for my help. I can only assume it has something to do with you. Can you confirm?

He stared at me. His eyes narrowed ever so slightly—or maybe I only imaged that they did.

Sunday, Miguel, and I are headed into the tiger's lair. We may need your help. We don't know if or when or how yet. Will you help us if we ask?

I waited for an answer.

Still, he said nothing. Aside from what I'd clearly imagined a minute ago, his expression betrayed no thought, no emotion.

You could just tell me to fuck off, I said.

The corners of his mouth curved ever so slightly. They were unnerving, these micro-movements, even if—especially because— they represented progress. He hadn't done even that much before.

Will you help us? I asked again.

He held my gaze. He opened his mouth to speak. I caught a glimpse of eternity beyond the fine edges of his white teeth.

I held my breath.

Wrong question, he said, and turned away.

That was more than he'd said to me in all the time we'd been entangled.

Wait, I said.

He paused his step.

I turned over thought fragments, weaving my words carefully. *If I were to ask you the right questions, would you answer them?*

He turned his head so that I could see him clearly, then nodded.

Why won't you help us? I asked.

If I do, your mentor will know for certain that I'm with you, he said.

You're hiding?

Strategically.

At that, he walked to the back of the cage, his edges blurring until I could no longer mark his form.

That was it, then. I needed to figure out what to ask. Fat lot of good that would do us now.

I shifted my consciousness, allowing my magic to ebb, and opened my physical eyes. It took a few seconds to focus again on Sunday and Miguel.

"Well?" he asked.

The sound of his voice re-grounded me in the here and now. "Well, nothing. The good news is that he talks now. The bad news is that he won't help."

I explained why.

Miguel studied his shoes a moment. "At least now we know."

We needed a tally of our resources, and now we had one. Three former operatives. No Angel of Death. "So," I said. "Plan."

Sunday lifted her foot from the desk and planted it on the floor again. "Just the basics."

"Find Lily," I said.

Every Order operative had an internal magical compass that pointed them home. Normally, that internal drive would steer them toward the closest headquarters, but it could be worked with to find other collectives anywhere in the world.

It took a mentor to set up a collective or HQ location.

The Order could also use a wayward operative's internal drive to locate them. All magic was about connection, after all—connection between the operative and the target, the healer and the one to be healed, the seeker and the location. Power mixed between them the way a river at its end mixed with the sea. It was impossible not to get a little of the other's magic or energy on you in the process.

When I'd left the Order, I'd done my best to magically disable my connection, to smash it enough to make it unusable, for that very reason. My guess was that Sunday had done the same, although we hadn't talked about it.

We still registered on the Order's radar as "alive," but our location could not be pinpointed or even guesstimated using that internal drive. That also meant that neither Sunday nor I could pinpoint the location of the Order HQ—or Lily.

I looked at Sunday. She shrugged. We both turned to look at Miguel.

He sighed. "I did what I could to throw them off, just like you guys."

"Doesn't sound definitive," Sunday said.

He pressed his lips into a thin line. "It's not, exactly."

I raised a brow.

"I kept part of the connection alive." He held up his hand, measuring a paper-thin space between his thumb and forefinger. "The thinnest thread."

"How?" Sunday asked.

I knew the answer. "Through the chameleons."

He nodded.

The chameleons maintained a connection with and presence inside the Order. They didn't share all their information with the Order, however. They kept their secrets to themselves.

Sunday gave him a pointed look. "How are they not out for your blood?"

He held up a hand. "Some of them are. But they have bigger fish to fry right now, and I'm small potatoes. They're not looking for the back-door connection that I left open."

"Does this connection have a name?" I asked.

He flashed a wry grin. "Tana."

Sunday sighed. "Friend or lover?"

"What's it matter?" he asked.

"True friends are forever. Lovers are forever sometimes."

"I trust her," he said.

"And we trust you," I said.

Sunday shrugged. "Night trusts you."

He snorted. "Not news to me."

Sunday slid to the front of her seat, resting her elbows on her knees. "What are they looking for, exactly?"

"A way to take down the Order," he said.

My eyebrows climbed to my hairline. "You didn't think we should know this before now?"

"I've been here a week, for chrissakes," he said. "I'm still recovering from getting my ass kicked. And I'm still trying to figure out where I fit here. Anyway, the chameleons won't move against the Order unless they have to. Their current play is strictly a contingency."

I took a minute to absorb what he'd said. "I get it. Really, I do. But we need to know what we're walking into."

He nodded. "Okay."

"Anything else we need to know?" I asked.

He shook his head.

Sunday met his gaze and held it. "You'll tell us if and when there is?"

The implication being that, if he didn't, there would be conse-quences.

"You got my word," he said.

That would have to be enough. "Moving on," I said. "Are all three of us going in?"

Miguel nodded. So did Sunday.

I met Miguel's gaze. "I need your word that if this goes sideways and you're the only one to make it out, you'll do what you can to protect my people."

He mulled the question. It was a lot to ask of someone I'd once known but had been separated from for years. He had no ties to the people I loved except that those people were tied to me. He'd spent his life avoiding connection with anyone and everyone because connection meant vulnerability and vulnerability meant destruction. Yet, more than anything, he wanted the kind of life I had, with people he cared about and who understood and cared about him.

If something happened to Sunday and me, my people would need his help. Beyond that, asking meant that I respected him, that I understood him, that I cared. Once upon a time, I'd gone into battle with other operatives without those things. I couldn't do it anymore. I refused.

"Okay," he said.

I nodded. "One more thing."

He waited.

"I need to know where you stand on the subject of the Angel," I said. "I don't mean whether the Angel lives inside of me or not, or whether someone else takes control of him. We've talked about that already. What I mean is, how will you react if the Angel does something to put the end of the world in motion?"

He held my gaze. "You have a preference?"

"I do," I said. "I'm asking you."

He didn't hesitate. "I want the world to keep existing. I want it to thrive. Anything I do, it's in that cause."

"Good," I said.

The corners of his mouth curved. "It's good to understand each other."

The stakes were as high as ever, and we would need each other to get through. I believed him as much as I could. It was a beginning, and a bridge.

I looked at Sunday. "We good?"

She nodded. "We're taking my car."

It was fast. It cornered well. It was conspicuous as hell—a Mustang in a city of Priuses.

"Can't blend into traffic in that thing if we need to," I said. "We'll take my Honda. Miguel drives."

The ride to the place where the Order had set up shop took twenty minutes. Far northeast side of town, in a warehouse just south of the Columbia River. By the time we arrived, the mist had stopped falling and rare winter sun peeked from behind the clouds. A seagull glided by overhead, its call half-stolen by the wind. There was no other sound but the slam of our car doors and the crush of gravel under our shoes as we headed for the warehouse.

The garage door that served as the entrance rolled up on its tracks just before we reached it, revealing an Order operative I didn't know —a Korean woman with her long, black hair pulled into French braids. She wore a brown leather sheath at her hip. The blade she carried had a bone handle. Her halo glowed with a pure golden light that reminded me of the sun.

Her magic shone light into dark places—natural shadows, secrets, intentional obfuscation. Nothing could be hidden from her, at least not for long.

She schooled her expression as she looked at me, the reason the Order had begun to unravel. I was a legend inside the Order for having left, for having lived. My exodus had inspired others, so much so that the Order had begun to magically chain its operatives' minds to prevent them from following in my footsteps. Once, loyalty would have been enough to keep operatives in line. No more.

Her gaze moved from me to Sunday, eyes flashing with recognition.

Sunday inclined her head. "Kat."

Kat returned the gesture, but said nothing. As her gaze moved over Miguel, her eyes widened, the corners of her mouth turning down.

Maybe she'd never seen a chameleon before. Maybe she knew him and wasn't happy to see him.

Miguel looked at her as if she were beneath him. It didn't feel personal, though. It felt like chameleon versus Order operative, and the chameleons had a high opinion of themselves.

We slowed to a halt, waiting for Kat's cue. She kept us there for a good fifteen seconds, scanning for hidden things. If she'd seen the Angel inside of me, she gave no sign.

I eyeballed the parts of the warehouse I could see. A small office tucked against the left wall, large windows providing a clear view inside. It was empty of everything except a metal desk, a folding chair, and a space heater. Shrink-wrapped cases stacked three deep on wooden pallets, with no signage on the boxes as to what they contained. My magical sight provided a clue, however—the items in those boxes gave off a dull green glow, a halo signature I hadn't seen before. Just looking at the halo made me feel nauseous, as if the magic had been specifically conjured to be anti-Night. Or anti-Angel.

No—that assessment felt slightly off. I shook my head to clear it.

The magic was…anti-magic.

As far as I knew, nothing could take away a person's magic. It was part of who they were, inextricably woven into their DNA. But blunt it for a while? Sure, that might be a possibility.

Beyond the pallets, a lot of empty space. Long fluorescents hung from the ceiling, chasing away shadows. There was a door in the far corner. All the windows were up high, at least five feet above the floor. I couldn't tell which of them might open, or which might be painted or nailed shut, from my vantage point.

No other exits or entrances. Some sightlines blocked by the pallets. No dark corners to duck into. Better than I'd expected, but not great.

I spotted Lily over by the back wall. Her tiger-striped halo stood out among those of the two of operatives with her, its surface rippling as if there were muscles beneath its skin. She sat behind another of the small metal desks, a laptop in front of her. The glow of the screen lit her face and burnished the unruly auburn hair that had escaped her ponytail. She glanced up, meeting my gaze over the distance.

She said something to the white male operative on her left, whose halo reminded me of a lion's pelt. His halo didn't move like hers. Mentor in training, maybe.

The operative to Lily's right had a human halo only—no magic at all. She had shaved, silver hair and dressed all in cherry-red from her turtleneck sweater down to her boots. She stayed behind as Lily and the lion operative rose and walked toward us.

I couldn't scan Lily or the other operatives to confirm their identities without slipping into their minds. Miguel could tell at a glance whether any of them were chameleons. He shook his head, letting me know we were clear on that point, at least.

Kat led us into the warehouse. Clearly, the plan was to meet Lily halfway.

As we passed the pallets, Miguel took a long look at the contents. He clenched his jaw.

He knew what was in those boxes. He considered them a threat.

I felt a fleeting mental touch from him. I opened my magic in his direction, sliding part of my consciousness into his mind, leaving the rest of it to navigate the walk and take in new information as it arose.

What's in there? I asked.

Very bad news, he said.

CHAPTER 3

A N IMAGE BLOOMED in Miguel's mind, one that made my
blood run cold. I kept my expression neutral, so no one around
me could see the chill that'd come over me. I marshaled my emotions
so that no one would pick up on my discomfort—or the rage that
ignited in my heart.

The shrink-wrapped cases on the wooden pallets contained
ammunition. Bullets, to be exact. Not regular bullets that had been
spelled, but bullets created entirely with magic, meant not only to
injure or kill physically, but to cut off a person's access to their magic
until any lodged bullet was removed. If the bullet remained in long
enough, it could permanently end the victim's magic.

Miguel fed me the fruit of his senses: I breathed in the stink of oil
and metal. I saw the life force in the concrete floor and walls, in the
long fluorescents hanging from the ceiling. That life force could be
manipulated for Miguel's ends. It could provide a way to hide in plain
sight if need be.

Through Miguel's eyes, our escort operative, Kat, became a collection of characteristics to be copied. From her braided black hair to
her steady, dark gaze, to the particular way she moved in space and

time, down to the balance of compact muscle on her lithe body and the slight bow of her legs, more pronounced when she walked.

Lily looked like dead meat to him. As in, she'd done something to make it impossible for any chameleon to copy her. Rare but powerful magic that was almost as anathema to him as the bullets.

Now that we'd grown near to Lily and her pet lion, Miguel could make out certain amount of triumph in her hazel eyes. She'd caught his examination of her, along with his conclusion.

He hated her so much that the force of it caused a hitch in my step. Not enough to knock me over, but enough to feel the raw power of his emotion. She'd done something to him—or to someone he cared about—that he refused share with me. It was enough to know that if he got the chance to slit her throat, he'd do it in a heartbeat.

Anything else? I asked.

Agree with what she's about to propose, he said.

I didn't understand. *Need to hear it first.*

No, he said. *It's the only way they'll let us out of here alive.*

He turned to look at the center of the room. It was shielded—something I hadn't caught with my own magical sight. Something only a mentor or chameleon could see. There was someone already trapped inside the field.

Miguel couldn't make out whom it might be. The shape and size suggested a man. A shine emanated from him, though the shield hid the character of his halo along with his features.

I don't think it's one of our people, Miguel said.

Not one of the family. Some other unlucky bastard.

I slipped out of his mind, returning all of my magic and my consciousness to their usual haunts. The floor and the walls and the lights became things again rather than resources. The shielded space became invisible to me, but now that I knew it was there, I could feel a tingling along the edges of my skin as we drew nearer to it.

I zeroed in on Lily and her people as she drew close and slowed to a stop. Lily believed she had an ace up her sleeve. The look she'd given Miguel had stoked the fire of my suspicion, and the way she looked at me now—as if I were the same woman she'd known before—confirmed it.

She wore black today as usual, accented with a teal jacket that had a small bulge in the pocket. Not gun-shaped or knife-shaped.

Her lion had a brown mane streaked with gold that fell to the middle of his back and proud, brown eyes. He filled out his black sweater and jeans like a cut Hollywood actor might. He gave off a chunk of smug self-confidence as well. He wore two blades, one sheathed on each side of his belt.

I glanced beyond them to the silver-and-red normal they'd left behind. She stood with her arms at her sides, hands curled into fists.

"Night," Lily said. "Thank you for coming."

I returned my attention to her and waited for the rest.

"I have an insurgency in my ranks," she said. "One I lay at your feet."

"I haven't been a part of the Order in years, Mentor," I said.

"You're mythic," she said. "As such, you've never left."

I shrugged.

"I'm cleaning house," she said. "Putting things in a new, refined order. From this point forward, we'll have only true believers. No more opportunists."

I raised a brow. "Are you suggesting that stealing kids off the street and promising them the world, only to make them into willing killers who obey your every instruction, creates opportunists?"

She flashed a quick, tight smile. "I'm suggesting that if you don't want those who believe in you more than they believe in the Order to be killed, you'll do what I ask."

An attempt to goad me into—what—sticking up for the traumatized and defenseless? I didn't need goading to go there. Also, in this case, her comments extended to Sunday and Miguel. And to rest of the team, including Faith.

Threatening my daughter was the wrong tack to take, regardless of the motivation.

I sighed. "What do you want, Lily?"

She kept a steady appearance, but her halo flinched when I called her by her name. First time for everything.

"I want you to take a contract job," she said.

I stared at her.

"I know, I know," she said. "You're not one of us anymore. Don't worry—it's not a hit. It's the jackpot solution you've been looking for already."

I sincerely doubted that.

She pulled the mystery object from her jacket pocket. A tiny black cube, two by two at the most. "This is a kind of cure, or a stop, at least. It will put the brakes on the transformation where it is right now, so that things never get any worse."

"What transformation?" I asked.

"Not what," Lily said. "Whose. I figured you'd have guessed outright."

"We have a lot of moving parts around here lately," I said.

She inclined her head, granting me the point. "I'm talking about Faith. I'm talking about the Awakened."

Hearing my kid's name roll out of her mouth ratcheted my rage up a notch.

Lily held up a hand. "Hear me out."

I flexed my fingers at my sides. "Talk."

"This was given to us by an Elder. You know what I mean by that?"

"Yes."

Elders: in the worlds since the beginning of time. Usually had titles rather than names, because they existed to fulfill a function, or a destiny. Their presence in the worlds made certain things possible. Like Shadow, the oldest Watcher, whom we'd defeated. Or the woman who'd for all intents and purposes been my *abuela*—

"Her name is Dream," Lily said.

My grandmother. Miguel's grandmother, too. Dream's purpose in the worlds was to enable people to envision what the worlds could be. What they, themselves, could be. Dream had a fondness for certain magical children. She searched them out. Marked them as children with a destiny.

"Dream gave you that?" I asked. "When did this happen?"

"A week ago," Lily said.

When Miguel had come to town to take me down and take the Angel for himself. When Shadow had tried to do the same. When we'd had the fight of our lives on the front lawn of a house in a quiet, oblivious neighborhood in the middle of the night, and the Angel of Death had, at least temporarily, chosen my side.

That couldn't be a coincidence. But was I going to believe Lily? Why would I ever?

I took a step closer to her. "She just dropped in at HQ and asked to see you?"

She hedged. "Not exactly. She didn't 'ask.' She demanded. She said I'd know what to do with this after she told me an interesting story about the girl you claim as your daughter. I learned all about the god known as the Awakened and how it's been showing signs of coming to life in Faith."

Lily couldn't have known that. Or that was what I told myself. The Order kept secrets at the high levels, things they didn't tell the operatives, like where they got their patronage, what chameleons were, and the ultimate purpose of the organization.

They could have had information about the Awakened and not shared it with the operatives. Not sharing it with the mentors would've been another thing.

I studied Lily's face. Her halo. Her body language. I didn't see a lie in there anywhere.

"So, you see, that's why I came here. That's why I showed up on your doorstep. Dream said that what's in this cube could halt Faith's transformation. I know that's what you want, too. I'm only asking you to implement this cure, for all our sakes."

She had me up until the end. "What do you mean, for all our sakes?"

"Dream told me that the rise of the Awakened will be catastrophic, not only for Faith herself and anyone close to her, but for all the worlds. It's the event that kicks off the Apocalypse."

Miguel leaned forward. "I gotta interrupt here. According to the book, the Apocalypse starts with the breaking of the first seal. Also, according to the book, that seal heralds the arrival of the first Horseman of the Apocalypse. There are two of them already in the worlds that I know of. The Angel of Death, for one."

Lily looked at him, stone-faced.

"Don't act like it's top secret anymore," he said. "I know what's up, and so do Sunday and Night. He's been your captain all along, steering your ship."

That was the information Miguel had brought to our table. The Angel had been in charge of the Order. The Angel had left in search of me, his vessel. What had happened after that wasn't public knowledge. As far as we knew, the Order was clueless as to the Angel's current whereabouts.

Lily's pet lion cocked his head. He had a voice that scratched bloody, like broken glass. "You know where he's gone to?"

"He's gone somewhere?" Miguel asked. "Last I knew, he was in his home place on the other side of the In Between."

"You're not a very well-informed chameleon, are you?" the lion asked.

Miguel gave him the side-eye. "The other Horseman—or Horse-woman, in this case—is the one they call Famine. She's been seen, out and about in the human world and in Faery. If these Horsemen are already on the board, then the Apocalypse has already begun, at least if we're following the book. So, which is it, Lily? If we're doing this thing you're asking, for all our sakes, then we deserve to know."

Sunday folded her arms beneath her breasts. "Share and share alike."

Lily narrowed her eyes at the three of us in turn, landing last with Miguel. "No idea."

"I thought you knew everything," Sunday said.

"We only get information when we need to have it," Lily said.

Miguel snorted. "Need to know. That's rich."

"It's the truth."

Again, I saw no lie in Lily.

If the Angel had doled out the information he wanted the Order to have, and only in quantities necessary for the mentors and operatives to do their jobs, then she really wouldn't know.

Miguel had a good point, and I felt grateful that he'd made it because those things needed to be said. I had something to say, too. Something that had been brewing inside of me since the night I made the choice to leave the Order behind.

At the time, the choice had been about what depths I allowed myself to sink to, and what I could no longer abide. It had been about saving the life of a child, and taking on the raising and care of that child, even though I had no experience and no decent examples to follow.

Since then, it'd become about widening the circle of care beyond Faith and me to include the people I now considered family. With the Angel, it had taken on a different dimension entirely. Having a part to play in the goddamn Apocalypse meant that the choices I made affected all the worlds.

That was a hard responsibility to realize, much less to take on.

I had my own opinion about what constituted an apocalypse, capital A or not.

"There's always been famine," I said. "All throughout time, in every world with the possible exception of the angelic realm. There's always been death. No one gets out of life alive. Same with the other Horsemen things. There have always been disease and war, martyrs and cruelty. Subjugation of people because of their skin color or religion or class. All of it. If we want to get Biblical, it goes back before Cain and Abel to the idea the knowledge was forbidden fruit.

"We are creatures of free will. Here's mine: I don't buy the crap about the seals—at least not that they're somehow special to the Apocalypse. If they were, then the worlds would be an ash heap already. I believe that the people who wrote those prophecies—or whatever you want to call them—were trying to describe a cataclysm so vast and so deep that it was beyond imagining, and that they used the words and concepts and tools they had at the time. Whatever they had, it was woefully inadequate.

"Whether that's true or not doesn't matter to me, because it looks from my view as if no one really knows, and people are jockeying for power and position. If the end goes down, the prophecies are fulfilled and the people who give a shit about that get what they want, fade to black. If the end never comes, people get to go on living, and we have second and third and fourth chances to get it right, to care about each other and help each other, I'm good with that."

Lily reached out a hand, the cube cupped in her palm. "This is how we get there."

We, my ass. Neither Lily nor the Order were on board with me and mine. But if what she said was true—if what the cube held could cure Faith, arrest the awakening of the god inside her—how could I not take it, regardless of who handed it to me?

I glanced at Sunday from the corner of my eye. She gave no sign, but kept her gaze focused on the lion.

Miguel had already given me his opinion. Say yes to whatever Lily asked. Only way we'd get out of here alive. We could decide what we were actually going to do later.

He wasn't looking my way either. He'd shifted his attention from Lily and her pet to the shielded form again. I could only guess he was teasing through the layers of light to get a better look.

I let my magic rise higher, scanning the cube for any overt, or more subtle, magical signs of danger or foul play. I saw none.

So I lifted my hand and plucked the cube from Lily's palm. It felt like nothing special to me. Light as a feather. Sharp edges, but not sharp enough to cut. It didn't zap me or turn me into a toad, nor did I feel the sudden flutter of the Angel's wings around my heart.

I looked more closely at the surface, realizing that it wasn't entirely black. It looked like a Watcher halo. Like the night sky, alive with stars.

"Let us know how it goes," Lily said.

Sunday turned to her. "You're sticking around?"

"No." Lily reached into her jacket pocket and pulled out a burner phone. "We're out of here tonight, but I'll be available for the next three days at the number programmed into this cell."

Three days wasn't a long time to make a decision and set in

motion something that could change the course of the future. Then again, I'd made decisions with serious consequences in less. The stakes kept ratcheting higher. The risks grew greater every day. I didn't want to have to rely on instinct, weighing every possibility as more horrible than the last. I only wanted to do what was right.

I didn't trust Lily as far as I could throw her. I didn't know whether I should trust my *abuela*, Dream.

If the magic in the cube could arrest the Awakened, it could save Faith. She could keep herself, and not lose it to another, more powerful being. She could be a girl, albeit a girl with a powerful magical gift. She could have the life she'd always wanted.

Sunday nudged my arm. "Let's go, Night."

I glanced up at her, startled. The cube might not have been spelled, but it had held me under a kind of spell. One where possibilities I'd dreamed of might come to pass.

Or, if we unlocked the spell and the whole thing went wrong, one where nightmares could become three-dimensional, bloody monsters.

CHAPTER 4

RED OPENED THE DOOR to Addie's yellow house as I stepped onto the wide porch, the cube burning a hole in the pocket of my hoodie. He took one look at me, then stepped back and out of the way to let Sunday, Miguel, and I file in.

The house looked the same as always, with the coat rack and shoe rack to the right of the door, the long dining table on the left with its silver bowl filled with clementine tangerines. The Christmas tree stood tall and proud on the far side of the table. An assembly of sofas huddled in front of the fireplace, family photos watching us with friendly eyes from their perch on the mantle. The exquisite perfume of meatloaf and mashed potatoes made my mouth water.

I wondered for a split second who Addie had cooked it for, given that if she had visitors or expected them, her cooking became as much of a spell as an inviting meal or snack. She always seemed to know what food would find the heart of a person, and therefore allow her to see more deeply into them than they might have bargained for.

Then I noticed something off. Way off.

However it looked, the place *felt* different. Where it had always before welcomed me after getting a sense, or a reminder, of who I was, this time the house spirit that guarded and defended the place surrounded me like white blood cells surrounding a contagion. The air around me filled with pressure that squeezed my skin and eyes and mouth. It lifted my feet from the hardwood floor and yanked me across the living room, into the heart of the house: the kitchen.

Where I'd been headed anyway. Where I'd find Addie. She was the one who might know something about the cube I carried.

Addie was bent over in front of the open oven, pulling out the meatloaf and setting it on the stovetop when I floated in. She had on a long brown dress made of jersey fabric that hugged her curves and warmed her brown skin. Her legs and feet were bare, but the house was warm enough. She wore her black hair in a bun on the top of her head, secured today with a pencil.

The house spirit dropped me unceremoniously on the floor, where my sneakers failed to catch. I hit the worn tile like a cartoon character —flat on my butt.

Addie turned around slowly, giving me the once-over, eyebrows rising above the silver frames of her glasses. She pulled off her bright yellow oven mitt and set her hand on her hip. "To what do I owe this indignity?"

"Your house did it, not me."

"Let me rephrase," she said. "What did you do, Night Sanchez?"

In the past, that question would've stung with anger. Not anymore. Addie had needed saving from Shadow, and the Angel and I had done the saving. She didn't have to like me, but she trusted me.

I met her inscrutable, brown-eyed gaze. "I brought something with me from the meeting with Lily." I plucked it from my pocket.

"Damn," Addie said. "Give that to me."

I clambered to standing, brushing off my backside, and handed the cube over to her.

She lifted her glasses to rest on top of her head and turned the cube with the tips of her fingers, eyeballing it closely.

Red rushed into the kitchen behind me, Sunday and Miguel in his wake.

"What just happened?" he asked.

Addie kept her eyes on the cube. "Night brought a Watcher artifact into the house, and not one that has permission to be here."

Sunday asked the question on the tip of my tongue. "Artifact? Permission?"

"Yes." Addie glanced up. "Permission. These things are alive, you know. Sentient. They have minds of their own and, as such, they require my say-so as to whether they're permitted in my home."

"I didn't know," I said.

"Obviously."

Footfalls sounded on the staircase at the other end of the hall beyond the kitchen. One set, one kid.

Faith burst into the kitchen, squeaking to a halt just before she ran into Sunday and Miguel. She looked at me with anxious eyes, and seemed to quiet once she saw that I was all right.

I'd done what I'd promised. I'd come back. I didn't know how she'd feel about what I'd brought with me.

"What's your verdict?" I asked Addie.

She met my gaze. "It can stay, but you and I are going to have talk right now, just the two of us."

Miguel shook his head. "This concerns all of us."

"You're lucky I let you in here at all," Addie said. "Chameleon."

Miguel couldn't say much about that. He'd been the enemy, after all. And Addie didn't like the Order, although she'd used it to do her dirty work. Order operatives, former or not, were viewed with suspicion.

He opened his mouth to reply, then thought better of it.

"Let's go," Addie said.

We couldn't talk outside, and both the main floor and the upstairs were occupied. That left the basement.

I let her lead the way past the others, into the hall and through the basement door. She pulled the string to light the bare bulb overhead, illuminating the staircase ahead all the way down to the gray-carpeted landing, and then shut the door behind us.

"I know I haven't thanked you for saving my life," she said.

I held up my hands. "It's not necessary."

"Yes, it is. I don't do well with unacknowledged debt. You remember that, in case next time it's you who owes me."

I nodded. "Fine."

She held up the cube. "Did the Order give you provenance on this thing?"

"Lily said she received it directly from Dream," I said.

Addie took a moment to digest that, then cocked her head toward the stairs.

I followed her down, the steps creaking underfoot. At the landing she turned left, stepping through the magical curtain that marked the safest space in the house, one she'd warded with every ounce of her power. That warding and the side door at the other end of the basement had allowed escape at a crucial moment last week. The place felt more than protected. It felt blessed.

Passing through the curtain cloaked me in silence and white light. When I emerged, I found Addie waiting for me in the dark, the handle of a camping lantern swinging from one hand and the cube in the other.

"What do you know about Dream?" she asked.

I gave her the bullet points Miguel had passed to me, as well as my memory of her—of the *posole* she used to make for me, which Addie recognized as the meal she prepared for me before our first meeting; the color blue that Dream favored, the contents of her pantry.

Addie nodded. "I met her when I was young."

"How young?" I asked.

"Nine," she said.

So young. "What did she tell you?"

"She told me the exact location of the house I would buy when I got older—this one, of course. She told me that one day I would meet someone I'd tried to kill, and that I should be watchful. Pay attention."

Addie was talking about me. I whistled. And waited, because there was a third thing Addie had been about to say.

"When it came time for my training, when I was about the age your daughter and my niece are now, she took me as her apprentice for the first year."

I stared at her.

"I know. It was baffling. I thought for sure I'd go to Shadow and his bunch." She made a face as if she was going to spit, then thought better of it. It was her basement, after all, and sacred space at that.

"What did she teach you?" I asked.

"Everything about the history of the Watchers, including the not-so-nice bits. Some things about what would be coming, including that one day I'd come into possession of a piece of magic she'd made."

"It's not yours," I said.

"No," Addie replied. "Not yet."

I narrowed my eyes.

"I'm not going to take it away from you," she said. "I just need you to know that neither you nor I will be able to unlock the magic inside of it. It will require a witch, and one of considerable power. That's just the way the magic works."

"How do you know?" I asked. "Is that part of what Dream told you?"

She shook her head. "Yes. And it's what I see when I look at it."

I closed the distance between us, peering into the cube again. "All I see are darkness and stars. Is it a Watcher thing?"

"As you say."

I met her gaze. "Can you tell whether it's what Lily said it was?"

"No," she said. "And that troubles me. It should trouble you, too."

It did, but my hope that it might work warred with my concern. "Did Dream ever lie to you?"

"She always told the truth," Addie said. "The truth wasn't always pretty, or kind, or comfortable. Occasionally, the truth had razor teeth."

"Cut you?"

"To ribbons," she said. "If Dream told Lily it could be a cure for the Awakened, I believe that. The rest of it—that working the magic will arrest a process already begun? I don't buy that at all. So the question becomes, what does 'cure' mean? And are you willing to risk finding out?"

I wanted to be willing, which wasn't the same thing at all. "It's not my decision. Not entirely."

"Yes, it is," Addie said.

I shook my head. "Faith should have a say. She's the one it's meant to change."

"Faith is a child, Night."

"She's almost grown. And she'll find a way to get what she wants whether I think she should have it or not. You know that. You've seen it, too."

Addie mulled that over. "She'll look to you for advice. They all will —like they always do. You'll have to weigh in. So if you need to talk about it some more with me, or with your man, or with the others, you do that now. Be sure. Because whatever you decide will take us down a road we may not be able to come back from."

A disturbance in the magical curtain told us we'd have company any second now, and we did. Red stepped through into the lantern-lit space, his jaw set and his own magic riding high in his green eyes.

"Addie," he said, "what's going on down here?"

"Having an honest talk with Night. You?"

"Wondering why there's two strangers from Texas on the front porch," he said.

Addie pursed her lips. "Two Texans? I only ordered one."

"Well, whoever they are, they're insisting they belong here and asked to be let in. I sent Faith upstairs and asked her and the others to stay there for now. Your strangers are sitting in your living room sipping cans of fizzy water I found in your fridge and giving Sunday and Miguel the side-eye. You want to come up and talk to 'em?"

She handed me the lantern. "You fill him in, and come up when you're finished. You only talk about this down here, inside the protections. You understand?"

Red furrowed his brow. "You're worried someone's listening in?"

"There's always someone listening," she said, and headed for the stairs, vanishing through the curtain.

I met Red's gaze.

"What's goin' on?" he asked.

I gave him every detail, from beginning to end, watching the emotions cross his face.

He was silent for a long while—so long, I wondered whether he would say anything, or whether I'd want to hear it when he did. Eventually, he hunkered down, then lowered himself to sit on the concrete floor. I went to sit beside him.

He took my hand in his, tracing the line of my fingertips with his own. "This is huge," he said. "It could be amazing. Or it could be a disaster."

I nodded, but I didn't say anything else. I could tell he wasn't finished.

"It's important to me that we talk with Faith about this," he said. "And that when we tell her about it, we make sure to talk about it like there's nothing wrong with her that needs fixing. I don't want that girl thinking that she's bad or evil again. I want her to know she has our support and that we love her, and that it's up to her and what she wants as much as we can give her that."

I let his words echo inside of me, all the way down to my marrow. He'd been good with Faith the way he was with all of the kids. He'd made sure she knew that he was there for whatever she needed.

Red and I were committed, but it was still early for us, and for him to talk about her in the way that he did—as if he were her father and not just my partner—made me feel a sense of wonder that shone like a light inside.

No one had ever said anything like that to me, or about me, when I was young. If they had, who knew what might've gone differently for me.

"I want that for her, too," I said.

He threaded his fingers through mine. "What happens if it goes pear-shaped?"

I took a deep breath. "The Awakened rises, and this time it's not for a minute, it's forever."

"Will she still be Faith?"

"I don't know," I said.

"What does the Awakened want? What is it, even?"

I shook my head. "No one knows."

"Not even the Angel?" he asked.

"Not that he's telling."

"I don't like it," he said.

"I don't either."

He met my gaze. "We're trusting in memories, here—Dream, Addie. I want to believe it will be all right. If Faith decides she wants this, and it doesn't go our way, what are we prepared to do?"

That was the thing I didn't want to hear. The implications made my blood curdle. "I won't let anything happen to her. I won't let anyone touch her."

"Even if she's the Devil?" he asked gently.

I considered the question, giving it the weight it deserved. I weighed right and wrong, and the size of the stakes, and what I might do if it were anyone else we were talking about. I'd done terrible things to people who deserved it, and to plenty of people who didn't. I knew what Red was asking.

"No," I said. "Not even then."

He lifted my hand to his lips and kissed it softly. "All right, then."

"You're not gonna argue with me?" I asked.

"Not even a little bit," he said.

I looked at him. "We should head upstairs and see what's going on with the visitors."

"I think they're here for this," he said. "One of 'em's a witch."

CHAPTER 5

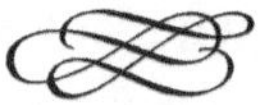

TWO GIRLS HAD COME. The first perched on the edge of the sofa that faced the door. She wore a long, flowing skirt, black with red roses printed all over, a matching peasant blouse, two red cardigans, and a velvet scarf. She had on black- and red-striped tights and black Mary Janes. Her blond curls had gone frizzy in the rain. And she was barely older than Faith and the others. Like a year older, maybe. Her halo looked like a very specific blue I remembered from a trip to the Oregon coast: the color of the waves rolling in at sunset on a clear night.

No way was she the witch powerful enough to decode Dream's cube.

The other one couldn't be either. She sprawled on the opposite sofa with one stocking foot tucked under her, surfing on her phone. She wore her long brown hair in braided pigtails that reached all the way down to her butt, and thick, black-framed glasses over her green eyes. She chewed gum as if her life depended on it, and she'd dressed in a long-sleeved denim shirt with the sleeves rolled neatly to the elbows, a pair of holey black jeans, and combat boots.

She had tattoos on her forearms. Nothing dainty, and not sleeves either, but glyphs and symbols that glowed to my magical sight. Her halo screamed orange, as if the brightest crayon in the box had exploded. Streaks of black undulated through the orange like snakes.

I had no problem with snakes in general, but I sure didn't like the look of that.

She looked younger than the other one, but felt older, as if she'd seen things no one her age should have to.

They were clearly waiting for Red and me, judging by the way they glanced up as we entered and locked their gazes on us, and then on me as Red peeled away to lean against the dining table for a wider view of the conversation.

I looked to Addie, who sat beside the frizzy-haired girl. She flashed a wry grin that was gone as quickly as it appeared.

So, frizzy hair was the witch.

I looked at Sunday, standing guard by the front door. She shrugged.

Miguel had taken up position at the opposite end of the living room, blocking the way to the kitchen and the back of the house. He nodded at the tattooed kid, and sent a mind touch my way. I answered his call, meeting him in the halls of his mind. This time, slipping in was easier than the last, as if by talking this way we were developing specific neural pathways for connection.

I know her, he said. *Not personally, but of her.*

How? I asked. *She's not an operative. Was she a target? Someone the Angel had an eye on?*

No, he said. *She's an apprentice to someone important.*

Who?

The serpent, he said. *You know, from the Garden of Eden.*

It took a moment to absorb that. I'd heard of the serpent—not just the one people read about as having tempted Eve, but the one who'd been condemned to human form and walked the earth, immortal. We'd been told about him in our training, although it was unlikely that we would run into him. The Order wanted us to steer clear. To say he was dangerous was an understatement. He had poison for blood, no respect for anyone but himself, and a twisted sense of poetic justice.

He took a human apprentice? I asked.

She's not entirely human anymore, Miguel said, *but, yeah. Story is that she got herself into some trouble with one of her local gods, and the serpent made her his apprentice to save her life.*

From what I'd been told about him, that didn't sound like the sort of thing the serpent would do. On the other hand, circumstances changed. People changed—even if the people in question were gods.

I slipped from Miguel's mind back into my own, focusing on the serpent's apprentice, reappraising. If he'd saved her life, if he'd been training her—she had to have something special.

The girl with the curly hair cleared her throat, turning her gaze toward me. "You're Night?"

"That's me. And you are?"

"Stacy." She cocked her thumb toward the serpent's apprentice. "This is Beth."

Beth tucked her phone into her back pocket, finally glancing around, sizing up each of us as I made introductions.

"Order operatives, huh? That's fucked up," she said.

"Yeah," I said. "It is."

"I never thought I'd get to meet one."

As if meeting one was a privilege. Or an adventure. Easy to see how this one might've gotten in the kind of trouble that required a god to save her.

Stacy rolled her eyes. "Well, now that that's out of the way, what am I here to witch?"

Down to business. I liked that.

Addie pulled the cube from her pocket. "This."

Stacy shifted in her seat to get a closer look. After a moment, she turned toward me. "Are you sure?"

"Why would you say that?" I asked.

"Things that old are better left alone," she said. "Working with them can have unforeseen consequences."

I knew all about those. And the girl wasn't stupid—I gave her that. "Are you willing?"

"Yes," she said.

"Just like that?"

She took her time answering, choosing her words carefully. "I've made hard choices before. I haven't much liked how things turned out most of the time. But I've chosen my side in this fight, and I'll do whatever it takes to win."

"All right," I said, turning to Beth. "What about you? What's your purpose here?"

"I'm her bodyguard," she said.

She was too small to be bodyguarding in the traditional manner and, as a witch, Stacy had plenty of magic to deal with unwanted attention. "How do you do that?"

Beth sighed. "I know things. Piece puzzles together. I see patterns that other people miss."

"That's not the same," I said.

"It's preventative," she said.

"That's it?" I asked.

She shook her head. "I'm also a deterrent. People leave me—and, by extension, the people I'm with—alone. Messing with me incurs my boss's wrath."

"I'm sure no one wants to incur that," I said, letting Beth know that I understood who her boss was. "What do you think?" I asked Stacy.

"I think she's annoying," Stacy said. "But also smart. And useful."

Beth folded her arms across her chest. She'd been told before that others didn't like her much.

"So, Beth," I said, "You're the serpent's eyes and ears, and you'll report to him what happens here."

She frowned at me. "I'm all the things. Malek likes Stacy. He doesn't want anything to happen to her. He also wants the deets on what goes down. All of the above."

Malek. That was the serpent's name. "Just say so next time."

"But I did," she said.

She was right. She had. Convolutedly. "Don't take so much time to get there."

"Fine," she said.

"What interest does Malek have in the fight?" I asked.

She took a deep breath, clearly gearing up to tell us a story. Then she took a look at my face and deflated a bit. "He's in the fight. He's helped save the human world more than once."

I was surprised to hear that. I let it show in my eyes.

"Don't judge a book, blah blah," Beth said.

I could see how Stacy found Beth annoying. I could also see how she endeared herself to someone like Malek. She was irreverent as hell. The very powerful didn't respect anyone who feared them. Sass was the opposite of fear.

"How long are you here?" I asked.

Stacy supplied the answer. "Until it's done."

I looked at Addie, who took over the questioning.

"You got another place to stay?" she asked.

Stacy shook her head.

"We're a little crowded here, but I'll make room for you. Who likes meatloaf and mashed potatoes?"

Beth raised her hand, a tinge of melancholy coloring her words. "My mom used to make it for me."

"Kitchen," Addie said. "We'll eat in there. Except you, Night. I'll put away plates for you and Faith."

"And me," Red said.

Addie gave him a nod of approval. "Send the rest of the kids down, will you?"

We waited for the parade of people to wind into the kitchen. The silence in the living room became a palpable thing.

Red walked over to me. "Ready?"

How could I ever be? I started to say something, then snapped my mouth shut as the Angel fluttered his wings around my heart. I pressed a palm between my breasts. I could feel the movement underneath the skin of my chest.

"Was that what I think it was?" Red asked.

I nodded.

"What does it mean?"

"I wish I knew."

Red hesitated. "You asked him?"

"I'd asked him everything I could think of, and he answered nothing except my questions at the gym. Those will do, but we could use more. I need to figure out how to ask the right thing in the right way."

"No," Red said. "You just need to keep asking until you get it right again."

I met his gaze. "Let go of frustration?"

"Is it helping?" he asked.

Frustration was good for nothing except signaling the need for a change of direction. So, no. I shook my head.

"There's your answer," he said. "Let's head up."

"I'm worried," I said. I'd meant every word I'd said to Addie about the final decision being Faith's, but the thought of actually telling Faith sent a shiver of fear up my spine.

"I know," he said. "Remember what you said to the kids back at the gym?"

"The only way out is through."

"That's it."

I sighed.

He leaned forward, resting his forehead against mine. He did not, bless him, say everything would be all right.

We found Faith in Jess's room, which, as usual, looked and smelled like a library. Walls covered with full bookshelves, mostly fiction. History and magic books stacked on the night table. Open schoolbooks stacked on the desk beside Jess's open laptop, where pics of Portland Trailblazers flashed as her screen saver.

Faith sat on the edge of the full size bed, picking at the hem of the purple comforter. She made room for Red and I to sit on either side of her.

"The thing the mentor wanted to see you about is me," she said.

Not a question. A statement. She knew. I'd wager she knew everything.

"I was listening," she said. "Well, not me."

The Awakened. How the god had gotten through the protections in Addie's basement was a mystery. Then again, it was a god.

"What do you think?" I asked.

"I think it's crazy that I have to think about it at all," she said. A heartbeat later, she burst into tears.

I wrapped my arms around her and rocked her as she sobbed and shook. Red held her hand, not saying a word even when she squeezed so hard, her knuckles bleached.

I'd been expecting her to break down, but she'd held it together. I'd wondered why and how—maybe I could've found out by slipping into her mind, but like lying, that was off-limits. Well, now I knew. She'd been pretending to be all right. I hoped like hell that she hadn't done that because she thought it was what we wanted or needed.

Nothing that had happened was okay. She didn't deserve to be the vessel for a god as an accident of birth or destiny. She'd never had a chance to give her consent. Not until now. And the pressure of choosing to give it or not was too much.

She let go of Red's hand, finally, and leaned back, wiping her eyes on her sleeve. Her silver halo swirled with gold. The motion was agitated.

She still had more tears in her, but she'd come to a stopping point.

"I want to try it," she said.

A question formed in my mind that I didn't know how to ask.

"You're wondering whether the god will let me," she said.

I met her gaze. "How did you know?"

"I know everything about the Awakened. Every conversation you have about the god. Every thought you try to protect me from. It's not something I can help. I know it because the god does."

"Jesus," Red whispered.

I knew what it was like to have another being inside of me, one with his own thoughts and motivations and plans.

"You want that to stop," I said.

"Yes," she said. "Whatever I have to do."

"Okay," I said.

She sniffed. "What's the worst that can happen?"

I glanced over her head at Red. The corners of his mouth turned down.

"The cure could have the opposite effect from what we intend," I said.

Faith took that in and turned it over in her mind. "That's the risk?"

I nodded.

"If I don't do it, I have no chance at all," she said.

I couldn't argue with that, and neither could Red.

"But let's do it tomorrow," she said. "It'll give me more time to get used to the idea."

I raised a brow, coaxing a soft laugh from her.

"As if that would ever happen," she said. "Right?"

I thought about Addie's admonition that this should be my choice, not Faith's. I thought about it hard. In the end, I came to the same conclusion as before.

I brushed the hair from her face. "We'll be right here with you."

"I know." She leaned her head against my shoulder.

I hoped it would be enough.

CHAPTER 6

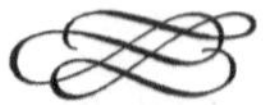

THE DREAM SWALLOWED me whole. I'd barely had time to take a breath after I closed my eyes before it captured me, drawing me down into unfamiliar territory. The images bore no resemblance to my usual nightmares—the greatest hits of tests the Order had forced me to undergo during my training. Instead, the landscape breathed white light. It streamed from the concrete beneath my feet toward a sky or ceiling I couldn't see.

When I breathed in, I tasted oil and metal and wood on my tongue. I drew in the scents of water and earth. The mournful cry of gulls pierced my heart.

I remembered those things from the warehouse, from the meeting with Lily and her operatives.

The white light had housed—or held—someone, but I hadn't been able to see them and Miguel hadn't been able to make out enough detail for an ID of any kind, only that the prisoner inside the light had been a man.

The Angel's wings fluttered inside of me. It felt as real in the dream as it did when I was awake. It had to mean something.

I'd ignored that feeling before. I'd wondered at it. I'd asked him about it, but he hadn't answered. I'd never slowed down to consider whether I could figure it out on my own.

I forced my breathing to slow and closed my eyes, not to try to escape the dream or to slip into another mind or to visit the Angel in his cage, but to slide deeper into my own mind. No—that wasn't the right place. I gathered all of my awareness into the shape of a ball and dropped it straight down, through my throat and into my expanding and contracting chest. Into my heart.

The rhythm of my heartbeat and the rush of air into and out of my lungs became my world. The pulse of blood through veins and arteries and capillaries. The Angel's sleek black feathers, wrapped around all of it.

I had a sudden vision of the Angel's body superimposed on mine, as if a creature as vast as he was had made himself my size and stepped into my body, enfolding my chest and belly—my internal organs—within his wings.

I understood now.

The Angel was protecting me. *Protecting. Me.* The woman who'd hurt him. Trapped him. He'd stayed when he could've gone, and he aimed to keep me safe.

If that was true, the movement of his wings had been a warning, or a sign that something important was about to happen and that I should take care.

The Angel's voice echoed in my head, as if I'd asked him the question directly.

Yes, he said.

Relief rushed through me, so strong it overwhelmed. This was a dream—not even mine—and whatever progress the Angel and I had made seemed too good to be true. Except that it wasn't. I couldn't explain it, but I had no doubt.

In this moment, the Angel had sent me a sign.

Someone—not the Angel—set their hand upon my shoulder.

I reacted instinctively. Stepped back into whoever it was, using my momentum to fuel an elbow strike to the gut.

My assailant sidestepped.

I spun to face them, and saw that they weren't an assailant at all, at least not a usual one. I stared into the face of the last person I expected to see. He wasn't a person at all, in the traditional sense. He was an archangel.

Michael.

I'd called for him in my moment of greatest danger and despair, hoping against all odds that he'd hear me. His blood ran in my veins, after all.

After the fight had ended, and we'd miraculously made it out alive, he'd shown his face. Not up close—he hadn't come over to help with the wreckage. He'd just taken a quick look and then gone on his way.

He looked exactly as I'd seen him last, standing down the street from the house where we'd faced down Shadow.

His hair was made of fire, writhing flames of orange, yellow, red, and blue. He had three eyes, two where I expected them to be and one in the center of his forehead. He wore golden armor that glittered like diamonds, and a sword with a golden hilt sheathed on his back.

Just as before, he became suddenly uninteresting. A regular-looking guy who threw off enough power to bend the air around his body—and, given how close he stood to me, the air around my body as well. He wore a pair of faded jeans and a black T-shirt embossed with faded white script that read *Ride the Lightning*. He had black hair, short and thick, and eyes the color of the sun.

His voice sounded like thunder to my ears, and like a tenor's whisper inside my head. "They need your help."

No *thanks for coming,* or even *hello.* "I needed your help. You declined to give it."

"This is not about me," he said. "It's about the children."

I blinked at him. "What children?"

He raised a hand. With a snap of his fingers, images appeared in my mind.

The street on which I'd grown up shrouded in darkness, the smoldering ruin of my parents' house down the way. Frogs sang in the shallow, over-grown ditches on either side of the road. I'd left Red's house and whatever salvation he'd offered. I didn't deserve salvation. I was bad. Everyone who was supposed to love me said so, and now they were dead.

The scene dissolved, another rising to take its place.

Sunday in the alley where she'd blinded and beaten her pimp to death, the smell of rotting trash and piss and stale wine tainting the air, the taste of blood in her mouth. She'd killed the only home she had now. She had nowhere to go. No one to turn to. Her heart—her soul—hurt so bad. She pressed a hand to her chest. A sob escaped her mouth.

The sob echoed until silence swallowed it, and the alley vanished like so much smoke.

Oak and ash trees appeared, their shadows stretching across a front yard full of itchy grass and dandelions. The huge, rhythmic chanting of cicadas made it hard to think. Miguel lay on the grass, head nestled atop his backpack. He'd sneaked out at two o'clock in the morning, intending to run somewhere—anywhere but here. But once he'd climbed out the window without waking either his aunt or the dog, he'd frozen. It'd taken every ounce of will he possessed to make it even as far as the middle of the yard. He'd hurt a friend this afternoon. Hospital-hurt him. He hadn't meant to. But Javier had —it didn't matter what Javier had done. It only mattered that Miguel had thrown a punch, and that his crazy strength had broken ribs and punctured a lung.

Lying here, he could hardly breathe. What if he hurt someone else? What if he hurt them worse?

The same big, black car that had come for me pulled up alongside the curb in front of him, brakes softly squealing as it stopped. It smelled of money and peril. Lily opened the door. She told him that he could belong somewhere. That he'd be safe there. That she could teach him. Hope kindled in his raw and broken heart.

The dream released me without warning. I flew back into myself as if I'd been launched from a slingshot. I sat bolt upright in bed, fist pressed to my chest.

Red came awake beside me, pushing up on his elbows. "Another nightmare?"

My breath came fast and hard. My heart pounded.

He pushed all the way to sitting. "The Angel?"

"Partly." I met his gaze. "I think it was a true dream."

I'd never experienced anything like it before. My dreams had never been more than just that—dreams. My nightmares had been thick of late, but it felt clear to me that what I saw in their depths was my subconscious working through discarded memories and reminding me of who I'd been during my early days in the fold of the Order, and what I'd felt before I'd grown to enjoy killing too much. If those nightmares were occasionally timely—I'd dreamed of Miguel only hours before he'd infiltrated my home—I'd never had an inkling that I could dream true.

"What did you see?" Red asked.

"Michael," I said. "He said there are children in trouble."

Red's eyes widened. "What children?"

I thought about the images Michael had placed in my mind. Miguel, Sunday, and me. The three of us had been children when the Order took us in. That was the way of things. Some magical children managed to make it on their own. The rest of us either died or went to the only place that would take us in and give us a place to belong.

"The ones the Order is gathering," I said.

He mulled that over. "I know what happened to you there because you've told me some of it. There's a lot of things wrong with what the Order does to kids. If it were up to me—if I could do it without dying —I'd burn the place down. If I could give every one of those kids a home, I'd do it."

I loved him for that. I could also feel a "but" coming. I waited.

"Why now? What's happening now that hasn't been happening since the Order came into being?"

"I don't know. Michael didn't say. But what he showed me—it was visceral. It feels urgent. When we met with Lily and the operatives at the warehouse, they were holding someone prisoner. We couldn't see who it was."

"Could've been a kid."

I nodded. "Could've been anybody."

I flicked the switch on the bedside lamp, illuminating the champagne- and white-striped wallpaper of Addie's guest bedroom, along with the pile of clothes I'd left there before crawling into bed.

The light helped me think. I didn't like the thought that came to me.

"I figured the Order had lost their reason for being when they lost the Angel," I said. "It's not that at all. It wasn't the Angel's agenda the Order was faithful to. It was his power."

"They lost their goddamn battery," Red said. "They need another."

"The kids—"

He interrupted. "They wouldn't do that. They need those kids, don't they? They'll become the operatives of tomorrow."

That was how it'd always been done. Maybe how the Order still ran things. Maybe not. All I could think of was my own kid, and where she would've ended up if she'd been any magical child. If she'd been raised by my parents, or Sunday's, or Miguel's.

Would the Order use the kids as a battery? Of course they would.

"Where is Miguel in all of this?" Red asked. "The chameleons?"

The chameleons would know about anything concerning the Angel—or his replacement. Which means that Miguel, as the one chosen by the chameleons to wrest control of the Angel from me, would have to have known. I frowned.

"Exactly," he said.

I climbed out of bed and searched my pile of clothes. I located my pants and pulled them on.

"You're gonna go talk to him now?" Red asked.

"Better now than later." I plucked my shirt from the pile and slipped it on, too. "We've got a big day tomorrow. Everything has to be on the table. If Miguel refuses to come clean with me—or to give me a satisfactory reason for not telling us earlier—I don't want him there."

Red swung his legs over the side of the bed and began to pull clothes from his own pile of castoffs.

"You're going, too?" I asked.

"Two of us who can tell what his shapeshifting ass is up to are better than one," he said.

Miguel and Sunday had been offered the sofas out front in the shuffle to make room for everyone who lived here in town and the additional two who'd come to help us. The temperature had dropped into the twenties after sundown, and they'd lit a fire before packing it in. The flames had burned down to glowing coals, the occasional spark breaking away to rise up the chimney.

Sunday lay facing toward the dining room—and any passersby—one arm propped behind her head. She hadn't bothered to undress for whatever reason—maybe she considered sleeping behind the front door to be guard duty.

She opened one eye to peer at us as we walked in. "Couldn't sleep?"

"The gods won't let me," I said.

She sat up. "What's going on?"

I inclined my head toward Miguel's sleeping form on the other couch.

"I knew it," she said.

I didn't want to hear that. "Don't tell me you told me so. Wake him up."

Sunday rolled to her feet, kicking the coffee table with her heel. The rug it sat on slid, and the table slammed, into the sofa where Miguel lay. He didn't move a muscle.

Sunday's brow furrowed. She reached for his arm and shook him.

He shook, all right. As if he were a hollow shell stuffed with straw.

She stared at him. "What the fuck?"

I bent and shoved the table out of the way. I laid a hand on Miguel's leg. For a second, it felt real. The feedback from my fingertips to my brain and what I saw aligned. But then the illusion fell apart.

A selection of throw pillows and blankets had been lined up on the sofa and spelled to look like Miguel. To feel like Miguel. The quick magic he'd created hadn't stood up to being played with for more than a minute.

He hadn't needed it to. He'd only needed us to believe he was there for as long as it took him to slip away.

"Sunday, how long have you been out?" I asked.

"Couple of hours," she said. "He's long gone."

Red had moved to check the door. "It's unlocked."

"Bastard left us vulnerable," Sunday said.

As if we weren't already—to Miguel in our midst, to the Order, to forces so big, we couldn't hope to stand against them. "The house spirit takes care of unwanted visitors. No one with bad intent can pass."

Sunday set her hands on her hips. "The house spirit didn't do a damn thing about Miguel."

Which meant what, exactly? "Any real threat should've awakened Addie."

"Unless he did something to her," Sunday said.

"No." No way something like that went down and no one knew a thing. But things I'd thought were settled fact seemed to be inverting at a scary rate. "I'll check on her."

I'd made it one step before Red's voice stopped me.

"Clever," he said.

"What is it—a booby trap?" Sunday asked.

He shook his head. "The deadbolt's not engaged, but there's a lock on the door all the same. A little piece of magic like the one Night keeps engaged on her own door, only with a lot shorter shelf-life. Only approved visitors allowed inside. No one could've walked through this door without getting blasted, and for sure not without us knowing."

So he'd lied to us, left in the middle of the night, and made sure we were safe? "That doesn't make sense."

Red turned the lock. "The magic will wear off by morning. Go on, Night."

"Check Sunday, will you?" I asked.

"Chameleon bullshit," she said.

"Sorry, darlin'."

"Just get it over with, Red."

I headed up the stairs and down the hall to the master suite, listening to them bicker.

Addie's door was shut. I knocked softly.

A moment later, she opened the door, glasses in hand. She slid them onto her nose. "What's wrong, Night?"

"I have to check you first," I said.

She said nothing, only waited while I slipped into her mind and riffled through her memories for one I didn't think Miguel would've had time to grasp in the time it would've taken to copy her.

I found something from her childhood, a moment in the afternoon sun on a family outing in the Ozarks. Seven years old—two years before she met Dream. She'd been out walking through the tall grass under the dappled shade of cedars when she'd come upon what looked to be a thick gray-brown stick lying in the grass. Only the stick also had hourglass markings all along the length of its body. Not a stick, but a snake in the grass. A venomous one at that.

I retreated from Addie's mind, not needing to know the outcome, given that she was standing right in front of me, wholly herself and healthy.

"I haven't thought about that day in a long time." She held up her thumb and forefinger, maybe a half inch apart. "I came this close to getting bitten. I couldn't tell you who was more afraid—me, or that copperhead."

"Lucky," I said.

"Mmm. You want to tell me why you're knocking on my door in the middle of the night and poring through my memories? This is Miguel, isn't it?"

I nodded. "He's gone."

"Left, did he?"

"You don't seem surprised," I said.

"He was worrying at something all through dinner. Some problem he couldn't solve. I could see it in his face."

Red and I had missed all of that, since we'd been with Faith. "There's more."

I told her about the dream I'd had and Red's and my suspicions.

"That tracks," she said. "And I agree it was a true dream."

"I have to do something about what I saw," I said.

"Yes, but it can't be reckless."

I shook my head.

"So Miguel's a traitor," she said. But her tone told me she still didn't seem convinced. "You were concerned he'd copied me."

"The house spirit didn't sound the alarm or eject him. We thought he'd done something to you, or to it."

"It's a she," Addie said, "so you should refer to her properly. And there's nothing wrong with her. She's here now. Can't you feel her?"

I quieted my mind a touch. Her presence became clearer. A touch on my skin. A caress of the back of my neck. The pressure in the air that I'd felt earlier, only dialed way down.

I nodded.

"I don't think there's anything to do about Miguel right now," she said.

"He could be on his way to Lily right now. He could be giving her every piece of information he's gleaned on us, including about the Angel. Including what he knows about Faith." I froze. "The spell we're performing tomorrow for Faith. It came from Lily."

Addie leaned against the doorframe. "You think Lily means to kill her?"

"Or steal her away and hook her up to the battery cables," I said.

She considered the problem, turning it over in her mind. "It's possible, but I don't think so. Did you sense any lie in Lily when she gave you the box?"

I shook my head.

"It sounds like your mentor is done with the Angel if they've got themselves a new source of power. And there's nothing that Miguel could possibly tell them about Faith that they don't already know or that they haven't guessed. Lily gave you that box for a reason, and not all of it has to do with Dream. They're hoping for something, too, although I seriously doubt it's the same thing you and I are hoping for. They're not going to interrupt the ritual tomorrow. In fact, I'd lay odds that they're out patrolling the neighborhood, making the place safe for life, liberty, and the pursuit of happiness."

I stared at her.

"You disagree?" she asked.

"No," I said. "But this whole thing is tainted worse than I gave it credit for. I don't want to do it at all."

"It's not up to you," she said. "You were right. Your daughter is almost grown. We've seen what she and the others can and will do without telling us, just like anyone else their age. If you don't allow her to do this in your presence, she'll find another way, and you won't be there to protect her."

I didn't want to hear her repeat my own words back to me. I couldn't deny them.

"What we need to worry about is what happens *after* the rite is over and we've either got Faith free of the Awakened or all hell has broken loose," Addie said. "Your Lily might come then."

"To take Faith, either way."

"Bingo."

"We need all the help we can get," I said.

"You'll have it, Night."

I combed my fingers through my hair. "I'll have Red check the kids, just in case."

"He's easier at it than you are."

"Yes, he is." Thank all the powers.

I didn't mind doing what needed to be done, but I was starting to mind spearing the private thoughts and memories of people I cared about. People ought to have some level of privacy, number one—a strange place for me to land after having spent so many years roiling through my targets' memories in order to kill them. But more than that, I knew that sooner or later I'd come across a memory or a thought I truly wouldn't want to know. Something that had been kept from me for a reason, or something so personal and private that my knowing would be hurtful.

"Then go to sleep," Addie said. "We're all going to need it."

Easier said than done.

The cries of children whose faces I couldn't see haunted me until daybreak.

CHAPTER 7

W E HAD A PLAN in place. Ben would add his shield to the house's already stellar protective capabilities—Addie was adamant that there was nothing wrong with the house spirit. Sunday would set traps at the entrances, with the strongest laid on the side door that connected the basement to the yard, and take watch while the rest of us were downstairs. That seemed like our best bet, whether or not Lily and her operatives came calling after the ritual.

Addie, Sunday, Red, and I had some discussion about letting our guests in on what had transpired or not, but in the end, full disclosure seemed like the best policy. What they didn't know could hurt us all.

By mid-afternoon, everyone except Sunday had gathered in the basement. Inside the curtain of Addie's protections, Stacy and Beth had positioned a nine-foot square of ocean-blue cloth, along with a pillow of the same color. Along the outside of the cloth, enough chairs for everyone had been placed in a circle, and outside of that, another circle of tea light candles, the last of which Stacy had just lit.

The witch wore white today, from her flowing lace top and skirt to the white polish on her bare toes. Beth wore black—leather vest and pants, along with her combat boots. The rest of us had been free to wear what we usually did. I'd added an additional item: a blade from

Addie's collection of magical objects, sheathed in the waistband of my black leggings.

It was the size of a pocketknife, and made from jade of all things, with symbols carved into its surface and leafed in gold. I had no idea what the symbols meant; they didn't come from any magical alphabet or system I knew. Addie insisted that the blade would be exactly what we needed, whatever that was.

I took her at her word. She knew I'd protect us with my life, and I knew she wouldn't let us down.

Melting wax perfumed the space, as did the herbs that Stacy had set into the tops of the candle—rosemary and lavender from Addie's front yard. Plants of protection, remembrance, cleansing. Stacy spoke prayers over the cloth and the cube, which Addie had given her. The gentle tone of her words seemed at odds with the power they contained. I could feel the magic that flowed from her tongue and emanated from her skin, calling down blessings and more protection, filling the circle with the juice she would need to unlock the cure for Faith.

Faith's friends milled near what would be the head of the ritual space. They whispered amongst each other, glancing my way from time to time. They'd already come by to hug Faith, who stood to my right, and to wish her well. She'd taken it all with as much grace as she could. The gold in her silver halo had dimmed because of her teenage human nerves. Her breathing came so shallow, I worried she might hyperventilate.

She'd dressed in white, just like Stacy, only on her that meant a white tank underneath a creamy cashmere sweater, white leggings, and white sneakers. The leggings were a little short since she'd borrowed them from Jess, but they fit just fine otherwise.

She'd knocked on my bedroom door early to ask a question that she wouldn't have asked if she wasn't terrified: could she borrow my hourglass pendant, the one Sunday had given me when we were still lovers, a symbol of what I'd been and what I'd become. My chance at a different life that I'd sworn never to waste.

I'd given it to her then and there. It was hers as long as she needed it.

She leaned into me, her muscles tense, nerves evident in the way she shook out her hands every few minutes.

I wished I could do the whole thing for her. That she could be safe and that the risk would be squarely on my shoulders.

Red stood on her right, and held her hand just like he had last night while she cried. He wouldn't let go until she asked him to.

He met my gaze. The ferocity in his eyes startled me, and filled me with the love I needed to keep myself grounded, to be what I needed to be for my daughter.

Addie, dressed all in white as well, stood behind the three of us. I felt her presence as life-affirming, and her power as a Watcher, monitoring the fabric of the space and the makings of all the people in it within her domain. She, too, spoke softly and with immense power, calling for blessings to rain down over the working.

Faith spoke low, her voice a harmony to Addie's melody, her words meant for me alone. "It's obvious that I'm scared."

I put my arm around her, pulling her closer.

"I need to know one thing," she said.

I waited.

"That whatever happens, you'll still love me."

My heart cracked open, the break sharp and painful. "Of course I'll still love you. You don't have to be anything, or do anything."

She released a breath she'd been holding in one long, slow exhale.

Stacy spoke the last of her prayers, then turned to us. "Time," she said.

Red pulled Faith into his arms, enveloping her in the solid, steady grass and earth of his magic. He hugged her tight and whispered in her ear.

"We got you," he said.

She held on to him, taking in his words and the truth behind them. When she pulled away and let go of his hand, she seemed stronger and he seemed a little less steady, as if he'd given her everything he had.

I turned to her, framing her face with my hands, letting the love I felt for her fill my eyes and breaking all over again to see that love reflected in hers. I kissed the top of her head.

"I'm right here," I said. Whatever fate had in store, I'd do every-thing in my power to make sure Faith was all right.

She nodded, then turned away.

Watching her walk away from me was the hardest thing. And watching Stacy take her hand to lead her onto the cloth, helping her to lie down.

As soon as Faith's head touched the pillow, she lost consciousness. Her nervousness, gone. Her tension, drained away.

Stacy placed the cube on the left side of Faith's chest, just over her heart. The candles around the circle flickered. Stacy spoke a word so thick with power that I couldn't make it out—then I realized that the word had not been in English or Spanish or any language of which I had command or understanding. She'd spoken in the language specific to Watchers, one that Addie had given to her.

The candles at the edge of the circle went out, trailing smoke into the air. For a moment, the space turned pitch black. I could see nothing and no one. Hear the huff of quick-drawn breaths and the shuffle of feet on the concrete floor. Across the circle, the kids mumbled to one another.

Then the cube began to glow, starlight rising from its night-velvet surface in all directions.

Stacy spoke the word once more. It echoed across the circle, rever-berating along the edges of the magical curtain, seeping in through my skin. Into the flow of my blood. Into the marrow of my bones. Into the heart of my cells.

The Angel's wings fluttered around my heart.

Time slowed. The molecules in the air seemed to separate, allowing me to see between them into the mystery happening before my eyes.

The black skin of the cube began to peel away from its core, folding itself into triangles, stacking one on top of the other until all that remained of the skin was a single, microscopic point. It hovered above the cube for an instant, then winked out of existence entirely, leaving only the sheer, shining starlight.

Stacy spoke the word a third time.

The starlight filled the room, turning all of us dark as night in its wake. Still the cube floated on Faith's chest, rising inch by inch until it hovered above her heart, waiting for one more thing. One essential thing.

Stacy's face turned ashen. She didn't know what it was.

Beth did.

The serpent's apprentice reached for her hand, twining her fingers with Stacy's, channeling the raw power of the serpent's blood inside of her, transferring the ancient magic to the one capable of completing the rite.

Stacy tilted her head back and screamed.

The starlight swallowed the sound whole. The cube sank like a stone through Faith's clothing. Through her skin. Into her chest.

She was my daughter. Not my blood, but something else—something better. She was my choice. I felt it when the starlight entered her heart. When it settled there. When it decided to stay.

Her halo shimmered with the light, the silver brightening to a blinding white.

Then it went dark.

A heartbeat later, it filled with gold.

The silver was gone. There was nothing left of it. Not a single thread.

My cracked heart shattered.

The candles around the circle flared to life again, the flames shooting high and filled with sparks.

Stacy passed out.

Beth caught her and pulled her away from Faith a moment before Faith sat up.

Beth laid Stacy down, then looked at Faith. "Hold," she said.

Faith pushed to her feet, wobbling before her balance settled. She still looked like herself, her long black hair and brown eyes and light brown skin. She still moved like herself, part awkward teenager and part woman. But her magic had shifted utterly.

The girl who met Beth's gaze was Faith—and not Faith.

Beth's bravado melted, her jaw falling open at what she saw in Faith's eyes.

"The Awakened," Beth whispered.

I pushed forward, but Addie moved around me, blocking my path. I raised my hand to push her out of the way.

She raised her voice. "Red!"

He wrapped his arms around me and dragged me back—not to comfort, but to hold me there.

I struggled against him. He gripped me tighter.

I could break his hold. He knew it. Addie knew it. They were counting on me not to.

As Addie stepped into the center of the circle, the overhead lights flared to life, washing away shadows and clearing the air of smoke and power. She slowed to a stop in front of Faith.

"You're here now," she said. "All the way."

Faith nodded. It looked the same as it always had, that gesture. But not the same. "All the way," she said, in her own voice.

Addie looked her up and down. "You take care of that child. You understand?"

Take care of my daughter, she meant.

"I will," Faith said, with the strength and promise of a sacred vow.

"You know what you have to do?" Addie asked.

"Gather them," Faith said. "I'll have to go away."

"I know," Addie said. "But I need you to do something for me first, please."

Faith seemed to know what Addie was talking about. I didn't understand.

Then Faith turned toward me, though she spoke to Red first. "Let her go. It's all right."

He did, reluctantly—and stayed close as a second skin.

"Night," Faith said.

I met her gaze and saw what Beth had seen. Raw power. Knowledge so ancient that it had no time, no place. And pure magic.

The Awakened *was* magic. She was the source. The place where all our sparks originated. She was home.

She was my daughter.

"I'm still here," she said.

Different words than she'd used with Addie, but then she'd been talking with her friend's aunt, and now she was talking to me.

"I'm whole," she said. "And I'm okay."

I stared at her. My voice shook. "Who are you gathering?"

"All those with the magic needed for the fight ahead."

That was a good thing, wasn't it? "You'll protect them?"

"I will."

The vow again. She would not break it.

"Do you have to go away?" I asked.

She nodded. "I know you don't want me to."

I didn't. I wanted to draw her close. Hold her tight. Keep her safe. Love her.

I'd promised to love her no matter what happened. I didn't know where we went from here, or how far she had to go, or how long she might be gone. I only knew what she needed to hear before she went.

"I love you," I said.

She heard me. I saw it in her eyes. And I saw that love reflected in her, shining back to me.

Then she vanished like so much smoke.

CHAPTER 8

"LET GO OF MY HEART," I said.

Red refused. He'd done something—no, something had happened while I'd been talking with Faith, who was no longer just Faith, but the Awakened as well. I could feel his heart beating in time with mine. I could feel his sadness and grief, tinged with red rage, as if it were my own. Wave after wave of it rolled over me, through me, pouring into and out of my heart.

I knew he felt everything I felt, too. The gut punch of loss. Terror at wondering where Faith had gone, what might happen to her there. Was she safe? Was she all right? And the building spiral of my own rage that threatened to overpower everything else.

I pushed a little, just enough to gain the physical space between us so that I could look at him. I marked the lines etched into his forehead, deeper than they'd been a half hour ago. His eyes had darkened so much, they were barely green now, and filled with unshed tears.

He met my gaze.

He wasn't holding on to me to keep me still any longer. He was holding on because he needed to.

I needed him, too. I made sure he saw that in my eyes. That he felt it, because I felt it. But we weren't the only two people in the room.

The terrible thing that had just happened affected more than just the two of us—the awe had rained down over all of us. And the confusion. And the loss. And it might not be over.

Lily and her people were out there.

"Please," I said.

He nodded, the first tear rolling down his cheek.

I brushed it away with my fingertips, cupping the nape of his neck and touching my forehead to his, breathing in his grass and earth. Then I let the emotional connection between us recede enough so that I could pull away.

I turned to face the others.

Corey had collapsed at the far edge of the circle. Ben had drawn her close, spooning behind her. Jess lay in front of her, brushing Corey's red hair from her face over and over again.

Stacy was still out cold in the center of the circle. Her ocean-blue halo faded and fragmented. Addie had laid her out where Faith had been a few minutes ago, in the center of the blue cloth, her head on the blue pillow. Beth knelt beside her friend, rocking back and forth. She'd taken Stacy's hand and pressed it against her own heart. Her face was a mask of grief. Her mouth moved—she chanted under her breath.

Stacy was in mortal danger.

Witching the cube had cost her everything.

I rushed toward her, shifting my consciousness to ask the Angel for what we needed as I moved.

He heard me, his wings unfolding, scraping the inside of my rib cage. He saw through my eyes, breathed the air I inhaled, tasted the aftermath of smoke and pain. He moved inside my body, his arms and hands within mine, his legs and feet moving us with increasing speed toward Stacy.

Addie glanced up and saw me—us—coming. She backpedaled out of the way.

The Angel and I knelt where she'd been, scanning Stacy's broken halo, taking stock of any injuries to her body. There were none.

The insult had been to her soul.

She'd pushed so hard to manage the final opening of the cube that she'd tapped the power of her soul in the process. She'd fed her goddamn soul to the thing, and now there was almost nothing left of her.

The Angel's voice rang in my heart. I knew what he would say before I heard it. Life and death were his domain, but souls were not.

There was nothing he could do for her.

Addie moved into the space beside us. She looked at me. Met my gaze.

I shook my head.

The Angel had saved her life, but he couldn't save Stacy's.

She closed her eyes, gathering her own power—her Watcher's magic that allowed her to tear apart or weave together the fabric of being. I knew what she was about to do because the Angel knew.

If she could find enough pieces of Stacy's soul out there some-where and weave them back together, she might be able to save Stacy —or most of her.

The girl would never be the same again. She'd never be whole.

I looked at Stacy and saw what Faith could've become had she been allowed to live a normal life. I didn't know whether I'd let Faith down, not taking more time to try to find another way—but we hadn't had the time. I would *not* let Stacy down. I'd find a way for her.

A way to lend my power to Addie. A way to lend the Angel's power. Something.

Beth leaned over Stacy's form and grabbed hold of Addie's wrist, interrupting the building of power, putting Stacy further at risk.

Addie opened her eyes. Stared at Beth.

"I can do this," Beth said.

Addie stared at her. "At what cost?"

Beth breathed in deep, her every word filled with a power greater than I thought she carried. "Whatever it takes. She's my responsibility. If there's a cost, I'll pay it."

"Not all of it," Addie said.

I didn't understand. Not until Beth turned to me.

"I need the jade knife," she said.

I pulled my blade and handed it to her. The jade wasn't sharp enough to do the job, not cleanly.

Beth took the blade to her wrist. It sliced through the skin like a razor. Her blood began to flow.

It had a halo of its own, a red glow that demanded respect—and distance.

Beth's blood contained the same venom as her master's, and she was going to use it to heal her friend. How could that be possible?

She smeared her hand red, and bent to draw on Stacy's brow. The symbol she drew—I didn't recognize it. But, like Beth's blood, it carried its own signature: a black halo, like my own.

The symbol sank into Stacy's skin, disappearing without a trace, and in that moment something extraordinary happened.

Stacy's halo began to knit itself together, its hue returning to its original ocean blue, then darkening to a deep indigo, so deep and dark and rich that it was almost black.

I exhaled a shaky breath.

The Angel spoke in my mind. *What she does for this one, the serpent did for her.*

That was how Beth had become the serpent's apprentice in the first place. He'd made her his in order to save her life. Did that mean that Stacy was bound now to Beth?

To Malek, the Angel said.

His blood—and Beth's—was poison. How could it have done this?

The working of it does not matter, the Angel said. *Malek has the power to bring a soul that has fled back into the body.*

Resurrection. How?

He ate all of the fruits of the Garden before he tempted Eve.

I couldn't go any further down that path at the moment. It was ephemeral esoterica. There was flesh and blood right in front of me.

I met Beth's gaze. "What now?"

The power in her seemed to be ebbing. "She'll sleep for a while. Then she'll wake up and want to kick my ass."

"You bound her to Malek," I said.

She pressed her lips into a thin line. "I have his permission."

"But did you have hers?" I asked.

"No," Beth said. "But tell me you wouldn't have done the same thing if you could've saved her."

The words stung after what had just happened to Faith.

Beth seemed to realize that a little late. "Sorry."

I glanced at Addie. "Did you know any of this would happen?"

She shook her head. "I only knew what to do in the moment afterwards."

There was blood spattered all over the cloth.

Beth licked my knife clean, then used it to cut a strip of the cloth to bind her wound. She handed it back to me carefully. "Clean that with alcohol as soon as you can. And step around anything red on the floor. Ms. Johnson, I'll need to burn this cloth."

"There's a grill out back," Addie said.

I pushed to my feet, leaving the logistical conversation behind. Red had headed over to help Corey and the others. He'd nudged Ben to let go of Corey, then slid his arms underneath hers to pull her to her feet. She leaned on Red, her legs unsteady.

I went to them. Whatever I could do, I would.

Ben and Jess looked at me with an equal measure of sorrow and pain. Corey turned her head when she heard me approach. Her face held no sadness, only rage.

She spoke low, her voice tight as a whip. "This is your fault."

I took the lashing. I said nothing. There was nothing I could say.

The thing that had been going on between Faith and Corey, the thing that I'd not yet taken the time to investigate, became obvious as hell. They were more than friends. What had happened to Faith had rocked Corey to the core like it had the others, but the wound was different. Deeper.

She threw an elbow into Red's ribs, shoving away from his grasp. She barreled into me as if she meant to tackle me, but she wasn't strong enough to topple me. She pivoted on one wobbly foot and punched me in the jaw, all the force of her emotion poured into her fist.

I braced for the blow and I took it. I did not return the punch.

She threw another that landed on my chest and a third strike to my gut before Red and Ben got hold of her and pulled her off of me.

She screamed at me. "Fight back!"

I shook my head.

"Fight back, damn it!"

I opened my mouth to speak, but no words flowed out. I could tell her that I was sorry. I could tell her my heart was broken. Neither would change a thing. It wouldn't make anything better. It would only hurt more.

Red and Ben penned her in, walking her through the protective curtain, heading for the basement stairs and into the house. Jess didn't follow them—not right away.

She closed the distance between us, her face unreadable, her halo pulsing with spiraling stars. I wondered whether she would hit me, too. Or worse, just leave me there.

She threw her arms around me and hugged me tight, surprising me so much that it took me a moment to hug her back. The gift of her warmth was a balm.

When she pulled away, her eyes were dry. She nodded at me, once. Then she made her way toward her aunt, offering to help move Stacy to a bed upstairs where she could sleep off what the witching and healing had done to her.

I turned to do the same, but didn't get the chance. Sunday stepped through the curtain, her halo dark and foreboding. The way she looked at me, Red had given her the summary.

"We have company," she said.

"Lily?" I asked.

She shook her head. "Her pet."

I'd expected him, but I'd also expected more. "What about the others?"

"Not here," she said.

I thought about the white light at the warehouse, and who might be imprisoned there. Whoever it was, they wouldn't have left him alone. "What's the pet want?"

"He's on the porch demanding to see Faith."

"Faith? He doesn't know?"

She shook her head.

I looked at Addie. "It's your house. I need your permission."

"You want to bring him down here," she said.

"Yes."

She looked me over, her Watcher's eyes missing nothing. She nodded. "Whatever you need, Night."

Between them, Beth and Jess hauled Stacy upright. Beth glanced my way. "If you want to use the knife, go ahead. Just don't let him cut you."

The blade still carried trace amounts of the poison in Beth's blood. Being cut by that blade would mean agony. It would certainly mean death.

I had my own ways of dealing death.

"I won't need the knife," I said.

I marshaled all of my feelings, condensing them into the finest point. I expected the Angel to retreat, but he did not.

He hadn't been able to help Stacy or Faith. I sure as hell didn't expect him to help me now. I didn't care one way or the other.

I met Sunday's gaze. "Bring him down."

CHAPTER 9

I STOOD ALONE in the basement, behind the shining protective curtain, amidst the remains of the magic that had transformed Faith and nearly killed Stacy. The hair on my arms stood on end. My heart beat faster. The circle of spent tea light candles on the concrete floor perfumed the air with wax and smoke, rosemary and lavender. I could still taste blood in the air, even though Addie had taken the blue cloth and pillow upstairs.

This time when Sunday stepped through the curtain, she had Lily's pet lion at her heels. She let him pass, taking up position at the edge of the circle, her magic risen and ready to strike.

The lion had pulled his gold-streaked, brown mane into a knot at the base of his skull. He wore the same black sweater and jeans that he'd had on the other day. They still fit him as if he were a fitness model. He still carried his knives, one sheathed on each side of his belt, and likely more concealed on his person. His halo glowed like a golden pelt in the sun.

The smug self-confidence I'd seen in his brown eyes before had muted a bit. But it was right there on the surface of his broken-glass voice.

He spoke over his shoulder to Sunday first. "I thought you were bringing me to her." Then, to me. "Where is she?"

"Gone," I said. "Where's Lily?"

He raised a brow. "Gone."

That had the ring of truth.

"You're taking an awful chance, coming down here alone." I paused, waiting for him to fill in a name.

"David," he said. "Did the ritual work? Did it cure the girl?"

I couldn't decide whether he truly didn't know, or whether he was stalling for time while the Order operatives he'd brought with him tried to find a way into the house. I took a second to reach for the house spirit, to feel her presence the way Addie had shown me last night. The pressure of her touch on my skin was all I needed to feel reassured that we were still under its protection.

I studied David's halo, which continued to shine—and which moved the same way that Lily's did, like skin over undulating muscle. The movement didn't seem coordinated, though, the way Lily's did. It wasn't discordant, either. Different parts of David's halo moved of their own accord.

I understood what he was a split-second before he struck—enough time for my magic to rise. Then he kicked me in the gut.

I let the momentum that forced me backwards carry me through a backward roll, rising to a crouch just as David's form shimmered and split into three, two copies flanking the original.

Three Davids. Three identical Order operatives.

Two were illusions, but those illusions could fight. They could kill.

Killing the original would not end the other two. All of them had to taken out.

David had meant for the odds to be three against one. He hadn't bargained on three against two, but he still had the numerical advantage. He had orders, and he would follow them. He had no doubt. No conflict in his mind. He had no grief or rage or despair.

I would give those to him. I would make him pay for Faith and Stacy and Corey. I would make him pay for the pain in my heart.

David One was already drawing a knife from his belt—balanced to throw.

I rolled forward as he launched the blade. It ricocheted off the concrete.

I caught sight of David Two charging to meet me at the end of my roll. I pushed off hard, driving a fist into his right knee. Taking him down with me.

The hairsbreadth of time and space I'd gained with that strike to the knee allowed me to slip into his mind. I seized upon the words he repeated to himself like a mantra.

You. Or her.

The words had come from Lily, who'd been his mentor. She'd locked him in a cage five days ago, intermittently withholding food and water, telling him he had no choice but to turn on his sister. She'd been brought into the fold with him. She was the only one he spent time with. The only person who knew why he woke every night, his face wet with tears.

It was either him or her. He knew what he had to do.

Lily pressured him daily—literally a magical wave of pressure that felt like a threat to survival, and was. He couldn't speak. He couldn't see. He couldn't breathe.

He couldn't face the choice. So he starved. And he thirsted. And he cried himself to sleep.

I pulled him into the memory, leaving him in his despair.

I rolled off of him, coming face to face again with David One. I could see past him now, catching a glimpse of Sunday as she broke Three's neck. He crumbled to dust as he fell. The dust disappeared before it hit the concrete.

David One pulled his second blade. He lunged at me—and simultaneously hitting me with the same pressure wave Lily had used on him. She'd used it on all of us.

I still managed to dodge most of the edge as it sliced across my stomach, slipping through shirt and skin as if I were made of paper. My blood welled. Spilled onto the floor. I couldn't move. I couldn't breathe.

My legs gave out. I fell to my knees.

Sunday kicked his hand. His blade went flying.

He kept his eyes averted from hers. He knew what she was. What she could do.

He threw a punch. She grabbed his arm and leveled a shot at his solar plexus that knocked him off balance.

When he lost his balance, he lost his pressure hold on me.

I sucked in air. I slipped into his mind.

He fought me, slippery where I tried to grab his thoughts and memories. But running from me meant running into hidden places where I might not be able to follow—places hidden for a reason. They were too painful to revisit. They were pain. They were destruction.

I had him, and I re-lived the memory with him.

Originally, Lily had wanted him to accuse her of murdering a fellow operative, one who'd already been culled. Once he'd agreed to do that, however, she'd upped the ante.

The night he killed his sister, he'd thought he could take her by surprise. He steeled himself against the betrayal, against the way she would scream, against the sight of her blood, of the light going out in her eyes.

He slid the blade into her gut—the most painful kill, the lingering death that Lily wanted. He looked into his sister's eyes as Lily had demanded, and he saw that she'd known what he'd been planning to do. Worse, she accepted that he had to do it.

It destroyed him. He'd never been the same. It didn't matter that she'd forgiven him. He couldn't grant the same grace to himself.

Some things were unforgivable. Some sins couldn't be prayed away.

I grabbed hold of his slippery mind and pinned him right there, in that moment. I grabbed him by the neck and squeezed.

Where's Lily? I asked.

I told you, he said. *Gone.*

I squeezed harder.

Gone to HQ, he said, gifting me with an image of the place where I'd come of age as a killer.

The Order hadn't bothered to move. No one would challenge its supremacy. It was legion, and we were few, fighting to survive.

What about the human? I asked. *The woman in red?*

With Lily, he said. *She's been stripped of her magic. Lily keeps her.*

I didn't know how someone's magic could be taken away utterly, but I'd heard David's tone when he'd said "keep." He meant "held," as in "held prisoner."

As in "pet," he said. *Lily treats her too good. Like she means something. Like she matters.*

I tucked that piece of information away to use later. Anyone who mattered to Lily could become my leverage.

Miguel?

He seemed confused by the question. *Your friend? Haven't seen him.*

I searched him for a lie, but found none. I had only one other question for him.

Who's trapped in the white light? I asked.

He stopped answering questions then. He went still and silent, and I saw that nothing I could say or do to him would change that.

I slid out of his mind, leaving him in the depths of his grief.

I came back to myself on all fours, my blood seeping from the wound in my belly to fall on the concrete. Sunday helped me to my feet, her hands moving the soaked fabric of my hoodie and tank to check the cut.

I pushed at her hands. "No."

She studied me. "I took care of the other one. He's the only one left."

"I've got everything from him we're gonna get," I said.

I pulled the jade knife from my pocket. I'd told Beth I wouldn't need it, and that remained true.

Inside me, the Angel fluttered his wings.

Put the operative out of his misery, he said.

I knelt over David. He was trapped in his memory. He had no ability to see his death coming, nor cause to fear me any longer. I slid the blade between his ribs.

I let him writhe for a long moment before I pierced his heart.

When I looked up again, Red had come through the curtain and frozen in place, his jaw hanging open. It took me a moment to grok that the emotional connection we'd spontaneously built after Faith had vanished had receded, but wasn't gone entirely.

He'd come running because I'd been in danger.

He'd seen what I'd done. He'd felt all of it—my fight to survive, my fierce anger, my lust for the kill. He'd felt the Angel urging me on, and the pleasure I'd taken in the operative's suffering.

I didn't regret any of it, and Red felt that, too.

He took a step toward me.

Sunday blocked his path. "Wait."

His voice trembled. "She's hurt."

"I'll see to her," Sunday said.

He shook his head. "She won't hurt me."

She clearly thought I might. My breath came hard. My magic was up. The Angel was close beneath my surface.

I left the jade knife in the operative and pushed to my feet. I met Sunday's gaze and held it.

There were things she understood that Red never would, things about me that she would always know better, see better, feel more deeply because she'd experienced them herself. I slowed my breathing as she watched, and ran my bloody hands through my hair.

"It's okay," I said.

She knew what I did—that it wasn't okay, and no amount of killing would change that. It might be all right again someday, but it would never be the same.

She moved out of Red's way, allowing him to reach me first, but she followed and made enough space to look at my wound.

"It's not bad," she said.

I tried to greet that as the good news it was. "Get me out of here."

Red placed his hand in the center of my back. "You okay to walk up the stairs?"

"If we go slow," I said.

I grabbed Sunday's wrist.

She shook her head. "Don't tell me to back off again."

"It's not about that," I said. "Don't touch the knife. Don't let anyone. Get Beth. It's her blade now. I don't think Addie would disagree."

"Ten-four." Her eyes filled with sadness.

I could tell she was on the verge of telling me how sorry she was about what had happened with Faith.

"Not now," I said.

She swallowed her words and swallowed her tears, too. "Ready?"

I nodded.

She and Red led me out of the curtain, up the stairs, and into the afternoon light.

The front room was empty. The kids had retreated to their room upstairs. Stacy was upstairs, too, sleeping in Addie's bed. Stacy might remain out for a few more hours, or through the night to morning. No way to tell.

Sunday went up to get Beth while Addie ushered me into the kitchen, where she'd set out the first aid kit and a pot of tea. She cut off my hoodie and my tank, refusing to let me try to pull them off the usual way, which might open the cut further. I didn't want to be ordered around. I didn't want to be touched, but I needed it. So I sat there in my bra while she took her sweet time cleaning and disinfecting the cut, which was not as deep as I'd feared and or as wide, and situated just south of my rib cage, left side.

Red leaned against the counter, sipping the tea from a mug the size of my head. He was a coffee man. He didn't even like tea. I could feel, though, that if he didn't keep his hands busy, they'd start to shake.

He'd pulled into himself, the magical connection between us broken. I couldn't feel what he felt. I could only imagine, and pay attention. And worry.

Sunday came back ten excruciating minutes later.

I opened my mouth to ask the questions that needed to be voiced, but Sunday interrupted me.

"Yes, Beth is handling the knife. Yes, I did a sweep. No holes in the defenses and no obvious Order activity outside. I think David was it—

at least for now. You get anything from him while you were in his noggin?"

"Lily and her human in red went back to HQ. Presumably, they took whoever was trapped inside the white light. David refused to give me an ID. That's the part that fits together."

"What's the other part?" she asked.

"Two things. One, he told me that the woman in red had her magic stripped."

Sunday's eyes widened.

"I know," I said. "Two, he said he hadn't seen Miguel. He wasn't lying."

She mulled that over. "Seems like that'd be the first place Miguel would go if he'd betrayed us."

Red cleared his throat. "I don't think he did."

I stared at him.

"Yeah, he left in the middle of the night, and he lied about what the Order was using the Angel for—or he conveniently left out parts of the truth. Same difference."

Sunday nudged him with her elbow. "You're not making your case."

He took a breath of air and patience, and went on. "He locked the door behind him. He didn't leave us vulnerable. He didn't outright tell us anything false—you know, something that having the wrong impression of could get us killed. He helped as much as he could. And he didn't go running to Lily. Maybe he's up to something else."

"Yeah," I said. "Maybe he went back to the chameleons."

Addie shook her head. "You think he's been playing that deep all this time?"

"It's been a little over a week, Addie," I said.

"You people are a goddamn eternity," she said.

Sunday nodded. "She's right. We are. Also, I don't think he could manufacture the type of connection he made with you the night of our showdown with Shadow. I think you'd have known. Which means he's on the up-and-up. He aborted his mission to kill us all and took up with us instead. The chameleons wouldn't take him back. They'd slit his throat and be done with it."

I bought every word. I still didn't want to believe it.

"You're just looking for someone to be angry with," Addie said.

I met her gaze and held it. "Yes. I am."

Killing David the lion had only helped temporarily.

Addie placed a piece of sterile gauze over the wound. "Hold this."

Once my hands were in place, she sat back in her chair and spoke over her shoulder to Sunday. "This needs stitches. We can take her to an urgent care, but this isn't *Honey, I had an accident with the carving knife.* They'll have questions, and they'll probably have to report it."

Sunday pushed off from her perch at the counter. "I'll take care of it."

Addie nodded. "There's a smaller kit inside this one. It's got everything you'll need. Make sure you disinfect—"

Sunday waved her off. "I know the drill."

"I'm sure you do." Addie rose to make room for Sunday to take her spot. "Red, why don't you come with me?"

"Where?" he asked.

Addie gave him a pointed look. "I want to talk to you."

He set down his mug with care and followed Addie out of the room without a word. I stared after him. Sunday did, too.

"He looks like he's ready to punch something," she said.

He did. I didn't know what Addie could possibly say to him to curtail that desire. "I know how he feels."

"I'll bet you do." She located the stitches kit and the alcohol to sterilize everything, then got to work.

I sat in silence while she prepped, holding myself together by the thinnest thread, until she sat down in front of me and gently pulled away the gauze.

"Got to rinse this out again, just to be sure," she said.

I gritted my teeth while she did. I gritted my teeth to keep from screaming.

She startled me when she lifted my chin with her fingertips.

"Sit up straight," she said. "This is going to be awful. No anesthetic."

"It's a shitty first aid kit."

"It's a first aid kit for people who don't have knife fights, but better than normal because it's Addie's," she said. "Sit up straight or I'll lay you out on the tabletop and tie you there."

I did what I was told, although I didn't much feel like being ordered around. Or like being alone with Sunday. I didn't want to hear all the things I knew she would say. I trembled when she made the first stitch, exhaling with a hitch in my breath.

She waited until I stilled, then made the second stitch. "It was always going to end this way."

I glared at her.

"The Angel told you so in the beginning. He tried to take Faith, not you. He told you that, by doing so, he'd be saving her from this fate. You said no. You had your epic battle. You locked him in your mind. But the Awakened's magic started to come alive in Faith and nothing any of us could do was going to stop it. It was inevitable."

My voice came out a whisper. "Don't say that."

"Someone has to, and you need to hear it. The worst case hasn't happened, Night. The Awakened didn't erase her the way the Angel would've. She's still in there. You can still talk to her. Get through to her."

Even if that was true, it didn't change how I felt.

I said nothing while Sunday finished the rest of the job, mostly holding my breath until she tied the knot and cut the end of the thread.

"There's a waterproof bandage in the box," she said. "How thoughtful."

She wiped the area around the wound clean one more time. After the alcohol had evaporated, she placed the bandage and pressed it to my skin. Her hands were gentle. Loving. It was more than I could take.

"She's gone," I said.

I felt Sunday's eyes on me. It took everything I had in that moment to look at her face.

"I know," she said.

I pushed back my chair and stood up. I felt a little woozy, gripping the edge of the table to catch my balance.

She shot out of her chair so quickly, the legs scraped the tile. "You got it?"

I nodded.

She didn't ask a second time. Sunday didn't go in for second guessing, even if she could see I needed more. She respected me enough to let me tell her what I needed. It was one of the reasons I loved her so much.

She still walked me to the guest room and saw me through the door.

"You can take a shower with that bandage," she said.

I gave her a small smile. "I know I've got blood in my hair."

"You've got blood in more places than that." She leaned me against the wall, because that was where I wanted to be, then pressed close and kissed me on the cheek. "You call me if you need me."

I reached down and took her hand in mine.

She studied my face for a moment. "I need to see to the operative."

Right. There was a dead body in the basement.

"See you in a while," she said. "Okay?"

"'Night," I said.

I didn't take a full breath until the door nicked shut behind her.

The room was silent, and the silence was deafening. Outside, the day was dying, the last of the light filtering in through the wooden blinds in the single window. The white shade on the night table lamp had been knocked askew. The bed Red and I had slept in last night lay unmade, as if we'd just climbed out of it, as if we had the whole day ahead of us. The red wool throw on top of the comforter felt too bright. It hurt my eyes.

I took careful steps to the bathroom, wishing like crazy that I'd asked Sunday to unhook my bra. I managed it very slowly. I avoided looking into the mirror above the porcelain sink and concentrated on logistics. Pulling back the yellow shower curtain. Hot water, but not too hot. Stepping into the tub without falling over.

The spray washed away the blood. The warmth penetrated the shell I held together by a thread. My legs gave out.

I hugged the wall. Turned around and slid down until I couldn't slide anymore. There was no one left to hide from. Nowhere left to go. Nowhere left to run.

The tears came.

CHAPTER 10

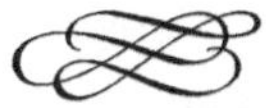

I SNAPPED AWAKE in darkness, with only a sliver of moonlight breaking through the window blinds, as Red climbed into bed beside me. I breathed in his grass and earth, the solidness of him, the scent of his skin.

I didn't remember how I'd gotten from the shower to the bed, or falling asleep, or dreams. I had no idea how I'd done any of that. My eyes felt swollen and painful. A dull throbbing had settled into the back of my skull, and the wound under my ribs stung. My heart ached.

"Didn't mean to wake you," Red said softly, rolling onto his side to face me.

A lock of hair fell across his face. I reached out with tentative fingers to brush it away.

He wrapped my hand in his and pressed it to his heart. "I checked on you earlier. You were passed out, and I just wanted to let you sleep."

How long had I been out? "What time is it?"

"Ten-thirty."

Five hours, give or take. I felt like I could sleep for days. I knew I wasn't the only one. "How's Stacy?"

"She's on the sofa out front stewing."

A wave of relief washed over me. "She's pissed at Beth?"

"Understatement," he said. "But she's alive."

The only person who'd died yesterday had been a man who'd deserved it. I wished that brought me more comfort. "Corey?"

"Jess talked her down. She's less angry, more heartbroken. She still blames you."

"I deserve it," I said.

He shook his head. "There was nothing you could've done. I know what I saw. I talked to Sunday. I know what she told you. Night, this whole thing is so far above anything any of us was prepared for—even you, with all your training. This is universe-spanning powers and fate and destiny and God only knows what else. How can any person, no matter how strong they are, or how smart, take the reins with this?"

I didn't want to hear any of that. I wanted there to be something I could've done. I turned it all over in my mind.

If I'd never met Faith, another operative would've killed her. If I hadn't taken her with me, hidden her—the same. If the Angel hadn't come to town…I could add everything that had happened since that day to the list.

The Awakened had been a part of Faith since birth.

Sunday had been right. Red was right. And blame never fixed a fucking thing. Getting off my ass, working a problem, solving it, making my choices and standing by them—that was the only thing that had ever worked.

I swallowed hard. I knew the answer to my next question before I asked it, but I had to ask. I had to hear it out loud. "Any sign or word from Faith?"

"No," he said. "It might be awhile."

"It might be forever," I said.

"Not likely." He stroked a thumb across the top of my hand. "She has a job to do, Night. She's the magic."

"She's sixteen," I said.

"She's *your* daughter."

I'd never trained her as well as I'd wanted to. But she had basic self-defense. She knew how to run. How to hide. And she had the Awakened.

"She'll be all right," he said. "We're in a fight—God, it's startling to even say it—we're in a fight for the whole world. For all the worlds. She's drawing forth people's power. She's gathering the troops. She'll be back, and not just because we're part of the fight."

I took in his words. I took them to heart. I thought, too, about what Sunday had said. "Faith is still in there."

He nodded.

I took a deep breath and let it flow out again. I studied his face. The lines on his face were still deep, and the color of his eyes had settled at an exhausted moss green.

"Have you slept?" I asked.

"What I could get on the other sofa," he said. "It'll do. You need to talk more?"

I shook my head. "It's enough for now."

"Close your eyes again?"

"No." Now that he was here, I wanted to be with him. "Can tell you something?"

He waited.

I'd seen his face, felt what he felt, after Faith had gone. I'd seen him try to keep his hands from shaking in the kitchen while Addie worked on me. He looked calm and solid on the surface, but I knew he didn't feel that way underneath.

"You don't have to pretend you're all right if you're not," I said.

He stared at me. The muscles in his jaw worked.

I thought I'd insulted him, or made him angry. But after a moment, a weight seemed to lift from him.

"I'm trying to be strong for you," he said. "For all of you."

"I know," I said. "You can only do that for so long before you break."

"I can't talk about it," he said. "I can listen to you, but I can't...."

He trailed off and averted his gaze.

"You don't have to," I said.

He stared at me. "You're talking about the magic between us. The connection."

I nodded. I didn't understand how it had happened the first time, on the night we'd fought Shadow. I didn't know how it'd happened this afternoon during the ritual. I only knew that if it'd happened twice, it could happen a third time.

He sighed. "I'm not proud of everything I'm feeling. I'm not sure about some of it."

I didn't want to step on that. "It's up to you."

"What do you want from me, Night?" he asked.

"What's real," I said.

He let go of my hand and pulled me close, smoothing my hair with his hands. I felt his magic reach for mine. My heart bloomed gradually, and then all at once, like a rose, the opening so painful, my breath caught in my throat.

I didn't hold anything back. The grief and love I felt flooded through the connection between us, still raw and wild, tempered only by exhaustion and sleep. It burned like a watch fire, sending flares into the dark.

He sent a flow of his own, wave after wave that threatened to overwhelm. I let them wash over me and through me. I let them be what they were, no more and no less. I made more room for him in my heart. I felt what he felt.

Fear for the child he'd begun to love as if she were his own. Grief at what had happened to her. Faith in her—that she might be the last, best hope we had.

Love for the others. Corey, Ben, Jess. The deep need to shelter them. To keep them from harm. To make the world better for them, whatever it took.

Fear of what he'd seen me do to the Order operative, and at what I'd felt while I'd done it. Fear of the Angel—that the Angel's endgame might be the destruction of everyone and everything he loved, that the Angel had hooks into me that I wouldn't be able to dislodge.

Lastly, love for me. Absolute trust.

He took me by the shoulders and drew back so that he could see my face, searching my eyes for a sign that I accepted what he'd shown me. That I didn't hold his fears against him. That I reflected the love and trust he felt.

I lifted a hand to cup his cheek and leaned close to show him, brushing his lips with mine. He returned the kiss, deepening what I'd started, drawing me to him until I couldn't tell where I ended and he began. His fingertips skimmed down my back, then followed the curve of my hip, rising along my waist. He reached to cup my breast.

Too close to the newly stitched wound. I winced.

He pulled away, his voice a whisper. "Sorry."

I shook my head. I wanted love. I wanted life. "I want you."

He looked at me in disbelief, even though I knew he could feel my heart as I felt his.

I took the hand he'd drawn away and kissed his fingertips. Then I slid his hand down my belly and between my legs, to show him I meant what I'd said.

He kissed me again. This time, he didn't stop. Worry and fear fled before desire like ghosts in the night.

I rolled him onto his back, tasting the sweetness of his mouth, the delicate skin of his eyelids, the salt skin of his neck and his chest. He fisted his hands in the sheets, holding onto control until he couldn't any longer. After that, I lost track of where I ended and he began.

I gave him all the fire I had—all the love, all the life—and he returned it in equal measure.

The morning would come soon enough.

CHAPTER 11

I DROVE EAST into the sunrise. I'd left a note about where I was headed and said I'd be back in an hour or two. I could think of better ideas than going out alone after what had happened yesterday. I could think of worse.

The clouds had blown away overnight, the sun blessing the sky for the first time in weeks. I cut over to Marine Drive as quickly as I could. The wide ribbon of the Columbia mirrored the fir trees on the other shore, and the sunlight glittered on the water. The mountain was out—Mt. Hood in all its snow-capped glory graced the horizon.

The beauty hurt my heart and at the same time felt like an offer of grace. I didn't quite know how to navigate the world I found myself in now. What was done could not be undone. I would have to learn. I cranked up the radio, pouring my hurt into Soundgarden's driving beat and soaring guitars.

A handful of miles east, I turned off toward the warehouse where we'd meet Lily and her people, parking in the lot and giving the place the once-over for any obvious or not-so-obvious magical or physical traps they might've left behind. I saw nothing. No evidence that anyone had been here at all.

David had told me that Lily and the woman in red had left town.

I'd believed him then, and I believed him now, but I'd awakened beside Red with the feeling that I'd missed something. I'd slipped from the warmth of our bed and out the door on the promise of that feeling.

I drove around back, parking on an empty side street. Gulls and crows wheeled overhead. A commercial plane roared past, flying out of PDX, destination unknown. A gust of wind whipped my unzipped black coat and black tee, chilling me to the bone.

The air smelled of water and warmth—and amber and vanilla.

I paused my step. "You've gotta be kidding me."

Sunday stepped from the shadow of the warehouse. I hadn't seen her in my initial scan, which freaked me out. She was good, but I was obviously off. I didn't belong out here. Not yet. My grief remained huge, flowing and ebbing like the tide. It did not, however, dwarf the impending Apocalypse.

Sunday carried two large coffees, one with pink lipstick imprinted on the lid. She handed the other to me. "Couldn't let you go alone."

"You kept an eye on my bedroom door?"

"I'd put a bell around your neck if I thought it would help." She sipped her drink and shrugged. "I asked the house spirit to let me know when you left."

"When, not if?"

She gave me side-eye. "I knew where you would go. I'd already walked half a mile for coffee, so I called a car. You're welcome."

The distance had taken its toll on my latte, but the thought counted for a lot. "Thanks. The house spirit calls long-distance?"

"Across a mile or so radius, according to Addie." She noted my change of clothes. "You went home?"

"I needed something fresh," I said. And a shower in my own bathroom.

"Did it go okay?" she asked.

"I can change my own shirt."

"I meant—"

"I know what you meant." I held up a hand. "Sorry. I'm raw as hell. I couldn't go into her room. I just did what I had to do and came here."

"It's okay," she said. "We can talk about it later."

Thank all the gods and powers in all the worlds. "Hallelujah."

"But we will talk about it."

I held her gaze for a moment. She wasn't going to take no for an answer. I didn't blame her in the least. I inclined my head toward the warehouse. "You been inside yet?"

She shook her head. "Doors are locked."

"I brought my tools," I said.

"Of course you did."

I winked at her, pulling the wee kit from the back pocket of my jeans. I picked the lock, no problems, and shoved the door open on creaking hinges. The place was mostly dark—except for the light that flowed in through the high windows. And except for one extremely bright column of white light situated in the same place we'd seen it before, in the center of the warehouse.

Sunday glanced my way. "What the fuck?"

I reached for the plate on the wall, flicking all the switches with one hand. The light chased away every shadow in the place. The desk that had been there the other day was gone. The office was empty. There was nothing except the column of white light.

"They left us a trap?" Sunday asked.

I couldn't see the point of that. Lily wouldn't have sent David after me as a distraction. He'd been meant to do real damage. If she expected me to be down for the count, there was no need for a trap.

I shook my head. "A message, maybe."

"If they expected us to come back," Sunday said.

"If you know me, Lily sure as hell does."

She gave me the point. "You know how to open one of those things?"

I started to say no, but the telltale flutter in my chest said otherwise. "The Angel does."

Sunday started toward the white column. "I'm not sure how I feel about that guy."

I goosed my step to catch up. "Me either."

"He's helpful, but also evil," she said.

I looked at her. "He's a natural force. That means he's evil under certain circumstances, but not all."

"Careful with how you're parsing that," she said.

We came to a halt in front of the light column—not wanting to be swept into it, so not too close.

"What now?" she asked.

I closed my eyes, allowing my magic to rise, reaching for the Angel. He lifted my hand and traced an equal-armed cross on the outermost layer of the light, imbuing it with his magic, not mine. I could taste the grave in it—wet earth and rot—but I couldn't make out anything else. It was too dense, too complex, to take apart in the moment.

When I opened my eyes again, Sunday stood at the ready, her magic on tap in case whatever—whoever—Lily had left us meant us harm.

"That's it?" she asked.

"Not quite," I said.

I curled my hand into a fist. When I glanced at it, it didn't look like my hand. It looked enormous, and ancient, and filled with the kind of strength only an elder or a god might possess. I settled on the balls of my feet, putting all of my weight and the Angel's weight into my fist, and punched the wall of light.

It shattered like glass.

Shards of light exploded upward and outward from the column, scattering along the concrete.

There was someone inside, all right.

Miguel collapsed into the spot where he'd been standing for the last forty-eight hours, fingers twitching and feet working as if he were trying to gain a hold and climb to his feet. After a moment, he gave up. His consciousness fled.

He looked exactly the same as when we'd last seen him except that his braid had been hacked off at the base of his neck.

Sunday pulled a blade from back pocket of her jeans.

"Wait," I said.

Sunday glanced at me. "I told you I didn't trust him. He's been with them the whole time."

"Imprisoned with them," I said. "Let's wake him up first. If you don't like his excuse, then you can stab him."

She lowered the knife, but didn't put it away.

One foot in front of the other. Next steps. Miguel.

I could simply slip into his mind, and I would if I needed to. But I'd also heard what Red had said about him, that Red didn't believe Miguel had betrayed us. I wanted to hear Miguel's explanation from his own mouth.

I hunkered down in front of him. I shook his shoulder. I slapped his cheek. Neither worked, so I finally pulled the lid off my coffee and poured it over him.

"I bought that especially for you," Sunday said.

"It's lukewarm."

Miguel sputtered, shaking off the coffee like a wet dog. He looked my direction, squinting at me, his eyes foggy. "Night?"

"Me, too." Sunday crouched beside me, brandishing the blade.

His brow furrowed. "What happened?"

"That's what we want you to tell us," I said.

"I remembered something about the white light," he said. "Something clicked in my mind about the Angel."

"What's that?" I asked.

"What the Order was using him for," he said. "That he wasn't there voluntarily."

I glanced at Sunday.

"You expect us to believe that?" she asked. "You're a chameleon, for crying out loud. You spent more than half your life being transformed into a magical being who could take care of the Angel. Serve him. And now you're all, 'I didn't know'?"

Miguel propped himself up on his elbows, trying to get the right angle to look her in the eye. "You ever serve in a religious order?"

Sunday rolled her eyes.

"Seriously," he said. "Do you understand what it means to be indoctrinated? To believe? There's no room for questions. You ask them, you're culled. And a being as powerful as the Angel? Who in the Order is strong enough to hold the Angel of Death against his will?

"Night did it. We've been over that already."

"Night has Michael's blood in her veins," Miguel said.

"Michael imprisoned the Angel?" Sunday shook her head.

"Come on," he said.

I stepped forward, offering him a hand. He took it, maneuvering to sit.

"When you initially told me about Michael, you mentioned that there was one other angel with the potential to trap and hold the Angel of Death," I said.

"Right," Sunday said. "Lucifer. He spends all his vacations from Hell topside, at the Order, jailing Horsemen of the Apocalypse. That's just ridiculous."

Miguel closed his eyes for a moment. When he opened them again, they were clear. "Lucifer doesn't live downstairs, Sunday. He's in the world, and he's not the Devil."

"Then who is?" she asked.

"I don't know, but I'm beginning to think that there is one."

Which was no answer at all—except that the Order clearly had a plan that we were only just discovering the existence of. They had to be marshaling their power for a greater purpose. Before, I'd been sure that it had involved the Angel's destiny. Now I knew better—or I suspected.

I didn't want to waste my time here arguing theology, especially since theology as I understood it bore no resemblance to Miguel's reality.

"Why did you come here?" I asked. "What triggered your curiosity?"

"Because the gate that led from the Order to the In Between to the angelic realm where the Angel lived was made of the same white light. I saw a kid inside the column when we were here before. I needed to know who they'd trapped. More than that, I needed to save him."

"Some random dude?" Sunday asked.

Miguel glared at her. "Can you give me the benefit of the doubt just once?"

"No," she said.

Miguel pressed his lips into a fine line. "Dude's not random. The Order doesn't do random. Lily doesn't do random."

Sunday nodded reluctantly. "So who was it?"

He rubbed his eyes with the heels of his hands. "I don't know, but I got the impression whoever he was, he wasn't from this time."

Sunday stood, pacing away from him. "This just keeps getting worse."

"Did you catch a glimpse? Get a name?" I asked.

"Charlie," Miguel said.

Sunday turned on her heel. "Last name?"

Miguel shook his head.

I looked at her. "What is it?"

"I got a chill," she said. "I'm thinking this is someone I know."

"From a different time," I said.

She nodded.

"How's that possible?" I asked.

She ignored my question, focusing on Miguel, a threat in her eyes. "Last name," she said again.

"It was a weird name," Miguel said. "Nobody."

I looked from him to Sunday. Her face had drained of color.

"What happened to him?" she asked.

"I think he got away," Miguel said. "When Lily opened the column of light to put me in there, he was waiting. He rushed her. They fought—it didn't take long for her to kick his ass. He was a kid, for chrissakes."

"She knocked him out," Sunday said.

"Yeah," Miguel said.

"And he vanished," she said.

Miguel nodded.

"That's how he travels." She pressed the heel of her hand to her brow. "He's from the past. Like, the 1930s past."

"You think the Order wants him because he can travel?" Miguel asked. "They want to know how he does it?"

"It makes sense," I said.

Miguel shook his head—not a disagreement so much as an acknowledgement of how in over our heads we were.

"Can you stand up?" I asked him.

He pushed to his feet very carefully. "You want into my head? Double-check my story?"

I studied his face. "At the house."

"Where Red can grill me, too," he said. "Great."

"You deserve it," I said.

He shrugged. He couldn't argue on that point.

"You're lucky I didn't let her stab you," I said.

He held up both hands in truce. "In my defense, I thought I'd be right back. It was just recon."

"In enemy territory?"

"I'm a chameleon," he said.

He should've been able to blend in. Wait for someone to step out of the space, do a quick copy, walk in and make an excuse to take another look at the light and who they'd trapped behind it. It should've been easy. "What went wrong?"

"The woman in red saw me," he said. "Then she took me down."

There was a way to spot a chameleon—a certain shimmer that could sometimes be seen if you weren't looking directly at them—but even that was dicey for anyone whose power didn't involve the ability to read a mind or a soul. Most magical people were soul-blind.

For a woman who had no magic, seeing through Miguel's disguise should've been impossible.

"What do you mean by 'took you down'?" I asked.

"I know it sounds like bullshit. But she fucking blinked at me, and two things happened." He ticked them off on his fingers. "My disguise went *poof*. The thing happened with Charlie. That's all. Next thing I knew, you'd broken me out of the light cage. How did you do that, by the way?"

I ignored his question and mulled his words.

I'd never heard of anything like what he'd described. I glanced at Sunday.

She shook her head. We were both at a loss.

"This is bad," I said.

"I know," he said. "It shouldn't have happened. I didn't think anyone, anywhere could do that to me."

Sunday flashed a wry grin. "Used to being the biggest kid on the block? The smartest kid in your class?"

"Pot calling the kettle," he said.

She had in fact been the Order's go-to operative for years before her exit.

"So we've got bad news all around," I said.

He nodded.

We needed information. We needed to be able to understand what was happening around us. We'd stepped onto a playing field with forces we couldn't possibly hope to understand. The scope was cosmic.

Cosmic. That sort of thing was a big part of what had brought me here this morning.

"One more question, Miguel," I said. "The realization you had before you came here—how did it come to you?"

He narrowed his eyes. "In a dream."

"Did Michael appear in this dream?"

"How'd you know?" he asked.

I held his gaze.

"You, too?" he asked.

Why had Michael come to Miguel in the first place if Miguel had known what the Order was doing to the kids they'd gathered? It didn't make sense. "Where are you, Miguel? Whose side are you on?"

"The kids inside the Order," he said.

"So you did know," I said.

He took his time answering. "I didn't work on that mission directly. I was being trained to take in the Angel, and that was a full-time thing. I was seeing someone, though. She never told me directly what was going on, but she hinted at it. It hurt her inside. She could barely deal."

I stared at him. "So you pretended not to know."

"What I said before about indoctrination—"

"It doesn't matter," I said.

He closed his eyes for a moment. When he looked at me again, they were filled with unshed tears. "No, it doesn't."

"You weren't going to tell us?" I asked.

"So you could lead a suicidal charge into the Order?" He shook his head.

He was right. I'd have done exactly that. "What would you do, Miguel?"

"I'd ask the only person who knows what the hell is going on," he said. "The only one who's been imprisoned in that place and drained of his power. He has the information we need."

I combed my fingers through my hair. Who'd been in a position to know what it felt like to serve as the power source for the Order? Who might know why they needed one in the first place? All the things we didn't know—or a good number of them.

"The Angel," I said.

"Exactly."

He seemed to relax a hairsbreadth, maybe because I'd let him get away with talking about us as a team. Maybe because we'd be taking him home with us to the only people in the world he knew who wouldn't want him dead.

Sunday didn't want him relaxed. She wanted to see the fear of God in him. Even if she believed him—and she seemed to now—she wasn't ready for bygones.

"Walk," Sunday said, pointing toward the door through which we'd entered.

He lead us out of the warehouse and into the morning light again, after which Sunday pointed to my Honda.

"Get in the car," she said. "And don't touch anything."

He did what she told him. We watched him settle into the passenger seat of my car gingerly, as if he was hurting.

"What?" I asked. She wouldn't have sent him ahead and out of earshot if she didn't have something to say privately.

"Did I see that right?" she asked.

"See what?" I asked.

"The part where the fucking Angel of Death used your body to draw a symbol on the column and break it?"

"Yeah," I said.

"That's not okay, Night."

"We needed his help. He came through. Job's done. What's not okay about that?"

Sunday met my gaze and held it. "Did you not hear me before?"

I sighed. "I heard you. But how am I not supposed to use a resource that's at our disposal when we need it?"

She raised a brow. "Who's using who?"

The question invaded me, passing through the rawness and pain, breaking up the funk that held me off-kilter. "Shit."

"Damn right," she said. "We're going to talk about that, too."

She set off toward the car, leaving me in her dust. By the time I slid behind the wheel, she'd belted into the backseat.

She leaned forward, tapping Miguel on the shoulder. "So, who cut off your braid?"

"I don't want to talk about it," he said.

"Lily? David?"

"How do you know his name?" Miguel asked.

"He paid us a visit," she said.

"Shit. I should've been there. I'm sorry."

"The magic words," she said.

He leaned his head back, bonking it into the headrest. "What happened?"

"Night killed him," Sunday said.

He glanced at me from the corner of his eye. "You okay?"

Sunday answered for me. "No, she's not."

He narrowed his eyes. "What's going on? Something else happened. I can feel it. You two are off—with each other, on your own."

Sunday didn't answer him.

I sighed, the pain welling as the words fell from my lips like stones.

His face turned ashen.

CHAPTER 12

THE BASEMENT BORE little resemblance to the way it had looked and felt yesterday. No evidence of the ritual remained, and no evidence remained of David either. The protective curtain had been taken down, the space swept, mopped with Addie's special floor wash, and smudged with Palo Santo. Then Addie had replaced the curtain with a new one with Jess's help.

They'd also put down an old Turkish rug that had been worn threadbare in spots, but served as a welcome layer over the concrete floor. Throw pillows had been brought down from upstairs.

The house spirit seemed soothed.

I sat cross-legged on a pillow in the center of the rug, across from Stacy, who'd wrapped herself in one of Addie's lush gray cardigans, the sequined hem of her long silver skirt hiked up to her thighs. She'd set out a purple cloth with a similarly sequined hem and pulled a deck of Tarot cards from a purple velvet pouch. She shuffled them with steady hands.

Her fragmented halo had knitted itself back together and stabilized at a dark indigo. She looked a little pale, her eyes tired, but her vitality had increased over the last twenty-four hours enough to be able to witch the cards for me.

She finished shuffling, and handed them to me. "Shuffle and cut."

The cards felt as well-worn as the rug, and as imbued with magic as any object I'd ever handled.

"What kind of information are you looking for?" Stacy asked.

"The kind I can't get any other way," I said.

Of course, that wasn't strictly true now, was it?

I handed her the cards. She began to lay them out in a traditional Celtic cross spread. The more cards, the more details. Details were what we needed.

"Everything Miguel, Sunday, and I—we've run into a roadblock. We'd always assumed the Order was one thing: a tool for the Angel of Death to fulfill his destiny, to accomplish his end game, but I don't think so anymore. We need to know what's really going on."

Stacy glanced at me through her lashes. "Beth told me about you and the Angel. I think it's bad news. I just thought you should know before you decide to say anything further."

"I had those conversations with my people weeks ago," I said. "No one's happy with the situation."

"But you're talking to him," she said. "You're letting him get to know you—and how to manipulate you—better."

I stared at her. "He saved my life. He saved Addie's life. I talk with him because he can help us."

"That's not the only reason," she said.

"Really?" I asked. "What's the other one?"

She shrugged. "Power. He has more than you, or he augments what you have, and you're leaning on that to get what you want."

She made it sound as if I was working the Angel to my own personal ends. "This isn't about greed. I'm working for the greater good."

"For now," she said, laying out the last card.

That felt too close for comfort—and too akin to what Sunday had said to me back at the warehouse parking lot. Was I using the Angel? Was he using me? How could I tell the difference?

"Everyone has an opinion," I said.

"Yeah," she said. "But you asked for mine."

I had, but only because she didn't know me well enough to have told me outright without prompting. I didn't need her good opinion or anyone else's, for that matter. I didn't need to be agreed with or liked. I knew I was loved regardless.

I also knew what felt right, both on the surface and in the depths of my patchwork soul. The problem was that I didn't know how much of what I felt originated with me, and how much originated with the Angel.

That was a scary fucking place to be. I understood scary. Fear had ruled a huge part of my life—juggling fear of Lily and the Order while I'd been under their sway, fear that they'd find Faith and me on the run.

Stacy turned her attention to the cards, concentrating on each in turn. I saw no change in her halo to indicate that she received messages from them. It took me a moment to realize that the cards were an extension of her. A part of her as surely as her heart and mind.

I studied her. The newly darkened halo. The way she moved her hands. The alt-hippie chick way she dressed. She didn't seem to belong with the serpent or his apprentice, but, if she'd ever had a choice, it had been taken from her.

"How's it feel?" I asked. "Your halo?"

She furrowed her brow for a second. "You mean my life force? My aura?"

I nodded.

"Like it shattered and got sewn back together," she said. "Like I'm Frankenstein's monster."

I sympathized, and not just because of the stitches beneath my ribs. "It'll get better."

"You know something about this?" she asked. "From experience, that is?"

I drew my knees to my chest, hooking them with one arm. "My soul is like that—made up of pieces of other people's souls, actually. The seams fit together like a jigsaw puzzle."

She looked up at me. "Whose souls?"

"My targets,'" I said. "From when I worked for the Order."

"Generous of them," she said. "They could've cursed you as they moved on."

I nodded.

"You know why they didn't?" she asked.

"No," I said. "No idea. I'm grateful, though."

"I'd like to get a look at it sometime," she said.

"For answers?"

"Not necessarily," she said. "There may not be any."

"True."

"For curiosity's sake," she said.

"All right. If we get through this." It was an unusual request, but then, she was an unusual girl.

When I'd first seen her perched on the sofa in Addie's living room, I could tell that she'd had to make hard choices. That she'd held the weight of the world on her shoulders and not broken beneath it.

"What was the hardest thing you've ever done?" I asked.

"I witched away a girl's memory. It was the only way to make her whole and save the people she loved."

I tried to wrap my head around that. As someone with the power to enter people's minds and draw them into memories and fears, it was quick jump to the idea of erasing a person's memory altogether. To do something like that meant stealing everything from a target. After all, we were nothing except the sum of our memories.

Amnesia happened as the result of trauma. People either healed from it, gradually recovering themselves, or they didn't—and if they rediscovered themselves at all, the life they uncovered must feel as if it belonged to a stranger.

"Did you do that with or without the girl's permission?" I asked.

"With," she said. "That made me feel marginally better. I hated myself for a few days. I felt so sad. I couldn't imagine having the guts to make the choice she made for the greater good."

"Did it work out for her?"

Stacy sighed. "That's her business, not mine."

I glanced down at the cards. I should've been more interested in them as a whole. Which card Stacy had pulled to represent me for the reading. What blocked my path. The cards that represented the past and present. Influences.

All I could see was the last card she'd placed, the one that signified the outcome.

Death.

In Stacy's deck, Death was a red-robed skeleton on a pale horse. I knew enough about Tarot to understand that drawing that particular card usually meant a big change on the horizon—something must die in order that something new be born. Rarely did it signify an actual, physical human death.

In my case, I knew what—or who—it meant.

"Well, shit," she said.

I looked at her.

"After what I just said to you, that card feels like a slap in the face," she said.

I nodded. "None of the others seem to matter much."

"No," she said. "You're going to have to ask the Angel. He has the answers you need, and if you're lucky, he'll give them to you without asking for anything in return. If you're unlucky..."

She trailed off.

"What?" I asked.

"If you're unlucky, asking him will be like stepping onto a patch of quicksand. He'll just drag you deeper, and you'll be fortunate if you manage to find a way out before you drown."

"Jesus," I said. "Are you always this direct?"

"I try to be," she said. "There's too much going on. Too much at stake. I don't want to screw something up because I don't say what I mean. I would've thought you of all people would appreciate it."

"I do," I said.

"Don't tell me you're not used to it?" She raised a brow.

"No," I said. "That's not it."

"Then what?"

I hated the idea of talking about my feelings—especially hard feelings—with someone I barely knew. On the other hand, denying the truth would get me nowhere. Honesty mattered.

"I'm scared," I said.

She nodded. "If you weren't, I'd want to know what was wrong with you."

Actually, *scared* was an understatement. I could see the quicksand she was talking about. The problem was, I couldn't tell whether I had an inch or a mile to go before I'd gone too far.

She picked up the cards, stacking them in a discard pile. She pulled a single additional card: a chariot driven by a prince and pulled by two sphinxes, one black and one white.

"What's that for?" I asked.

"Faith," she said.

I stared at her.

"What?" she asked. "If she was my daughter, I'd want to know."

It took me a second to recover. "I'd have gotten there eventually."

"I know," she said. "I'm just proactive. In this case, it's probably going to get me in trouble."

I cocked my head. I didn't quite understand.

"There's a place back home, in Houston. It's an alley in the southeast part of downtown, near the baseball field. Sometimes there's a yellow school bus parked there. The bus travels back and forth to Faery."

I shook my head. "What's a yellow school bus have to do with Faith?"

"Something's going to happen there over Christmas," she said. "I don't know what yet, but it has something to do with her. With what she is now."

"She'll be there?" I asked.

"I think so, yes. But you know how divination works, right?"

I nodded. It was a snapshot in time of what would happen if things continued along their current path. If I stepped off of that path and made even one different decision—or if Faith, or any number of others, did—Stacy's prediction went out the window.

"I'm glad to have the info, just the same," I said.

She folded the Chariot into the discard pile. "Anything else?"

"Yeah," I said. "But you won't need to the cards in order to answer. How long are you and Beth planning to stay? I'm not trying to kick you to the curb, but Addie asked you to come because of Faith and the Awakened, and that work is tied off."

Her lips curved. "We're sticking around. It feels like you still need our help."

"That's what I hoped you'd say."

"Whatever it takes." She rocked back and then forward again, using the momentum to roll into a squat, scooping up the cards and cloth and returning them to the pouch. "Why don't you stay down here a while?"

"Talk to the Angel," I said.

"Looks like you should. I'll send Beth to check on you in a while."

I met her gaze. "Why would you do that?"

"Because, out of all of us, she understands what's going on with you best."

"Because she's bound to someone powerful," I said. "And evil."

"Malek is powerful. But evil?" She mulled the idea for a moment. "He looks human, but he's not. He lives among us, but he doesn't have human morals or ethics. He's helped us save each other—save the world—but lie to him and you're in a world of hurt. Betray him and you're dead."

"Doesn't sound traditionally evil," I said.

She nodded. "The best word is 'complicated.'"

"Why's he helping at all?" I asked.

"He doesn't say so in his out loud voice," she said, "but I think it's because he cares."

"You never asked him?"

She chuckled. "If you'd met him, you'd understand."

The serpent from the Garden of Eden. The bogeyman responsible for the supposed fall of humanity. He probably radiated some combination of raw power and back-the-fuck-off.

I'd always had a hard time believing that any one powerful being was responsible for human beings' separation from the sacred. I'd seen too much. I'd done too much. I knew what evil was. I knew what it meant to lose my soul.

Human beings didn't need anyone else to intervene between them and the sacred. We fucked things up just fine all by ourselves.

"He scares you?" I asked.

She shook her head. "That's not it. When I'm around him, I see myself too clearly. I can't pretend I'm anything less or more than I really am. There's no room for guilt or shame or self-pity. I have to stand like I'm as powerful as him, but in my own way. I have to take that kind of responsibility. It's hard."

She was a kid, like Faith, drawn into cosmic, worlds-shattering events. She shouldn't have to be thinking about how to stand side by side or toe to toe with a being who'd been alive since the beginning of time. She was obviously committed, though.

"You came because he sent you," I said. "And now you're bound to him without so much as a please and thank you. How do you feel about that?"

"Doesn't matter," she said.

I raised a brow.

She twisted her mouth. "Okay, it does. I'm worried about what that means short-term and long-term—all the terms. I'm worried I won't measure up. And…."

"And what?"

"I feel proud."

"Pride before a fall? Pride, one of the seven deadlies?"

She rolled her eyes. "With my luck, both of those."

She tightened the drawstring on the pouch and headed out through the new curtain.

A couple of moments later, although I couldn't hear her footfalls on the steps or the open and shut of the basement door, I knew I was alone. Just the Angel and me.

In the best of circumstances, the basement was chilled. Unheated, underground rooms usually were. But I felt colder than I had a moment ago, as if Stacy's leaving triggered the Angel's rise in me.

It felt different this time than it had before. It felt alien. It felt like —death.

My fingers grew icy, the moons of my fingernails and my brown skin taking on a bluish cast. The same chill seemed to freeze my heart. I rubbed the heel of my hand against the cold there, but it didn't help. In the space it took to draw a deep breath, the ice spread to the rest of my body. My exhale rattled. The flames of panic ignited in my belly, but they couldn't dispel the ice. I rolled onto my back, no longer able to hold my knees to my chest.

I tried to ask the Angel what he was doing. My mind felt sluggish.

The panic in my belly flared. Then it, too, banked down to glowing coals, smoking as their heat dissipated.

It had never been like this. This was him taking control against my will. This was him showing me who was boss—the thing I'd feared from the moment we'd first faced off.

My magic rose in defense, but it could only move so fast and so far against the Angel's ice. I managed a single push of magic. I couldn't aim it. I couldn't connect with any one person's mind. I sent it wild. A single word.

Angel.

If anyone heard, they'd know what had happened—what was happening right now. They'd put up a shield or prep some other magic before running down here and ending up trapped in the ice themselves—or worse.

The Angel had control of my body. He could make me do whatever he wanted.

I want you to watch. To listen, he said. *Ask your questions.*

Can you confirm that the Order held you against your will?

He hesitated. *We had the same end for much of the time I was there.*

And then you didn't.

He nodded. *They continued to take from me.*

His energy. His spark. They'd used him up, slowly but surely. The question was, did what they take replenish itself? Or was it gone forever?

What they took—did it come back? I asked.

Not entirely, he said.

Will it, eventually?

Eventually, he said.

Meaning that he was stronger now than he'd been a month ago, but he still wasn't as strong right now as he could be. That in the future, he'd be more powerful.

I couldn't handle him now. Thinking about how much worse that could get—Jesus.

Is the Order draining magical children's power? Can you confirm?

Confirmed, he said. *They can't be allowed to continue.*

I couldn't help but think this was on me. I'd been there. I should've asked more questions. I should've opened my eyes beyond my own pain and rage. I should've known what was going on under my nose. If I had, I'd never have made it as far as rescuing Faith. I'd have died trying to take down the Order. And if I'd discovered all of this before now, I'd have done whatever I could to stop it, even if I died trying.

You would've died trying, the Angel said. *You weren't strong enough then. Now, you can do something.*

I would do everything.

He responded to my thought. *I know you will. I respect your reason why. I will help you.*

Respect my reason? The Angel had never given a crap about what I'd thought.

There's more, the Angel said. *They are using the children to kill magic. Extinguish it utterly.*

I shook my head, not understanding. It didn't seem possible. *How can children kill magic?*

Their power is one ingredient in the spell the Order is casting. They need one more. An archangel's blood, the Angel said.

They don't have that already, they won't get it, I said.

The Angel shook his head. *Not that simple. They may never find a way to trap Michael, but they don't need him. One of his descendants is good enough.*

I was Michael's descendant. Jesus H. Christ.

This whole thing—the Order wanting to destroy magic—it didn't make any sense. The Order gathered magical children. Raised them. Turned them into trained killers. Remade some of them into chameleons and who knew what else. It was all about magic. Magic used as a means to an end. Using magic to kill magic? It didn't add up.

Unless—

What happens when the magic is dead and gone? I asked.

The world ends, he said. *All the worlds end.*

I sucked in a breath.

Don't let it happen, Night.

You're the fucking Angel of Death. What do you care if the worlds end? Isn't that what you've been after the whole time? Your reason for being?

He didn't answer for a long moment. When he did, I heard more than his voice. I heard the power in it. He'd existed from the beginning of time, from the moment life had been breathed into the worlds.

What makes you think that death is all I am?

It's in your name, I said.

What is my name?

La Muerte. The Angel of Death. Those were titles, like all the Elders used in place of names.

It's my function, he said.

Like the other Elders, he had a job to do, and he walked across space and time to deliver. Whether he did it all himself or had a bunch of little deaths who worked for him, he didn't kill indiscriminately.

You take people's souls when their time comes, I said.

Yes.

That wasn't evil. That was what needed to happen in the natural order of things. People died, their souls shuffled off the mortal coil. People were born. That was the cycle of life.

In service of life, the Angel said.

I listened for a lie in what he said. I heard none.

He'd come after Faith and me in the beginning. After I'd defeated him, he'd saved my life. He'd been free to leave at that point, but he'd chosen to stay. And now he was telling me he was on the side of life, whatever that meant.

Tell me the truth about what's going on, I said.

You already know why I came for you, he said. *I needed you.*

Because he needed a human body in which to walk the world in corporeal form, and he needed one with enough juice to be able to hold his form. That was Faith, or it was me. I'd made the choice to spare Faith that fate and taken it on myself.

Why did you stay? I asked.

For the same reason. I need you—and you need me.

What do I need from you? Power? Magic?

The ability to survive in a fight against Elders. Make no mistake—that's where the battle ahead lies if we're going to save all the worlds.

I took that in, listening carefully, and still hearing only truth.

I don't understand the fight, I said. *Who's on which side. Why people are doing what they're doing. I can't make decisions based on half-assed information.*

He mulled that over. *You'd believe what I tell you?*

Not necessarily, but it would be a start.

He answered my thoughts, not waiting for words.

There are many players, all of them great powers. They were created along with all the worlds at the beginning of time. The worlds will not live forever, but the time at which they will end is not yet written, nor is it fore-told. There are Elders who want the worlds to live on, and those who want it to die—those Elders who side with life, and those who side with death. It's that simple.

Why would any of them want the worlds to end?

They believe the worlds have fallen into shadow, like the story people seem so enamored of. Adam and Eve. Eve, who disobeyed God and, as a consequence, fell from grace. Those events didn't happen that way, but people believe they did. They believe that, ever since, humans have sinned—more than that, that humans are sin. These Elders who want the worlds to end believe similar things about the worlds and everyone in them, but they believe that the worlds are beyond redemption. They would rather create new worlds in the hope of fixing the errors they see as responsible for the sin.

That wasn't hard to understand at all. From my vantage, having both taken and saved lives, I got it.

These Elders who want death—they have a leader? I asked.

The End, he said.

A title. A function.

The Angel showed me an image that stole my breath.

A halo with no color. Not white. Not black. Nothing in between. Just...nothing at all. He wasn't Satan, at least not the way that being was thought of traditionally. He was literally the opposite of creation. Not destruction, but the void where no oxygen—no creation, no life, no love—could live.

The End is the being at the heart of the Order's mission, the Angel said. *The Elder they serve.*

That was what was waiting for us at the end of all things.

If I wanted to pin the label of evil on something or someone, that was who I ought to choose. If I wanted to fight in the service of life— the living, breathing, loving, lusting heartbeat in every created being, animate and inanimate, conscious or not, embodied or not—that was who to take the fight to.

You see? the Angel asked.

I did.

This is not about a foretold battle, he said. *This is not about who's right and who's wrong. This is about everything.*

I let that sink in. I let it all sink in.

The Order served the End. The Order wanted to kill all magic.

One of the earliest lessons I'd learned during my time there blossomed in my mind. My mentor, Lily, had explained to me that magic wasn't evil. It just was. That magic existed because the world existed. It was the ultimate expression of creation, wild and true to the souls of those who'd been graced with it. True to the soul of the world.

Magic *was* the soul of all the worlds.

Yes, the Angel said.

My stomach rolled over. I choked back the sickness that rose in my throat. Swallowed hard.

How will Michael's blood be used to kill magic? I asked.

The Angel's wings fluttered against the inside of my rib cage. *He's the protector.*

I dredged up what I knew of Michael. The Angel and I had spent a bunch of time talking about titles. Functions. Michael's was the fiery sword of protection. Or maybe Michael actually *was* the sword. He was the right hand of God. He—

What is God if not creation itself? the Angel asked.

Someone had to do the creating.

Yes, the Angel said. *Creation.*

He wasn't buying my creator/creation angle. I'd never thought about this stuff any other way, when I'd thought about it at all. If I took the Angel's words as truth—and what the hell reason would he have for lying to me?—then the world I lived in and all the other worlds and everything and everyone in them were a part of God. Of creator and creation.

How many descendants are there? I asked.

Unknown.

Unknown? *But more than just me.*

Yes.

Some number of magicians out there, in the Order's crosshairs. Or in the Order's custody. The Order could already be bleeding them. How long did we have until magic began to fade from the world?

Then there was the central problem. The children. I refused to leave them. If I went in to get them and the Order captured me, I would've played right into their hands.

A sharp pain pierced my head, as if someone had taken an axe to it. As if someone had split open a ripe fruit.

The Angel rifled through my memories, drawing forth a flood of scents and feelings and images from places I'd never looked—not places or things or people I'd purposely locked away, but a memory I was unaware existed at all.

The flood of memory slammed into me. Roared through me like storm-tossed waves crashed to shore under gray skies threaded with lightning. The flash lit the horizon, tinted orange with the last rays of the dying sun.

The broad expanse of the Galveston Bay stretched in front of me. The lights of a faraway ship blinked in the distance. The beach was empty on either side of me for as far as I could see, as were the sidewalk and street at the top of the seventeen-foot seawall behind me. There was a hurricane closing in.

The sticky air weighed on my skin. I tasted brine. Wet sand shifted under my bare feet, toes digging in as dark water and foam rushed and swirled around my calves, soaking the hem of my pink-and-white flowered halter dress. I braced myself as the water ebbed, feeling the fierce draw of the undertow. Spray stung my eyes. I'd pulled my hair back, but the wind had whipped half of it free. It snaked around my face, making me feel like an ancient goddess, the one who turned every person she saw to stone.

I felt like stone.

Mi abuela had taken me on an outing here. She'd picked me up from home, spiriting me away from my father's sullen stares and sizzle-pop of the chicken that my mother fried single-mindedly in the kitchen.

Neither of them wanted to talk to me. I'd done something wrong, but no one would tell me what it was. I'd begun to wonder whether the something wrong wasn't a thing I'd done. Maybe the wrong thing was me.

If I stayed at the water's edge long enough, the storm would roll in and I would roll out, and then no one would have to wonder anymore.

My grandmother wrapped her strong arms around me from behind and hauled me backwards, out of the water. She sat down as she pulled us into the dry dunes, tucking me into the V between her legs and keeping her hold on me as if she feared I'd run back to the bay.

She'd rolled her khakis to her knees. Her white sneakers and socks were wet. Water beaded on her long, frosted-pink fingernails and the gold links of her watch. The rolled, powder-blue sleeves of her shirt looked darker, as if they'd taken on the colors of the looming storm.

Being held by her wasn't like being hugged by either of my parents. It was like being hugged by God.

The wind stole her words as soon as they rolled off her tongue, but somehow I heard them anyway. "No, Rosa," she said.

"But the—"

She interrupted. "No."

I wanted to tell her what I felt, but I knew that she knew, and nothing I could say would change her verdict.

"You'll be needed," she said. "People will count on you. You don't want to let them down, do you?"

"Of course not," I said automatically, even as I wondered who these mysterious people were and what on earth they'd count on me for—and why they'd even want to. I was just a girl. A wrong girl.

"You're not wrong," she said.

"Are you reading my mind again?" I asked.

"Always, *nena*."

"What am I, then?" She would tell me. She always told me the truth, even when I didn't want to hear it. My stomach clenched with sudden fear that she would tell me something bad—that I was bad.

"*Mi cielito*," she said.

Her little heaven. Nothing she hadn't said to me before. Relief poured through me, but didn't wash away all my fear. This time, I felt something different behind her words—images, fleeing across my mind of stars like pearls in the black night sky.

I asked my question not about what she'd said, but what I'd seen. "What does that mean?"

"It's beautiful," she said. "You're beautiful. It looks like one thing, but it's made up of many stars, many clouds, and the black mirror of space is so very vast. The moon. All the planets. You're like that, Rosa —or you will be."

Impossible. "I'm not like you."

She was special. Not like any other person I'd ever known. She felt bigger. More.

"If I had to choose a granddaughter from all the little girls in the world, I would choose you every time," she said. "You are the night."

I tilted my head back so that I could see her face. Her eyes were dark and filled with stars. It should've scared me, but it didn't.

"You're the quiet," she said. "When shadow falls over everything and we can't see anything except our own thoughts and feelings, and the thoughts and feelings of those closest to us. When love matters more than anything else. When we huddle close to the light to keep ourselves safe, but most of the time fail to understand that the light we should seek is the light within ourselves. When we rest and sleep. When we dream."

She no longer seemed to be talking to a girl like me, but to someone older. Someone who could understand the words that flowed from her tongue.

Her voice deepened, as if she'd grown older as we sat in the sand. "Do you hear me, Night?"

I did. And I understood in that moment that she hadn't been a stranger who'd dropped in when she needed something from me. She wasn't some Elder who looked at me as if I were a chess piece in a mighty, millennia-old game.

She'd known me. She'd loved me. *Mi abuelita.*

I drew a sharp breath.

The sand and waves and cloudy sky, the wind and spray and the solidness of her arms dissolved around me into so much smoke. They left me utterly in the dark, no longer small, but grown. In the basement. In the cold. With *la Muerte.*

I shook my head to clear it, struggling to find my voice. I spoke out loud, my words ringing against the concrete and magic all around. "What the hell was that?"

The answer, the Angel said.

To the name I'd chosen for myself, which I'd done according to instinct and desire. Now, I knew why. The rest of it, I couldn't wrap my head around.

The Angel responded to my unasked question. *What are you?*

A woman. A former operative. Mother. Lover. Friend.

Night.

Dream had told me exactly what I was.

I waited for the Angel to say something more. After a moment, he let go of me. My magic shot high like a geyser. My senses roared back to life. I cherished the weight of my body on the floor, the cool of the concrete as the chill receded.

The Angel remained, sharp in my consciousness, watching me

process what had just happened, like a fucking shrink. Or a teacher. He was neither to me. If I could've hurt him, I'd have done it. Hell, I'd done it once before. I'd just never figured out how.

The fuck did you do? I asked.

I showed you what you needed to know, he said. *Your place in all of this. From the many, one.*

That was what creation was: All beings. All worlds. One creation.

I'd been made that way as well, crafted during my time with the Order. My soul had died a little with every life I'd taken until nothing remained. And the nothingness—the end—inside of me had been inexplicably filled with the soul parts of my victims. They'd granted me the grace of a soul again.

From the many, one.

I had no idea how that tied in. What it all meant, only that it meant something important.

It's your choice, the Angel said. *You decide what to do.*

He turned away, retreating into the cage, pulling the door shut with a clang that reverberated through my bones.

I stared after him, thinking about our complicated...relationship. Things between us had begun with a life-or-death battle when he'd tried to take Faith as his human vessel and I'd refused. He'd tried to break me, and it hadn't gone his way.

He'd fought the oldest Watcher, Shadow, when the Watcher had tried to end me. Maybe that'd been for the Angel's own benefit, and I'd only been a collateral rescue. But instead of walking free from the mental prison I'd locked him in, he'd chosen to stay. He'd healed Addie of a mortal wound. He'd helped me every step of the way with the Order, demystifying its aims.

He'd shown me a glimpse of my childhood—of who I'd once been, how that had survived all the trauma and death in my life. He'd given me what I hoped was the key to springing the children. He'd walk back into Hell with me, knowing that if our magic failed he'd be taken and drained until there was nothing left of him.

Did it matter whether his reasons were always the same as mine? Did it matter more where he stood?

My body shook with awe and shock for a long minute, gradually growing still enough that I could attempt to push to my feet. My legs wobbled while they decided whether to hold me up. After another long moment, I managed to walk.

I passed through the membrane of magic on my way to the stairs, glancing up to mark Beth as she stood at the top of the steps. As I started the climb, she moved to block my exit.

I narrowed my eyes.

I was in no mood to deal with her—or with anyone else right now, expected or unexpected. I felt goddamn shaky, and I needed to go somewhere to think. Or not think at all, but just be. Let everything the Angel had told me and shown me sink in.

Beth noted the way I held myself. The tension in my arms and shoulders.

"I just need a minute. Promise." She crossed her heart with her index finger, then threw up a Scout's honor hand signal.

It was ridiculous and annoying and endearing. It dissuaded me from shoving her out of my way.

She'd added braids to her hair, making it look like a nest of snakes. She wore a black tank with a glass of whiskey printed on the front, with a black-and-blue flannel long-sleeve over it. She met my gaze and held it, looking at me as if she could see more than my physical form—as if she could see through me, all the way to the Angel. I'd have bet my last dollar that she could.

"Stacy said you'd be coming down," I said.

"I know about the Angel."

"I figured. You disapprove, just like she does. Am I right?"

She shook her head. "He's a Horseman."

I nodded.

"I know one of the others," she said. "Famine."

I cocked my head, considering. I hadn't thought much about the others. Having the one to deal with took up all of my time and bandwidth. I'd looked at the Angel as the driving force behind the apocalypse, forgetting that he was one of four. If the others were also walking the world, that meant things were worse than I knew.

"Just Famine?" I asked.

"As far as I know," Beth said. "She has a hate-on for me."

"She?"

"She's as old as your Angel, but she looks like a kid. Pigtails, tortoiseshell glasses. Navy blue dress. Mary Janes. I thought you should know, just in case."

"You tell the others?" I asked.

"Not yet."

"Why not?"

She sighed. "You're in charge."

"I'm not the only one capable of handling the information."

"You're the only one who understands it," she said. "You know what a Horseman is. Hell, push comes to shove, you might even become one."

I raised a brow.

"Please. We both know what's up. You don't have control. You've got powers you don't even know you have. It's, like, an explosion waiting to happen." She made an explosion sound and waved her fingers like flying debris for effect.

"Why does she hate you?" I asked. "Famine."

"I play a part," she said. "Just like you. My guess is I'm meant to hurt or kill her. I mean, it's a *guess*. And also she deserves it. She killed me once already. Karma."

That wasn't how karma worked. "Killed you."

"Bloodbath," she said.

"Your boss bring you back?"

She nodded. "His magic is powerful."

"All magic is powerful if you know how to use it," I said.

"Truth. Just be careful."

"I don't think there's such a thing as careful anymore." That was more honest than I'd intended to be. I winced on the inside.

"Yeah," she said. "But try."

I didn't want to end up the Angel's puppet. I sure as hell didn't want to become a Horseman—if something like that was even possible. "I will."

She took a step back, clearing my path to the door. "Dinner in fifteen minutes. That's what Addie said."

"What are we having?" I asked.

"Roast beast with Brussels sprouts and mashed potatoes."

A lot fancier than I was used to. "Thanks."

As I moved for the door, she stood very still, watching me go. As I stepped into the hall, I glanced back just in time to catch her silhouette as she plucked her phone from her pocket and dialed.

I had a good idea who she might be calling. I didn't like it. I didn't like it at all.

I shot her a glare that said as much before I made my way into the hall and through the kitchen, bypassing Addie's turned back as she stood at the stove. A quick flip of the back door lock and I stepped out onto the small patio in my stocking feet, into falling mist and cold.

No coat, so the wet seeped into my clothes. Gusting wind turned my skin to gooseflesh. It felt good—the shock my system needed to bring me back to the place I'd been before I'd headed down to have my fortune told.

I breathed in the perfume of Addie's roast beef and of biscuits rising in the oven and wondered who she'd made it for specifically. A magical meal if I'd ever smelled one.

I took in the fall of the mist on the looming Douglas firs to my left, and the smattering of earth and grass underneath them. The wooden privacy fence at the back of the yard, looking for all the world like a collection of stakes meant to pierce the hearts of giant vampires. The blue and green trash bins lined up like soldiers on my right, and the chain-link fence beyond them like poorly constructed armor. A crow cawed in the distance.

This was the world. Stupid world full of thoughts and feelings and things that both made sense and didn't. Full of people who made horrible mistakes and terrible choices and could still at any moment choose to be better. Full of children who deserved every chance. A world worth saving.

And every single thing in it that I saw seemed imbued with light and life force, even the things I wouldn't normally have thought of as alive. Everything had a halo, no matter how faint. And a web of light, reminiscent of the webs in Stacy's halo, that tied it to every other thing.

It was fucking beautiful. It was overwhelming.

I closed my eyes so hard, I saw stars. When I looked out again, nothing had changed.

Maybe it would fade with time and maybe it wouldn't. Didn't matter. The Angel had shown me what was up. I couldn't unsee what I'd seen. I couldn't unknow it, either.

I could wish I didn't understand what we had to face, but wishes weren't horses, and my dream would remain just that unless I rode into Hell to fight for what I believed in.

CHAPTER 13

SILENCE REIGNED at the table. At first, because we'd dived into the meal Addie had prepared as if we'd been starved, wolfing down roast beef and Brussels sprouts and mashed potatoes, sopping up the leftover gravy with biscuits. After that, we continued to sit quietly, the stillness taking on an electric quality.

The house spirit kept watch over everyone and everything inside, and over the front and back yards as well. I trusted it to tell me if anyone intruded, but I still kept an eye on the back door and my ears open for unexpected sounds in the front of the house.

Red sat to my left, his hand resting on my thigh as I rested mine on his. He looked older than he had yesterday, the lines around his eyes and mouth deepened, his salt-and-pepper hair shaded a little more toward salt. Sunday sprawled in the chair to my right, feet stretched far underneath the table. She held my hand, occasionally brushing her thumb across my knuckles. She'd twined her fingers with mine as if she needed reassurance. Miguel kept his hands and his thoughts to himself. His bruised-purple halo swirled faster than usual, betraying his nerves.

Addie, dressed all in ghostly white, poured coffee from a glass carafe. When she finished with our side of the table, she moved on to serve the kids.

One was missing. Not forever, though. I refused to let it be forever.

I swallowed my grief. We had too much to do. Too much risk to take. If I was ever going to see Faith again, I'd need to live through the next twenty-four hours. We were going to need everyone this time. No hanging back. No *this is too dangerous.* It was all hands on deck.

There'd been no time to discuss the plan that had been forming in my mind during the meal with any of them. Chances were, no one would like it. But I needed as many of them on board as I could get. All of them, if possible.

The adults I felt pretty sure of. I gave the kids a critical eye.

Stacy and Beth huddled together in the corner, whispering so low all I could hear was the hiss of their voices. Ben, all in gray, the same color as his halo, his mouth set hard and thin. Jess hugged her knees, heels braced on the edge of her seat, brown eyes full of sorrow and steadfast determination. Corey, dressed in black, her red hair darker than usual, the color of blood. She didn't look ready to mourn. She looked ready to go to war.

No child should ever have to feel what Corey felt. War was a place to channel her grief. A way to strike back at the forces that had taken over innocent lives. That had broken relationships. That had broken hearts—and people.

War was the only thing that made sense.

There was the other thing: the memory the Angel had shown me. The one he'd said told me everything I needed to know. The vision of Dream and me on the beach. The words she'd said. What the Angel had told me afterwards.

When I placed the puzzle pieces, they slid together in one way, and one way only. They pointed toward the path we needed to take.

Addie set the carafe down in the center of the table with a clink that demanded attention, then took her seat at the head. She met my gaze.

"Tell us," she said. "I can see it eating a hole in you."

I took a deep breath and blew it out slow. "I haven't had a chance to talk with everyone about what happened yesterday. My heart is broken. I know I'm not the only one."

I looked at each of the kids, landing finally on Corey. The corners of her mouth turned down.

"I don't yet know what we can do for Faith, but I want you to understand that I intend to find her. Fight for her."

"Not by yourself," Corey said.

I nodded. "I know."

She rubbed her eyes with the heels of her hands, then settled back in her chair as if a small weight had been lifted. She still carried too much, but understanding that she didn't carry it alone seemed to have helped.

"When do we leave?" she asked.

"Not yet," I said. "There's something we—I—need to do first."

Corey closed her eyes for a second. When she opened them again, she directed the spark of her anger at me. "Something more important than Faith?"

"Not more important to me." I meant it. There was nothing more urgent than finding my daughter. "I have no doubt that the Awakened will keep her safe. But safety isn't everything."

"Agreed," Corey said. "So what the fuck takes precedence over Faith?"

"The Angel—"

She interrupted. "The Angel this. The Angel that. I'm sick of the Angel. Everything's a battle since he came on the scene. And for what? To stop the world from ending? I mean, that's what it's all about, right? What if I don't want to live in a world without Faith in it?"

Every word she spoke raised an alarm inside me, the klaxon growing louder and the lights flashing brighter as she went on. Even raising the specter that she might hurt herself if Faith couldn't be recovered—or if Corey couldn't find a way to live with what Faith had become—I didn't dare discount what she said.

I could stop her. I could slip into her mind and alter her thoughts, her memories. It would be a violation of the soul to do something like that. I would still do it if I thought for a minute that self-harm was imminent. I wasn't the only one at this table who felt that way, or who had the capability to change Corey from the inside out. I didn't have to glance at Addie to feel the way her eyes narrowed or know the calculations that went on behind them. And Red's grip on my leg tightened for the same reason.

I held Corey's gaze.

"I know," she said. "I know what you're thinking because I would be thinking it, too. But that's not the point."

"It's everything, Corey," I said. "You want to talk about it now or later? Because we will talk about it."

"Later. For now, I need to know you understand."

"That you're hurting, and why," I said.

She nodded.

"I get it." How could I not? I swallowed hard. "I don't expect things to get easier. I expect them to get harder from here on out. We might have some peaceful times, but it's not always up to us how long those last or what we might have to face. None of us are the kind to stick our heads in the sand and pretend the world's not on fire. The question is, what kind of world are we saving? What are we saving it for? What kind of world do we want it to be?"

Corey's eyes welled. She blinked back her sudden tears. "Thank you."

"It has to be both," I said. "We have to be in it for the world and for each other."

Corey leaned forward. "How do we do that?"

"We handle the situation we've got. We have one terrible event—what's happening to Faith. We have to find her. We will find her."

"What's the other thing?" Corey asked—this time, with less anger.

I laid out the facts as the Angel had given them to me. The Order's purpose in the world: to destroy magic. How they'd been using the Angel as their own personal power source to fuel that mission, and how, now that the Angel was gone, they were using the children to accomplish the same goal.

Corey listened carefully. "We need more information."

"And I'm going to give it to you," I said.

"How?" she asked.

"Let me show you."

Showing her meant using my magic, entering her mind and opening my private conversation with the Angel, letting her see what he'd shown me with all the raw emotion, sight, and sound I'd experienced. I held her gaze.

"Everything," she said. "Holding nothing back."

I wanted to hold the memory of Dream and me on the beach close, to keep it to myself. But if I had to bare that to Corey—to all of them—in order for her trust what I brought to the table, I'd do it.

"Yes," I sad.

"Okay." She opened herself to me, waiting.

My magic rose in response to her opening, threading its way into her mind, setting the scene, and gifting her with everything I'd seen from the moment I'd walked down the basement stairs to see Stacy for the reading until the moment I'd started to climb them again and seen Beth blocking my path on the landing.

When I was done, I took the magic back into myself, watching the awe and shock play across her face. My heart hurt at the way she reached for Jess, wrapping her fingers around Jess's arm, and the way she shook from the inside out. The tremors calmed after a long minute. Corey took a deep breath and looked my way.

She shook her head. "You have to show them. All of them."

I nodded.

Not everyone wanted me inside their minds. Not everyone wanted to be that close to the Angel, either. But every one of them let me in. They took in what I gave them and tried to make sense of it as best they could.

After it was all said and done, Sunday spoke first. "Sorry."

I raised a brow.

"I'm apologizing for doubting you," she said. "If all of this is true, then I get it."

"You were just being careful," I said. "You were right to be."

Miguel cleared his throat. "I want to talk logistics, because there's no way we're not doing something here, is there?"

"Agreed," Sunday said.

Miguel took a breath and blew it out slowly. "I can see only one way to handle this."

Corey shook her head. "I know what you're thinking. You're thinking that we have to go in. No."

"You got a better idea?" Miguel asked.

"There has to be a different way," Corey said. "Someone on the inside who can jailbreak the kids. This is a trap, for fuck's sake."

Sunday sighed. "You're not wrong, Corey. It's an ingenious trap."

The Angel's voice echoed in my head. I let it fade again before I spoke. "Yeah, it is. Because I have to go in there. Even if we could spring the kids without me, we can't do it without the Angel."

"You of all people can't go in there, Night," Corey said. "What if you get caught? The risk is too great. Can't the Angel just tell us what to do?"

If only that were all we needed. "We need his power to break the cage."

Corey's face fell.

I swallowed hard. "If we had the time, we could maybe come up with another plan. Something more elaborate. A long game. Who here thinks we have that time?"

No one answered.

No one liked it—and that included me. But I wouldn't shy away from what had to be done because of that. I watched Corey come to the same place, her eyes turning fierce, her jaw set.

"So we go in," Red said.

I took a sip of my coffee, setting the mug down. "We go in. But not all of us."

"I hope to Christ not," Red said.

Corey shook her head. "I'm not just going to sit around and wait."

Ben bent to rest his elbows on the table. "That goes for me, too."

"Three," Jess said.

At the head of the table, Addie held up a hand to stop the avalanche.

"Please don't," Jess said. "I'm a part of this, too. You can't protect me my whole life, Aunt Addie."

Addie pressed her lips together. "You're awfully quick to jump into the fire."

Jess folded her arms across her chest. "It's like Night said, sometimes the fire comes to us."

Addie inclined her head, giving Jess the point, although the likelihood that she and Addie would have words later was high.

I didn't blame either of them for feeling the way they did. They were both right.

"I'm not intending for any of us to sit this out." I glanced at Stacy and Beth, the newcomers to our table. I had no right to expect anything from either of them. "Except maybe you two."

Beth held up both hands. "Hey, I'm in. I want to know what's going on too much to back out. Also, if I went home without helping you, Malek would kick my ass."

Malek would want every piece of intel Beth could get her hands on. And I wouldn't feel surprised if she had marching orders from him—actions to take or things to say in case of certain contingencies.

Stacy flashed a wry grin. "I'm thinking I'm needed here, whether my new boss wants it or not."

"All right," I said. "I think Sunday and Miguel will back me up here when I say that the three of us should be the ones to go inside."

Beside me, Red tensed. Corey flushed red, ready to blow her top.

I headed their objections off at the pass. "Hear me out."

Red took a deep breath and then nodded.

"We're gonna want Red and Beth, too," I said. "We need your skills, Red. We're going into chameleon territory."

He ran his free hand through his hair. Didn't say a word.

"Beth, we need you because—"

"The connection to Malek," she said.

"Good guess," I said.

"Seems obvious to me," she said.

I nodded. "Addie, I'm thinking you and Stacy should stay back here, with the others."

Jess shook her head. "We don't need a babysitter." As soon as the words rolled off her tongue, she winced. Addie didn't brook sassing. "Sorry. I didn't mean it like that."

"Yes, you did," Addie said. "That's all right—for now. What did you have in mind, Night?"

"We're gonna need magical backup," I said. "We're gonna need everyone's magic. Everyone's insights. We're talking about breaking into a magical fortress."

Sunday grinned. She could see where I was heading before the others. It had always been that way.

"What are we supposed to do?" Ben asked. "I mean, how are we supposed to help if we're not there. I don't get it."

"Two ways," I said. "One, those of us who're going in will need a spell to allow your magic to work through us."

Ben blinked at me. "Is that possible?"

Stacy's wry smile shaded to genuine. "I think so. There's just one thing."

"A magical conduit," I said. "Someone who can be open to channel the spell and, collectively, all of the magic."

She nodded.

"I don't need line of sight to use my mind magic. So, I should be able to serve as the conduit."

"It might take more than your usual standard operating procedure to make this happen," Stacy said. "Unless you've done this before and you know?"

"Nope. Never." I thought about what the Angel had shown me. What Dream had shown me. I could still taste the salt spray. Feel her arms around me. "We'll figure it out."

The kids looked intrigued. Addie looked relieved. Her niece would be going into battle, but not into the direct line of fire.

Miguel whistled.

I turned to look at him. "What do you think?"

"Goddamn ambitious, Night."

I waited for the rest of his verdict.

"But I can't think of a better idea," he said. "And we have my connection to lean on."

What was her name? Tana. Miguel's lover.

"You're sure about that?" I asked.

"One hundred percent."

Sunday took a deep breath and blew it out slowly. "So, we're set."

Nods of agreement across the board.

"When do we go?" Red asked.

"Best time to hit the Order is in the middle of the night," I said. "Two, three a.m."

"We need a day," Addie said. "More would be better."

"One day," Sunday said. "We can't take the chance that we're being watched. Or that the Order locates the rest of Michael's descendants."

"Who's watching?" Ben asked.

"The Order," Sunday said.

He shook his head. "They left."

"They did—at least, my mentor and her remaining people left," I said. "If you were them, wouldn't you keep a weather eye? They gave us the cube that was supposed to stop Faith's transformation. Instead, the cube accelerated it. We're pissed. We're grieving. Some of us want answers. Some of us want revenge. If I were them, I'd be expecting an attack. Only a matter of time. The only questions would be when and how."

He tossed the long hair from his eyes. "Can they hear us in here?"

I glanced at Addie.

"The house spirit has us locked down solid," she said.

Sunday pushed away from the table and stood. "Let's get started. Stacy, Corey, Jess, Ben, Addie—come downstairs with me? I need to start filling you in on what to expect."

"You want my help?" Miguel asked.

"Chameleons," she said. "Yeah."

"I can lay out the details."

"Come on, then."

They rose as a group and headed toward the basement.

As their footsteps faded, I stood and started to clear the table. The clatter of plates and clink of glasses and flatware felt very loud in the renewed silence. Red hadn't moved a muscle.

"What?" I asked.

He turned in his seat, hanging one arm over the back of his chair. His gaze followed me from the table to the counter. "Don't get me wrong. I'm glad to be doing something to help instead of running a protection detail for the kids. I figured the time would come when I'd be needed."

"Not this soon?"

He laughed. "Timing's not the issue. It's the where."

"The Order," I said.

"Bingo."

"You're scared?" I asked—without an ounce of judgment.

"Yes," he said.

"I'd worry if you weren't."

"I know that, Night."

I made my way back to the table, stacking more plates and cups. "What's on your mind, specifically?"

He pushed to his feet, closing the short distance between us. His green eyes clouded with worry. "I know how to take care of myself. I've been doing it a long time. I'm decent in a bar brawl. I'm strong. But my magic is about seeing, knowing. It's not a weapon. We didn't get around to training me. What I'm trying to say is that you and Sunday and Miguel are gonna have to watch my back in addition to your own."

"We've got you," I said. "We won't let anything happen to you."

"That's a promise you can't make," he said. "And I'm not asking you to make it. I'm not worried that I'm gonna die."

I furrowed my brow.

"If you're concerned I'm gonna get hurt—if you're watching me— you might miss something vital," he said. "You could be the one who ends up getting hurt."

"You're not wrong," I said. "It's a possibility. But it's one I'm willing to risk."

"Because you need me," he said.

Miguel was a chameleon, with all of their inherent talents. I could unmask a chameleon, but not as quickly as Red could. Sunday was soul-blind. The idea of going in there without Red—it felt like courting disaster.

"Yeah," I said. "We do."

He planted a soft kiss on my lips. The green-and-earth taste of him was my home.

"Since that's settled," he said, "let me help."

I reached for the stack of dirty dishes and handed them over.

He grinned.

By the time we flipped the lights off in the kitchen, the only sound we heard was the tick of the clock over the stove. The others were still downstairs listening to Sunday and Miguel or running through whatever drills those two had managed to devise.

"You want to join 'em?" Red asked.

I shook my head. "If Sunday had wanted us down there, she'd have said so. I know every word she's saying anyway."

"Because they're the words you'd say?"

"They are."

He cocked his head. "You get any rest last night?"

"Not really. I passed out, but my heart…."

He took my hand in his. "I know."

He didn't—not like I did. He'd slipped into Faith's life seamlessly, but they'd only begun to get to know each other. She'd been my reason for years. My true north. I wanted to say that much. To do exactly what I'd described to Ben—take out my grief and rage on someone. If not Lily, then the nearest target.

I muzzled the urge, holding tight as it strained for release. I held my breath for a long moment, finally forcing an exhale.

Red didn't deserve to be treated like that. He loved Faith, too, even if his love was shiny new.

"Sorry," he said.

"You've got nothing to be sorry for."

He held my gaze. "You want to turn in?"

I felt exhausted. Wrung out. I needed to be on top of my game as much as possible if we were going to have a fighting chance of making my goddamn ambitious plan work.

I nodded.

He led me down the hall to our room, the floorboards creaking under our feet. He offered for me to go inside ahead of him.

"You go," I said. "I'll be right in."

He left me at the threshold. After a minute, I heard the spray of the shower.

I swept the living room with my gaze, listening carefully past the sound of falling water, sensing the house. Solid. Locked up tight. The house spirit, vigilant.

No one and nothing here that shouldn't be.

I stepped into the bedroom and closed the door behind me. The kiss of steam from the shower made it easier to breathe—and harder. Because closing the door to the rest of the world didn't make it go away. If the plan I'd put forth didn't work, there would be consequences. Consequences involving the death of people I loved.

A week ago, I'd have never placed my most vulnerable to be in a position to get hurt or killed, not like this. Sure, Sunday, Miguel, Red, and I would bear the most direct risk. The former operatives? We could accept that, knowing exactly what it meant. Red could only guess, but he was a grown-ass man and he was willing to lay down his life if it came to that.

Even the thought of that happening made me shake inside, yet still I'd suggested it.

The kids were worse. Technically, they'd be a lot safer, removed from the action on the ground and protected by a powerful Watcher and a badass witch linked to the serpent. But a technicality was all that it was. If the Order managed to take me while I was linked to them and had someone at the ready who could trace my magical line back to Stacy, they could pinpoint the kids' physical location easy. I'd considered asking Stacy to set up an additional barrier by putting some physical distance between herself and the other kids, but a) I didn't know whether her magic would work at all or well enough over that distance, and b) I refused to take the chance of leaving the kids without enough protection in the room with them.

A week ago, all of this would've been unthinkable. What the fuck was wrong with me that it wasn't unthinkable now?

Because of the children.

And because the stakes felt catastrophically higher once the Angel had revealed the Order's true reason for being. The Angel had flexed his magical muscles, showing me just how easy it would be to take me over and never let go. What else had he been up to while I'd been busy staying alive, keeping my people alive?

I rubbed my eyes with the heels of my hands.

I let my hands fall, seeing stars. When the stars faded, I met Red's green gaze. He stood in front of me, naked and warm, the fire of his sacred heart tattoo glowing with his magic. I breathed in his grass and earth.

"You all right?" he asked.

I wanted to say yes. The burden of the mission was mine to bear. I didn't want to bleed it all over him. But I didn't want to lie, either.

"I don't know how to answer that," I said.

"You worried you'll fall apart if you let go of everything you're holding?" he asked.

I let loose a sad laugh. "That's not it."

"No?"

I shook my head. "I don't know how to let it go. I'm used to—I *used to be* used to—working alone."

He took a deep breath. "All the risk was yours."

"If I fucked up or something went pear-shaped, I'd be the only one lost."

He mulled that for a moment. "How'd you feel when Sunday was out on a mission?"

I stared at him. "Fine on the surface. Ball of nerves underneath."

"She felt the same when you were out?"

"I don't know," I said. "She never told me."

"But you knew."

I'd loved her. She'd loved me. We were all each other had. I nodded.

"I'm not talking here about risk," he said.

No, he wasn't. "You're talking about consequences."

"Every choice we make—sometimes the small ones, but almost always the big ones—there's someone else who has to shoulder those, too. It's not just us."

What he said was true. I couldn't argue that. "It's not the same."

"No," he said.

But it was something. It was important to remember.

"You all right with my taking your mind off where we're headed?" he asked.

I held his gaze, searching for any sense of fatalism in his eyes, any acceptance of the very real possibility that one of us might die tomorrow. I didn't even catch a glimmer. This wasn't about death. It was about life. We were right here, right now.

I reached for the hem of my T-shirt and lifted it over my head, letting it fall to the floor behind me.

"Good answer," he said.

He leaned in to kiss me, chasing fear and blame away, filling me up with the sweetness of his mouth. His fingers worked the clasp of my bra and then the zipper of my jeans, making me as naked and raw as he was and drawing me close, into his heat.

The magical link between us opened wide. I felt everything he felt.

Despite what his eyes gave away, he harbored fear and lightning nerves of his own. But the love that he felt licked over them with its strong flame. If he couldn't burn them away completely, he could keep them at bay. It was his choice. Love over fear. Every time. Always.

It was exactly that—a choice.

I'd learned a long time ago how to feel fear, even terror, and do what needed to be done anyway. I'd chosen again and again with Faith, and with Red, to let love win over fear. I could do that now, too.

If I did that right here and right now, I might lose control. Fall apart.

If I had to keep such a tight rein on my emotions, what kind of control did I have?

None at all. Control was an illusion. And my trying to hold on too tightly could, above all, be the one thing that hurt us all.

I opened the floodgates of my heart, allowing everything I'd pent up there to flow through the link, allowing Red to feel what I felt. He caught his breath for a moment, then fisted his hands in my hair and deepened the kiss, pulling me so close that I could no longer say where I ended and he began.

For a moment, I felt awestruck as to how he could handle feeling everything I sent to him. Everything I gave. Surely, it was too much. But he took it all and, more, he sent his own to me.

He didn't try to calm me. He didn't try to change a single thing. He laid his own heart bare.

Raw grief for Faith's transformation and worry about what would happen to her. Fear that things would go horribly wrong for one or all of us tomorrow. Hope that we'd pull out all the stops without anyone getting hurt too badly, and that maybe we'd finally find a way to get free of the Order. Need for control and coming to terms with having none at all.

Desire for me, right here and right now.

I pulled away, framing his face with my hands and gazing into his eyes, reflecting that desire back to him.

He took my hands in his, leading me into the steam of the shower. The water slicked our bodies, running in rivers down our skin. He ran his fingertips along the curve of my side, tracing the edges of the bandage, then slowly slid them down the hollow of my back, pulling me tight against him. I let go of everything—every thought, every worry—until there was nothing left but his grass and earth, the salt of his skin, the need in his touch. I poured myself into him in waves of lust and love.

The magic between us flashed like lightning, pulsing between us with the roar of thunder. We rode the storm until the last wave crashed against the shore.

CHAPTER 14

I FOLLOWED THE heavenly aroma of coffee into the kitchen. Morning light flooded the old oak table, rimming Sunday's blond curls with sparks and brightening her bloodred tee. She'd taken Addie's chair at the head of the table, one black-legging-clad leg tucked under her. Her free foot swung free, her black-painted toes not quite brushing the tile. For a second, she looked like a much younger version of herself, the way she'd looked when I'd first met her—all bravado and survival-at-any-cost. Then I blinked, and noticed the dark circles under her eyes and the white-knuckle grip she'd wrapped around her steaming mug.

"You sleep at all?" I asked.

"Enough," she said. "You?"

That would do for me, too. "Same."

She cocked her head toward the counter, where a new pot of joe had just finished brewing. She'd set out a single mug—for me. Just like that, old times were new again.

"You drink a whole pot by yourself?" I asked.

She nodded.

"Did it help?"

She shrugged. "We had a good session last night. Stacy laid it down for the kids—what the magical conduit would be like, how it would feel, what the blowback might be. You know, having someone else in your head, which would probably feel like a grape under someone's boot, and how if and/or when things got bloody at HQ, they'd probably feel whatever you feel when you fight and kill."

It was what it was, full of dangerous edges and ruthless magic. Corey and Jess and Ben had never seen me fight all-out. They'd been protected from that. Now, they'd be getting the goods up too close and way too personal. I winced.

"My feelings exactly," she said.

I filled my mug. "How'd they take it?"

"Like champs," she said. "If champs were terrified and trying to hide it."

I set the pot back on its burner and leaned into the counter. "You think we're doing the wrong thing."

"Nope." She shifted her weight, scooting her chair out from the table so she could meet my gaze. "I think we're doing the necessary thing, but those kids are going to grow up in ways they never wanted to."

I thought about what they'd already endured. "What's Miguel think?"

"He thinks we're all probably going to die, so whatever."

Well. "I asked, didn't I?"

She flashed a quick, wry grin. "What about you?"

"It's necessary." I'd been sure about it last night, and I still was. But there was something else now that my head felt clear and my heart felt centered again.

They'd be as prepared as they could if an Order operative or two came calling. They'd have Addie and Stacy and each other, and although they were young, they were badass personally and magically. I loved them and trusted them, and I knew they'd be all right, at least physically.

"We're taking them into Hell," I said. "Showing them a glimpse of what our world was like when we were their age."

"Making sure they really understand what we're up against," Sunday said. "You worried they won't be able to handle it?"

"No," I said. "I just wish we didn't have to do it."

"It's time. Like you said, you wouldn't have put it on the table if we didn't need them."

I nodded.

She looked away, studying her mug. "You're taking point, Night. And Miguel's going to need everything he's got to deal with the chameleons. I think I should take responsibility for Red."

Her words sank into me like stones. She was asking me to let go of any and all considerations about Red's safety. To depend on her utterly to keep him alive and whole.

"Tall order?" she asked.

It was, for a whole host of reasons, not the least of which was that for all of Red's talk about how he'd feel if worrying after him got one of us hurt or killed, I felt the same way. If I didn't watch him closely enough, if I couldn't get to him in time, if I miscalculated in the middle of a fight—he could end up dead on my account. Like Sunday said, I'd be taking point. I needed to focus on one thing and one thing only: what stood in front of us. I couldn't watch Red and do that.

Sunday and Red more than got along—they'd become friends in a way I hadn't expected. She'd been my lover all the years we'd been under the Order's roof, and Red had taken her place in my bed. He hadn't replaced her in my heart, though; I'd made a new place for him, one that belonged to him, and him alone.

I still loved Sunday, and she loved me. She'd never do anything to hurt me, and that included allowing Red to get himself killed.

"I can see all of that on your face, you know," she said.

"Not hiding it."

She caught the leg of the chair next to hers with her free foot and pushed it out from the table. I grabbed my cup and headed over, lowering myself slowly into the seat.

"Number one," she said. "I'm a big girl, and I've had other lovers since you left me. None of them 'the one,' or 'the next one,' but I'm okay with that. Also, I think Red's good for you. And you're good for him."

"Is that number two?"

She waved away my question. "Why don't you ask me what you really want to ask me?"

I beetled my brows. "I don't have an ulterior motive—or ulterior question."

"Well, then let me," she said. "What you really want to know is whether, if the Order begged me to come back and I could stomach the mission, would I have them?"

I stared at her.

"I see the way you look at me every so often, Not Hiding It. You're wondering whether I've still got the thirst. Whether killing's more important to me than anything else, the way it used to be."

I couldn't help but remember what I knew about her entry into the Order—where she'd been when the mentors had come calling. She'd been the same age as I'd been. Young, but not innocent any longer. Victim and perpetrator.

She'd gone to the Order gladly. She'd killed with precision and passion, and sometimes with relish. She always would. That had been her nature all her life.

Here and now, in Addie's kitchen, with the morning sun bleeding through the clouds and the beginnings of rain pattering the window over the sink, she held my gaze.

"I left them," she said. "I did it of my own free will. Yes, it had something to do with finding out the Angel had come here, and how I figured that yours and Faith's presence here was no coincidence. I wanted to keep you safe. But I came for me, too. I needed the fight to mean something. What I did with the Order—it stopped being about taking revenge on my parents for hurting me, for throwing me away a long time before I officially left. It stopped being about killing that bastard who turned me out and all the other bastards who used me. I took out my pain on my targets until I realized I didn't have any pain left. You understand what I'm saying?"

She knew I did. I got it all too well.

"I like it because I'm good at it," she said. "Killing."

I knew that, too.

"Doesn't mean it rules my world. Or that I have any illusions about what kind of afterlife I'm going to have, if there's an afterlife to be had."

"You're talking about going to Hell?"

She didn't answer.

"You believe in that?" I asked.

She tilted her cup to glance at what remained of her coffee, then pushed the cup away. "I don't know. I used to think all of it was bull-shit, but then some things turned out to be real."

Like the Horsemen of the Apocalypse.

"I wanted to be clear, Night. About who I am. Where I'm at. You want to come clean with me?"

I slid my chair closer to the table, leaning forward to rest my elbows on the oak. "Which part do you want to hear first?"

"Red," she said.

The easy stuff. "I love him."

"You tell him?"

I nodded.

"He better have said he loves you, too."

"No need to kick his ass," I said.

She folded her arms across her chest. "Good man."

"He is." And that was the end of the easy part. "I'm not gonna be able to leave what happened to Faith alone—or leave her alone. I don't care what anybody says about how she has the Awakened's protection or how I won't be able to find her if she doesn't want to be found. I don't care about her evolution as a god."

"You're going to look for her after all of this is done," Sunday said.

"Yes."

"Good," she said. "Next?"

I sighed. "The Angel."

She leaned back in her chair. "You give any more thought to what I said back at the warehouse?"

"Who's using who?"

She nodded.

"He's stronger than I am," I said.

"Not a surprise."

I steepled my fingers. "He wanted to show me something. An important memory. One that held the key to what we're about to do. How to make it work. He took over for a handful of minutes."

Again, she didn't seem surprised. "He tell you what his ulterior motive is?"

"Not a word." I could only think of one reason he wouldn't let me in on that. "I'm pretty sure I won't like it."

"Having you compliant beats the hell out of having to fight you."

Exactly. "Maybe he could subdue me now, or maybe I still have— or I can find—some kind of edge."

"No way to know," she said.

I shook my head. "If he takes over while we're inside—"

"I'm not going to promise to kill you, Night."

I clasped my hands. "Not asking you to. Just keep an eye out. Make sure I don't get out of line. That I don't jeopardize the mission."

"I'm still not going to kill you," she said.

"Make sure I don't kill anyone I shouldn't. That's all I'm asking."

"Will do," she said. "Is that all?"

Of my confession? Yes. But it wasn't everything. "If I don't make it back, find Faith. Make sure she's all right."

"You have my word," she said.

A knock sounded behind us. I glanced over my shoulder to see Miguel rapping his knuckles against the door jamb.

"Private party?" he asked.

"Nah," Sunday said. "Get a cup and sit."

He looked slightly better rested than we did. His hair stuck up in five directions. His white T-shirt and gray sweatpants were rumpled. He studied the collection of mugs in the cabinet before choosing a bright yellow one with smiley face and the words *DON'T PANIC!* written underneath.

"Sugar?" he asked.

"The cabinet next door," Sunday said. "Same place it's always been."

He rolled his eyes.

When he'd doctored his drink, he headed for the seat on Sunday's other side, closest to the wall. He set his mug down, flipped the chair around, and straddled the seat.

"We're planning?" he asked.

"Now that you're here," she said.

"If we can get to Tana, she'll help us. She can't get us in the door or into the chameleons' domain. That's on us."

"Are all the chameleons with her in that?" I asked.

He shook his head. "I don't know how many she's got on her side or how many opposed."

"I'll take what we can get," I said.

He sipped his coffee. "But you're carrying the Angel. The chameleons as a rule worship the Angel."

Sunday nodded. "That's our advantage."

"If we can get that far," he reminded.

They looked at me.

I considered all the angles. We couldn't account for every contingency, and we'd need enough space and grace to respond in the moment to whatever happened. "There's only one way in."

"Then we'll have to go that way," Miguel said.

A shadow darkened the doorway. I glanced in that direction to see Beth wiping sleep from her eyes. She'd left her glasses behind. Her brown hair hung long, all the way to her waist. She wore purple pajamas peppered with pictures of smiling tuxedo cats.

"I smelled the coffee," she said, just before her mouth opened in a spectacular yawn.

The yawn was contagious.

"Join the party," I said.

"Not my idea of a party," she said. "It's a planning session, right? Logistics, contingencies. You haven't gotten to my part yet, have you?"

I shook my head.

Sunday sighed. "You sure you can handle it?"

Beth scowled. "The big magic? Of course. Big magic is my middle name. I've got our transport into enemy territory locked."

Miguel met her gaze. "You'll have the hardest job. You'll have to hold a circle of protection around us and make sure the Order doesn't break it in those first crucial moments. We'll be vulnerable."

"I know, I know." She headed for the counter and the coffeepot. "I'm not a member of your once-upon-an-assassin club, but I won't let you down."

I traced the rim of my mug with my index finger. "I trust you, Beth."

To have our backs. To fight for us and with us.

"I trust you, too, Night," Beth said.

Sunday poured on the sarcasm, pushing to her feet. "Fantastic. I saw bacon in the fridge. Who wants breakfast?"

Miguel downed the rest of his coffee in one fell swoop. "Make enough for everyone. That salty goodness will wake the dead."

I laughed at his joke, but his tone made me shiver on the inside.

CHAPTER 15

T HE MOON ROSE after midnight. I caught a glimmer of its pregnant belly through the swiftly moving clouds, and a glimpse of the stars in the velvet fist of the night. We stood in the piney woods that encircled the Order's compound—which, from the outside, looked like climate-controlled storage facility—outside of the electrified chain-link fence that marked the perimeter.

Beth had cast the spell to bring herself here, along with Miguel, Sunday, Red, and me.

Spell wasn't exactly the right word. Her magic wasn't like any other kind I'd ever encountered. She'd triggered it by touching a tattoo on the inside of her right wrist and focusing her intention. What was more, the ink writhed beneath the surface of her skin, as if it were not a thing but a living creature.

The serpent's magic, empowered with his poisoned blood.

The air here didn't hold the same chill as Portland's. It emanated a warmth that I recognized from the kind of memories that couldn't be stolen by the Order or disintegrated through years of sanctioned killing—memories that lived in the body, that sang to the senses. The humidity that hugged my skin. The faded scent of brine that conjured up the memory of my *abuelita* on the beach all over again. The satisfying crunch of pine needles underfoot and the perfume of their sap. The wind was turning, bringing us the kiss of a cold front that would be here by morning.

Red had some of the same memories, but then he'd never had his laid to waste.

"Texas," he said softly. "East Texas."

"Out here, it is," Sunday said. "Inside the fence, it's something else."

Red nodded. "Hell."

Miguel shook his head. "Purgatory."

The rightness of that hit close to the bone.

"They're watching," Red said. "Will they see us at all?"

"Nope," Beth said.

Not with the force field with which Beth had shielded us. *Force field* wasn't even the right description. Neither was *shield*. It was more like a very strong *don't look or hear or smell or otherwise magically sense here.* She'd conjured this one from a different tattoo further up on the same arm, near her shoulder.

Maybe it wouldn't work as well as she figured, and a couple of operatives would move in any second. Or maybe, like me, the Order hadn't experienced her magic before and, not knowing what it was, would have no defense against it, allowing a handful of insurgents decked out in black to infiltrate the area adjacent to their boundaries.

I hoped it was the latter, because we had one more thing left to do here for which we'd need a minute. An uninterrupted minute. Stacy had insisted that we had to do it here in order for our magical conduit to span the distance between here and where the others had set up shop in Addie's basement. It had to do with the physical connection to the land, and the powers of that land.

If the land wasn't on our side, our magic would falter. And the land, Stacy emphasized, was emphatically on the side of life. She said more that I didn't understand, though I would try later. In the meantime, I could damn sure follow instructions.

I looked at Beth. "You got this?"

"Do what you need to do," she said. "Let me know when it's done."

For the few minutes it would take to complete the spell, we would all be vulnerable. I couldn't keep watch at the same time. None of us could. Except for Beth, who would remain outside the scope of this magic for that purpose.

I nodded to her and held out my hands. Red, Sunday, and Miguel circled up with me, Beth watching our perimeter for any movement, mundane or magical.

We'd run through the whole sequence this afternoon, first while we stood in the same room, then repeating the experiment with the kids and Addie in the basement and the rest of us across town. No hiccups. No shorts in the magical wiring.

This was a lot more distance to encompass. It shouldn't be a factor in theory. Neither should the Order's magical technology. Once our magic set, nothing should be able to challenge or cancel it. We'd see what reality had to say.

I met Red's gaze first, then Sunday's and Miguel's. "Ready?"

They nodded.

I closed my eyes, opening my mind and allowing my magic to rise. I sent a tendril of magic to my left and into Miguel, following the same communication pathway we'd used before, slipping into his mind quickly and easily. For an instant, I tasted the sharp tang of crushed pine needles in the air the same way he did, like a sour memory. The water that hung in the air, thick and claustrophobia-inducing. The strong, reassuring feel of Sunday's hand in his. Our connection was stable. Solid.

I heard his voice in my mind. *You got this.*

Hope so, I said.

Hope wouldn't be enough. I had to know. The entire plan depended on it. I let my *abuelita's* words fill my head and my heart.

It looks like one thing, but it's made up of many stars, many clouds, and the black mirror of space is so very vast. The moon. All the planets.

She'd said I would be like that one day, as if she'd known that I'd lose my soul to blood and death and that, inexplicably, the shattered souls of those I'd killed would join together as one within me. From the many, one.

I'd never known why. I'd been too awed and grateful to delve too deeply.

Miguel squeezed my hand. *Time to find out.*

I held on to our connection, bringing a piece of his chameleon magic with me, sliding my magic left again, into Sunday's mind. She let me in as if I belonged there—because I did. She was my friend in the truest sense, as I was hers. The connection locked instantly, settling into the spaces that years of loving and working together had worn. She glowed in my sight, the rose-gold of her halo warm and steady, lending me a part of her ability to blind anyone she saw.

Red held his breath as I moved my magic into his mind and wove it into his thoughts and senses, the sacred heart flaring on his chest. He opened his sight to me, allowing me to see what he saw. Not the halos my own magic made visible, but the deeper evidence of who each of us was inside—our souls. My own, black as my namesake, built to hold the weight of the world and strong enough to allow the stars to shine. Miguel's, white as a blank canvas. Sunday's, like a pillar of red fire. I breathed in Red's grass and earth, and his ability to see souls. To know who they were and what that meant. Potential. Possibility. Truth.

My magic followed the arc I'd sent it on, returning to me, holding the connections between the others and me, and something unexpected.

The connections between each other.

This feels a little more intimate than back at the house, Miguel said. *What's different?*

Maybe because that had been practice and this was the real-world application. Heightened senses. Wired nerves.

Sunday grinned. *Useful. Easier to watch each others' backs.*

Now, the others, Red said.

Because it wasn't just the three of them I had to encompass, it was everyone back at Addie's house. We'd need everyone's magic if we were going to have a chance against the power of the Order, the chameleons.

No guarantees. No way to recon. We were doing all of this because the Angel insisted that it was the only way. If he was wrong—or if he somehow screwed us over—there'd be hell to pay, for all of us.

The others didn't trust him. I did.

They trusted me. That would have to be good enough.

I smoothed the doubt from my thoughts, marshaling them to my will. As I did so, the established connections grew stronger and suppler. Before I conjured the question in my mind, Red, Sunday, and Miguel answered it—their knees bent, their centers of gravity lowering, anchoring us to the spot. Anchoring me.

I sent my magic across the distance Beth had transported us. Thousands of miles, to the yellow house surrounded by rosemary and lavender. From balmy air to rain-soaked chill. From piney woods to city. To Stacy.

I focused on her faraway black-and-blue halo, the echo of her magic. I saw her face behind my eyes. Blond hair, frizzy from the weather. Blue eyes that missed nothing. I whispered her name. Reached for her with my magic.

Across the miles, Stacy grabbed hold of the thread of my magic and let me in through the magical trapdoor we'd carefully crafted this afternoon with the permission of Addie's house spirit. I tasted her connection to the land there, the youth and wildness of mountain ranges. Of volcanoes. Of damp and lush green growing things and winding rivers. I sensed the hard concrete of the basement floor underfoot, the cold seeping in through the walls.

Stacy channeled her power cleanly, with ruthless intention. Some of that ruthlessness belonged to her, and some of it had come to her brand-new because of what Beth had done to save her life. Black webbing had grown, shiny and new, along the outside of her halo— that was what had darkened her native ocean blue. The webs clearly touched something outside of her, but I couldn't tell how or see the elder to whom she'd been connected. I could feel him, though, waiting in the wings with a patience as ancient and enduring as the deepest stone within the earth. He smelled like old paper. Like knowledge.

Much as I felt him, he sensed me, too. I couldn't see his eyes, only feel his gaze like a thousand eyes boring through my skin and into my marrow. They read everything on my surface in the space of a breath, but stopped before they delved too deeply.

As if from respect.

He was there. I expected him to be. I couldn't dwell on him. I had a job to do, and he would choose to help or not.

I forced myself to move on. My magic—and my mind—along with the connections I carried had entered fully into Stacy, and therefore fully into the basement at Addie's house.

The barrier that protected the space had been taken down in order to facilitate my entry, but the house spirit had reinforced its own mighty, protective intelligence, its senses razor keen and intimately connected to Addie's.

She circled the space, the rhythm of her steps strong and even, a kind of heartbeat. She'd dressed like one of us—all in black and for ease of movement—in case of trouble. Her halo looked like the Milky Way, swirling with stars and planets.

In the center of the room, the kids sat on the threadbare Turkish rug, propped up on throw pillows and fidgeting with nerves. Corey tucked her fire-engine red hair repeatedly behind her ears. Her bone-white halo shimmered. Jess played with the silver hoops that dangled from her ears, the stars in the night sky of her halo flashing. Ben used both hands to brush his long bangs back from his forehead, pressing his palms to the crown of his head. His stone-gray halo looked fortress-tight.

Normal nerves. Nothing out of the ordinary. Their haloes were strong. Unwavering. They were ready.

Stacy's voice echoed as she spoke a single word. "Now."

Addie went still.

I aimed my magic in her direction, entering her mind and linking immediately into her senses. The power that flowed through her welled, vast and beautiful and terrifying. If she allowed it to flow through her hands in its full measure, she could unmake the fabric of reality or weave it together again.

My magic from Addie into Corey, whose wellspring of grief and rage fueled her own power. For a moment, I saw through her eyes and gasped.

There were dead people in the basement. Ghosts. I knew instantly that all of them belonged in some way to Addie. Her ancestors. People she'd loved. They'd come to help her. To help us. None of them had spoken to the girl with the red hair who wore skulls on her earlobes and on her fingers, but they marked her presence and the magic she'd connected with. They fed her what power they could in streams of pale smoke.

Corey reached out to touch Jess's arm. I let my magic flow through the physical connection between them, sliding into Jess's body and mind, noting her magic as a not-quite-yet-as-powerful version of her aunt's. She could amplify whatever Addie did—and vice versa.

She had her own conduit to Ben, a connection of the heart. I tripped along that thread toward Ben's mind, but couldn't go all the way until he opened to me of his own volition, forcing a path through the shield that surrounded and protected him.

His magic cut him off from the world in ways I hadn't even imagined. He could sense the magic in the room, and even to some degree the presence of the ghosts, but only as a light brush against his shield-armored skin.

As my magic found its way back to me again, holding and carrying the connections between and among all of us, I had to pause. Take a deep breath. Make my own halo larger, able to hold more than just myself.

Ben's deep voice sounded in my head. *How does it feel?*

Their minds. Their senses. Their magic. Their memories, if I needed them. I held a piece of all of them, many parts that within me became one unified power. It felt strong. I knew the others felt the same way.

We could access any and all of it. We could—and would—use it against the Order, the chameleons, and anything else we had to in order to accomplish the mission.

I'd never done anything like this before, going into a fight with my magic hooked into the minds of people I didn't intend to target— connecting with other magicians, combining our forces. If it worked, they'd be able to track me. My thoughts. Feelings. Physical motion. They'd be able to see what I saw. To deploy their magic through me. If I needed to, I'd be able to use their magic myself to defend or attack.

That was the feature. The bug was that they could access everything. My memories. My secrets. The Angel of Death.

The tips of the Angel's wings brushed against the inside of my ribs. After a moment, I felt his wings fold across the front and back of my heart, his wingtips closing the gaps in between, protecting my heart completely against incoming magic or mundane weapons. Against things I couldn't possibly yet know.

He was always a step ahead. I couldn't make assumptions. I could only follow his lead.

The last time we'd teamed up against an enemy, my heart had been the key. The pulsing, beating love that had kept me alive under an onslaught of magic I'd had no right to survive. Without the Angel, I wouldn't have.

He'd never done or said anything without a purpose. I marked his words and his motion. He had a reason for that. Maybe one I couldn't see.

"Okay, Beth," I said.

She touched the ink on her arm, deactivating the shield she'd surrounded us with, leaving us open to the Order's surveillance. Three or four minutes later, a twig snapped nearby, the crack of the wood so faint it should've melded with every other sound in the woods.

Company's here, I said through the mind-link. Then aloud: "Beth."

"See 'em," she said. "No time to add me to the circle now."

Sunday scanned the trees. *Six operatives. They've got us surrounded.*

Like clockwork, just as we'd known they would.

Red's grip on my hand tightened. He was the only one who didn't know what to expect. He had reason to be afraid for himself, and for the first time I felt a little of that in him. It was normal. If he hadn't been afraid, I'd have worried about his connection to reality. I sent reassurance to him through the link and squeezed his hand as well.

The only way to get inside a place like the Order's HQ was to allow ourselves to be taken. Fighting our way in was a suicide mission. We hadn't had the time to secure a way in with the help of some rebellious operative and, even if we had, chances were high that the Order would be monitoring that operative.

They'll separate us, Miguel said.

Eventually, I said. *Not right away.*

Sunday shook her head. *We're not separate. Not really.*

Not with the link connecting us. We could use it to find each other if we needed to. And we had our wild card in Beth and her boss. I keenly felt the lack of magical connection to her. There was nothing I could do about it. Not yet.

They'll use dampers, Sunday said. For Red's benefit, she sent a mental image of silver collars carved with runes. *They don't shut off your magical current entirely—that's impossible. They make it hurt to use what's left, though.*

How much? he asked.

Somewhere between the pain of I've been shot *and* I've been electro-cuted, Miguel said.

Red had neither of those experiences for reference. *It'll knock you out,* I said. *And if you're stupid enough to try to remove it without the proper tools, you die.*

He took a minute to absorb that. *Will the Order sense the link between us?*

My gut said no—even though they'd have every kind of magical detection available to them. They'd have operatives with talents similar to Red's and mine able to look beyond the surface and read inside.

The link connected all of us, but it lived inside of me. My magic was mind-magic, but it didn't originate in my mind; it was born in my heart, which the Angel had just shielded. The Angel's wings should be stronger than any magic the Order would use.

I shook my head.

A moment later, an operative materialized behind me. I let go of Miguel's and Red's hands. Sunday met my gaze. The corners of her mouth curved.

I raised my hands, lacing my fingers across the back of my head before I felt the barrel of the operative's handgun between my shoulder blades.

"Knees," he said.

I didn't recognize his voice. None of us did.

The man had the privilege of carrying a gun, and probably a knife as well, because he'd drawn guard duty. The gun wasn't his primary weapon, though—his magic was. I couldn't see his halo or its flavor with my back turned, but I could feel it like a looming shadow. His power, primed and ready.

He'd given me an order. I complied, sinking into the loam. The sharp ends of the pine needles pierced the fabric of my pants, pricking my skin. He slipped the collar around my neck, locking it into place with a snap.

Enochian, the Angel said.

The runes on the collar, carved in the language of his kind. That would've been how the Order held him in the first place. Dampers. Chains. Enochian runes.

There was nothing in the runes around my neck designed to damp my magic, only the Angel's. Stupid.

Unless the Order had someone to counter my magic at the ready. Or they thought that the Angel had taken me over completely, and his was the only operational power.

The Angel's wings remained wrapped tightly around my heart. No cracks in the protection. No sign that his strength waned.

How are you affected? I asked.

Shielded, he said.

Ben's shield.

The Angel sent an affirmation.

Neither the operative behind me nor any of the others seemed to notice.

I looked at my people—Red and Sunday and Miguel—their faces drawn, a lost look in their eyes. Ben hadn't shielded them through me. Maybe he hadn't had time.

Strategy, he said.

Allowing some of us to be incapacitated. I would rather have had some of us pretend to be incapacitated.

Wouldn't they know? Ben asked.

Maybe. I'd never tested the effectiveness of the dampers' magic or seen anyone try to counter it. So much of the Order's rules and control during my time there had been enforced with a combination of gratitude for a place to belong and straight-up fear of stepping out of line. It'd been very effective.

I glanced at Beth from the corner of my eye. The operative behind her had placed the damper around her neck, but she didn't look subdued. She looked, of all things, amused.

I shot her a look. She toned down her expression.

The operatives walked us fifty yards along the perimeter to the next access point. The one on me kept one hand on his weapon and one hand wrapped around my upper arm, fingers gripping tight enough to bruise.

I didn't feel the pain of it at all. I felt only the fear rising in Red and his valiant attempts to rein it in and climb on top of it. He trained his gaze on me, following my lead, unable to read me the way he normally would have. The damper had belayed his power completely —except for one shining thing it hadn't touched. The connection between us, separate and above the link I'd forged. The connection our magic had made on its own, his heart to mine. I sent a push of magic through that line. He returned it, quick and strong.

Sunday fantasized about killing the operative who'd collared her, the color of her thoughts so strong I could smell death and taste the copper-penny-stain of blood on the back of my tongue. She let her intent show on her face. Once the operative had seen it, he couldn't help but glance at her expression every few seconds, expecting the trouble she promised. With his attention captured, she turned hers to the formation the group walked in, the body language of each opera-tive, the tensions among them, searching for possibilities. For a moment she could exploit.

Miguel studied the operative closest to him, absorbing the way he walked and talked and grunted, getting a feel for the flavor of the man's magic—he could compel with his voice.

Perfect power for an operative in his position to have. Whether he served as a perimeter guard on the daily or had other assignments—interrogating prisoners, sanctioning operatives-in-training who didn't make the cut or full-fledged operatives who fucked up beyond redemption—he'd be effective as hell.

Miguel copied the man's magic, allowing it to settle into his own cells. He made sure he had it all, and that he had it right. Then he moved on to the next operative.

All of that was inherent in his nature, down to his DNA. My guess was that he couldn't actively change, though, with the damper around his neck.

Bingo, he said, answering my thought.

I'd take what we could get for now.

No difference in the woods or in the fence, but the air in this spot held a charge that had nothing to do with the electrified fence—a permanent spell set into a circle of earth, one that worked a lot like the spell Beth had cast to send us twenty-two hundred miles. The moment the whole group entered the circumference, the one operative with his hands and attention free pressed a hand over his heart, triggering the spell.

The magic hit me like a fist to the gut, stealing my air and knocking me off balance. The operative who guarded me stepped into the back of me, yanking on my arm, making sure I kept my feet. Before I could blink, the magic let us go, depositing us in an empty white room. No physical equipment, no visible entry or exit. A clean, blank slate.

Our state of togetherness wouldn't last long. We'd be taken away, one by one, or sent to separate rooms once the mentors had seen us. And it would be the mentors themselves, not proxies. Not for three former operatives. Not for the serpent's apprentice. And certainly not for the Angel of Death.

Where? Red asked.

The basement, I said. *Otherwise known as Interrogation.*

He sighed. *Just like you said.*

Sunday had described the compound for the non-operatives among us, with Miguel filling in any changes he knew of that had occurred after Sunday's exit from the Order. The storage facility façade promoted the illusion of a large, contained structure. On one hand, because humans without magic were unable to notice it, most people wouldn't see it at all. It was in the middle of nowhere, number one, with no roads that led to it. It appeared on no maps.

Anyone with enough magic to be able to see the facility might wonder why someone would build a thing like that in a place like this. The Order had placed a deflection on the compound and the surrounding land to counter just that kind of thing. As soon as the question entered a passerby's mind, it would fade away.

If a magician sought out the Order, they would either be incorporated or dealt with.

So maybe going to the trouble of camouflaging the place was unnecessary, but the Order believed in preparedness. Never assume superiority over an enemy. Never assume that the laws governing magic will remain a constant. Above all, never underestimate an opponent's audacity, training, or conviction.

Therefore: camouflage.

In reality, most of the Order's facility existed below ground, thirteen floors of training, mission planning, sleeping and living quarters, arms storage, and more. That didn't account for the parts of the Order housed in other planes, like the Order bastions in the in-Between or the angelic realm, where the Angel had been held. The place was a vast maze of hallways well known to the people who belonged here.

I'd expected us to be brought to the basement. It was the safest place for intake. We couldn't damage anything down here, nor would we be able to easily gain access to other parts of HQ from here. Or so the mentors would believe—just as they believed the dampers had sufficiently dealt with our powers.

Even with the blow the transport magic had dealt, I still felt Red, Sunday, and Miguel. I still heard their thoughts and sensed what they did. I'd retained a hold on Stacy—or she'd kept her hold on me—but it felt fainter. The only one of the kids I could still feel strongly was Ben, because of the shield he'd thrown up to keep the Angel and me whole.

I reached for Ben. I felt his mind-touch in return.

Cut off from Jess and Corey and the others, he said. *They're working on it.*

Not great news, but not the worst case, either. My rational brain said that. The rest of me—the part of me that could still smell the salt of Galveston Bay and feel the pressure of incoming wind- and storm-tossed wave, who could still feel my *abuelita*'s arms around me—her gut churned. We needed the others. The force of that need overwhelmed every other consideration.

Ben felt that. The urgency took hold of him as it had me.

Hurry, I said.

I heard the echo of his voice as he spoke that word in Addie's basement. I couldn't see or feel farther than that. It would have to be enough.

A door appeared in the wall in front of us. Lily walked in, the silver-haired woman in red at her heels.

Lily's tiger-striped halo rippled, magic over well-honed muscle. Her auburn hair hung in waves to her waist. She wore a pristine white button-down, sleeves rolled up to the elbow, white jeans, and white boots, as if she were just an extension of the room.

She narrowed her eyes and looked me over, scanning my current magical state. I couldn't tell whether she picked up the shield or whether she missed it. She schooled her expression, keeping her thoughts to herself.

The woman with the silver hair measured everyone else, her face not quite as neutral as her boss's. Her eyes gave away a healthy contempt for Sunday and Miguel—they were traitors, after all. Red might as well have been an ant. And Beth? Well, Beth was a mystery. Beth intrigued.

Lily cleared her throat. "We've been expecting you."

She didn't sound as if she was talking to me. The tone was all wrong.

As for expecting us, we hadn't counted on the element of surprise.

I'd meant it when I'd talked earlier about the Order keeping a watch on us. The house spirit wouldn't have allowed them to actually tap our conversations, but it was easy to see that there were conversations going on. Easy to tell that the people inside the Watcher's house were preparing for something important.

"I'm sorry about Faith," she said.

It didn't matter whether Lily had brought the Awakened into full awareness on purpose or whether she'd intended the opposite, but her plan had backfired. It only mattered that her magic had been the final push for Faith.

I said nothing, because nothing needed to be said. Lily knew I'd kill her. Maybe die trying. The question was, did she believe I'd come here to do that?

"Why did you come back?" she asked.

The strangeness in her words and tone again. The damper warded with only the Enochian, but nothing to contain me. She was speaking to the Angel, and the Angel alone. As if I didn't exist inside my own skin. Couldn't she see me? Didn't she know?

The answer, clearly and unequivocally, was no. How?

Hiding you, the Angel said.

"You know we can hold you," Lily said. "Damp your powers when we want to. Hook you back up to our draw and use you as a power source until there's nothing left. Your escape was one a million. It won't happen again. You can see it and feel it right here and now—we have the power. We have control."

I opened my mouth, but whatever I'd meant to say fell aside. The Angel spoke with my voice.

"Control is everything to you," he said.

Through the magical link I'd forged and the heart connection between us, I felt Red recoil. He understood at a level the others didn't what was happening here. The Angel, taking me over, as easy as breathing.

"Trust is everything," Lily said. "The operatives under my command trust that I'll kill them if they step out of line. Control is an auxiliary. A side effect."

Word games. What the fuck was she playing at?

"Let's talk about trust," she said. "How can the people you led into Hell trust you—I mean, is it you they think they're trusting? Or is it Night? They think they're following their lover, their friend. But she can't hold a candle to you. She can't hold a defense against you. Is she in there somewhere, fighting to be seen and heard? Or did you reap her soul the way you're destined to reap the world's at the end of all things?"

Red gasped.

I caught a glimpse of his face from the corner of my eye, and my heart cracked to see the wariness that filled his eyes—until I grasped that the feeling went only skin-deep. The heart connection between us stayed whole. Strong.

He played the trust angle because that was exactly what Lily wanted. Whether Lily could tell that he faked it? That was another story.

Sunday played my knight in shining armor, backing my play regardless. Also what Lily would've expected. Beth—I could see her the most clearly. She glared at Lily as if we'd come here for her. As if ending Lily was Beth's personal mission in life.

Miguel grinned like an idiot. As if he was enjoying all of this. He truly was. For a heartbeat, I didn't understand, but then the reason became clear as he peeled a mask away from the surface of his emotions. He'd hidden something from me. From us. Something crucial.

I'd missed it because he'd wanted me to. He'd tried to kill me a handful of days ago. He'd been sent to do just that, but he hadn't been able to complete his mission. He'd thrown in with us against the enemy. He'd risked his life. I'd trusted him little at first, but oh, so much more afterwards.

He was a chameleon. He wove and wore disguises like no one else, and those disguises went deep. Deep cover.

I'd sent a last, desperate plea in my panicked state down in the basement yesterday, and he'd been the one to hear it. He'd never let on that he had. But he'd used it.

He'd been in contact with the Order in the last twenty-four hours —with Tana. He'd told her about the Angel taking me over. He'd told her to expect us, and to deliver that message to Lily.

The Enochian damper. The way Lily addressed me. The way the Angel took over once again, seamlessly, as if he'd never let go. It all added up.

Miguel had been playing a longer game. He'd planted seeds in Lily —in the Order—that discounted me completely. Making sure that I had unfettered access to my magic, and making sure the Order knew we were on the way. He'd told them when we would arrive, give or take. He'd set us up brilliantly.

I didn't know whether to kiss him or kill him.

Through my eyes, the Angel watched Lily carefully as she looked from Miguel to Sunday to Red, measuring. After a moment, she spoke to the operatives who guarded us, training her gaze on the one behind me.

"Take them all to Level Thirteen—except this one." She pointed at Red.

The Angel kept my expression neutral, but on the inside, fear for Red quickened like a flame in the bowl of my belly.

He refused to show fear. He raised a brow. "I'm the hostage?"

"You're the weak link," Lily said.

Lily had extensive experience shattering the strongest will. She'd break him if she could, and the odds favored her.

I got this, he said.

I prayed that was true.

I love you, I said.

He sent a wave of love through the heart link to me, but focused his words on Lily. "Where you taking 'em?"

"We'll hook them all up," she said. "Bleed all of their magic dry. Except Night's—bleed her body, but not enough to kill her. We won't need all of her blood, but we will need her body to live so that she can continue to house the Angel."

If I could've cut Lily from stem to stern, I'd have done it. I'd have taken joy in watching her bleed bone dry. The feeling ignited a lust for violence and vengeance as deep as my marrow—I hadn't felt anything like it since my early days with the Order, when the world was black and white and had no room for gray. When things felt clear and easy, and I'd started down the road that had destroyed my soul.

I strained at the Angel's leash, but he kept my ill will in the background, pinned down.

Not yet, he said.

Lily cocked her head toward the door, which opened once again like a wide, hungry mouth. The operatives shoved us forward to our doom.

CHAPTER 16

THE OPERATIVES LED us through plain white corridors. No landmarks to latch on to. No signs or even scratches in the paint. I built a map in my head as best I could as we headed further underground, one I intended to use to return to the basement, to get Red and get out once we completed our mission.

Chances were, Lily would move him. SOP for any situation with a possibility of escape. In our case, not only would Lily make sure Red couldn't lock down his location, she'd make sure that if the unthinkable happened and I made it back, I wouldn't be able to find him either.

I concentrated on the mind link and the heart link between Red and me. As long as I felt the vibrant strength of those bonds, I'd know he was still alive.

I held that close and tight to my heart, forcing my attention outward again to the white walls and the clock of our footfalls on the tile floor and the growing reek of sulfur as we neared our destination.

The sulfur stink of the In-Between. The space between this world and all the others.

The stench made my eyes water and my breath catch in my throat. It made it hard to think. If I had to act or react fast, it would slow me down—maybe at a crucial moment. I tried to absorb it. To get used to it. To get past it. Finally, I managed to climb on top of it as we stepped across the threshold of the single room that served as the entry to chameleon territory.

The smell permeated the limestone bricks that had been set into the wall of the entry into chameleon territory, the dark oak planks of the floor, and the skin and clothes the chameleon who met us inside the door.

Her bruised halo resembled Miguel's, the purple in it shifting and shading like ink flowing through water. She wore a pair of polished black combat boots, gray men's trousers with a shiny black leather belt, and a dove-gray button-down shirt with a black tank layered underneath. A Star of David on a silver chain glinted in the hollow of her throat. Her long brown hair hung in an elegant French braid to the middle of her back.

She blocked the single door that led deeper into the chameleons' territory in a purposeful manner. She caught my eye as I checked for sightlines and noted the lack of weapons—or anything that could be used as a weapon—in the vicinity. Her lips curved ever so slightly, and so quickly that her grin vanished as if it'd never existed.

She'd seen the Angel in me.

She marked Sunday with her gaze. She looked at Beth for a long minute, eyes narrowing. Lastly, she looked at Miguel.

Had she sent him on the mission to kill me and take the Angel? How had she felt when he'd not only failed, but disappeared? She didn't look angry. She looked a little sad. It showed on her face for a split-second before it vanished like her smile had.

She addressed my guard in a voice that sounded like black silk. "Leave."

He stood his ground. "The orders are—"

She interrupted. "I know the orders. Lily called down."

My guard nodded curtly and turned on his heel, taking the other operatives with him.

I watched them go with a sense of disbelief. Number one, that the operatives had obeyed Silk with barely a question. She wasn't their commander. She had no power over them. But they were afraid of her.

Number two, Silk had just sent away six armed operatives, tipping the odds in our favor, four to one. Five, with the Angel. We still wore the dampers, but we didn't need our magic to fight. Silk didn't seem bothered.

Someone else was, though.

Miguel locked his gaze on her face, on her dark brown eyes. He looked as if he'd seen a ghost. I felt what he felt. Wonder. Shame. Regret.

"I didn't think you'd make it," she said.

Miguel's voice cracked. "Ye of little faith."

I narrowed my eyes. The way she spoke to Miguel, the way he was with her—they still felt for each other.

"Thanks for helping us, Tana," he said.

"We've been siphoning off as many children as we can without alerting the mentors. We sent them to another realm via the In-Between."

Beth cocked her head. "Which realm?"

"The realm of Faery," Tana said.

"You talk to the Faery King about that?" Beth asked.

"We're in negotiations."

Beth nodded. "And the rest of the kids? The ones you couldn't siphon?"

"Culled," Tana said. "Or in the cage."

Miguel took a step forward, closing the distance between himself and Tana. "Where are the other chameleons?"

"Before I call them in, I need to know something. Not from you. From the Angel." She met my gaze. "Are you here to destroy us?"

The Angel spoke. In this place, his voice reverberated off the walls and the floor and every living being. It vibrated my bones. It was damn unnerving.

"The Order can be salvaged," the Angel said. "It can be turned toward a greater purpose."

"Your purpose," Tana said. A statement, not a question.

The Angel nodded.

She folded her arms across her chest. "There are factions within the chameleons. My team will obey me. The others will follow their mentors or choose for themselves, but the most likely outcome is that they will follow you. You're the reason they were made. The problem is the old ones."

I felt the Angel recede enough for me to be able to use my own voice. To reveal my existence as a whole person, physically present and able and dangerous in my own right. The damper around my neck didn't touch my magic. It didn't even threaten to. I was unbound inside the heart of the Order, connected with the minds and magic of my friends, and the Angel of Death had my back.

I took a deep breath of my own choice and steadied my feet on the floor, allowing my center of gravity to anchor me. My people noticed the change as it happened. Credit to Tana for catching a clue a split second before I spoke.

"How many old ones?" I asked.

Tana blinked at me. "You're Night."

I stared at her, waiting for her answer.

She asked a question instead. "How are you doing that—sharing a body with the Angel of Death? All the lore we have indicates that it's impossible. Your soul should've long since disintegrated, even with the bloodline you carry."

I met Tana's gaze. There was only one answer to her question, really. "Because the Angel wants it that way."

She pressed her lips into a thin line. "Fifty old ones. Chameleons of great strength and power. The moment you and your friends entered the compound, they made their way through the In-Between to the angelic realm. They're guarding the cage, and they'll be ready and waiting for you."

I considered what I understood about the Order's goals. What the old ones were really defending, because it sure as hell wasn't the children. "Your most powerful are going to bat for the Elder who aims to destroy all the worlds. They're clear on that?"

"The End," she said, naming that being. "They're more focused on the magic the End offers. The power. It makes them feel less like the Order's Frankenstein monsters and more like they've got some control over who they are. What they are. What they do."

"You're kidding," I said. "They can't be reasoned with?"

Tana shook her head. "They don't have anything else to hold on to."

"Not even the Angel's promise to build something new here?"

"The Angel left," she said.

The finality in her voice left no room for argument.

If the old chameleons had worshipped him before, they did no longer. If they'd trusted in him before, he'd betrayed that trust. There was no going back. They would take what they could for themselves and go down with the Order if they had to.

The Order had made them. They'd never fit anywhere else. They couldn't be anyone else.

There would be a fight, one with terrible odds. Fifty against the four of us and the Angel. "How many chameleons will back our play?"

"Twenty-five," she said. "That's all of us who're still here."

Based on what Sunday and Miguel had said about the chameleons, there should be more of them. "Where are the rest?"

"In Faery with the children," she said.

Because although the realm of Faery offered a chance of survival, dangers still lurked. The children would need to be protected. The chameleons had done the right thing. Even so, that meant almost twice as many of the old ones as we'd be bringing to the fight.

"They ready now?" I asked.

Tana nodded. "Like the old ones, they've been ready since you walked into the compound. That was our promise to you. We keep our word."

"Get them," I said.

She raised a hand to point at the damper around Miguel's neck. "You can't fight with these things strangling your magic."

We wouldn't. "We'll take care of it."

She measured me with her gaze again, then turned on her heel and strode through the door.

"Who's 'we'?" Miguel asked.

I turned my voice inward, toward the Angel. *We need these dampers gone now. You can do this, right?*

Ye of little faith, he said, echoing Miguel's words to Tana.

The Angel and I started with Sunday.

His power rose in me the same way my own magic did. I'd felt it before, but I'd never seen it—not until now. He'd always possessed someone else, or been locked deep inside of me. I caught a glimpse from the corners of my eyes.

His halo looked just like mine. Coal black.

As before, the rise of his power came with the chill of the grave. It filled my hands. I reached for the ends of the damper Sunday wore and wrapped my fingers around them. The cold froze the damper's magic. It iced the silver straight through. Then, in the space of a heartbeat, the damper shattered into a dozen pieces that fell to the floor.

Sunday stepped away from the mess, wanting to get as far from it as she could in one stride. She looked back and down at the iced silver pellets and then at my hands. When she met my gaze, her mouth quirked into a half-smile.

The Angel and I took care of Miguel's damper, and then Beth's.

Of all of us, Beth had the best shot at removing the damper from around my neck. She had the serpent's magic, and the serpent might just have enough juice to take on the carved Enochian. She squinted at the damper, then searched the small tattoos on her arms, zeroing in on a symbol I didn't recognize, but whose magic struck me immediately as "unlocking." She focused her will through the symbol and then looked once more at the damper.

When she spoke, I heard more than her voice. I heard Malek's, weighted with millennia and sparked with knowledge.

"Open."

The single hinge in the silver clicked open at the nape of my neck. I tilted my shoulders back, providing just enough of an angle for the damper to slip off and plummet to the floor. It didn't break on impact, but it cracked underneath the force of Beth's stomping bootheel.

"Can't leave that thing lying around," she said.

I laughed. It sounded hollow. I turned my attention to the fight. "This will be bad."

Beth nodded. "I won't be much good at throwing punches. But I've got the resurrection arts down if one of you kicks it."

Sunday shook her head. "Not planning on dying."

Neither did I. "We'll need more than your healing skills, Beth. Can you replicate the shield you gave us outside the compound?"

Beth's eyes twinkled. "You mean, prevent the old ones from raising any kind of alarm that the rest of the Order could hear?"

"Better than having a horde of enemies join the battle," I said. "If we can hold them off that long, we'll have a better shot of figuring a way out."

Beth raised a brow. "You're worried about making it topside again."

"Even with the shield, chances are good that the mentors will know when we free the children," I said.

"Fail-safes?" she asked.

"Fail-safes," I said. "And that's assuming you don't get hurt and your magic blows up."

She gave me the point, then furrowed her brow. "The In-Between isn't secure. As in, there's no way to lock down any part of it. Being a gateway to other realms is its whole purpose. We have to go through there to get to the angelic realm, right?"

I nodded.

"When we get out of the angelic realm again, we can go from the In-Between to someplace else. Somewhere safe. That has to be how the chameleons have been sending the kids to Faery."

"That'll work for you and the children," I said.

She scowled. "But not you."

"Red," I said. Just the one word. Just his name.

Her face fell, then brightened again just as quickly. "The Watchers. They can unmake whatever bars our way. Weave us a path out of here."

"Assuming our connections reboot and remain true," I said. "We've got a lot of static right now."

Sunday shook her head. "*Assume* is the wrong thing to do here. The ideas are good, but we'll see what happens. We can't plan everything. Just know that I won't leave anyone behind."

Miguel combed his hair back with his fingers. "Agreed."

"Let's reset," I said. "I lost touch with everyone at home except Ben. We need all of us."

Sunday reached for my hand. I twined my fingers with hers. The mind link between us grew stronger with the touch. I pulled Miguel in as well, slipping my hand into his. It felt good, and the link with Ben and the others seemed closer.

"Beth," I said. "You, too, this time."

She took Miguel's and Sunday's hands, closing the circuit. The moment she did, I slipped into her mind, tying her to the rest of us.

Her orange-and-black halo expanded as she connected, and her jaw dropped. Her mind felt overloaded, as if she spent her days filling it up with facts that only seemed useless at first blush. The desire for more knowledge overwhelmed, but she'd tempered it with a healthy respect for what could happen if she overindulged. She felt human to me—and not, at the same time. As if the serpent's magic inside of her changed her DNA day by day. Her magic rose to meet mine, and it tasted of poison and manifestation—creating something from nothing.

I met her gaze, grateful for her presence and her magic. She grasped the magic, holding fast to the connection.

I closed my eyes and concentrated on Ben. *Everything okay there?*

No problems. His voice echoed softly in my mind. *We're ready. Can you feel us?*

I held the image of his magic—the gray shield—in my mind's eye, and he became solid and real, as if he stood right next to me. I reached beyond him, touching the spark of Addie's and Jess's Watcher's magic, their power to unmake and recreate the fabric of reality. Corey's bone-white ancestor magic felt close and vital. And Stacy's witchcraft held us all together the way a goddess held the world in the cupped palm of her hand.

Would the connection hold through between and across worlds?

Yes, Stacy said.

Even though the connection had wavered before.

She showed me an image of the serpent's face: Parchment-pale skin. Bald head. Gray eyes. Strong angles. Sharp intelligence. He was in the game, his power holding our magic together where it might otherwise fall apart.

I left any second thoughts about him at the proverbial door. I didn't have the time for them. I had to trust.

Got you, I said, and listened as the others absorbed the same vision of the serpent and made their own choices to trust. They chimed in along the mind link—everyone except Red.

I could still feel him through our heart link, but the fact that he didn't—or couldn't—respond sent a spike of fear through me.

I opened my eyes, gazing straight into Sunday's.

"He needs Ben's shield more than we do," she said.

Her words weren't a kindness. It was one-hundred-percent false that Red needed Ben's magic more than we did. In a handful of minutes, we'd walk into a fight that might end one or more of us. That shield could save us.

But I was distracted. Distraction got people killed. I'd need every ounce of my focus and will to do what needed to be done. If asking Ben to concentrate his shield around Red allowed me to do what I had to do, then so be it.

I reached for Ben, highlighting the question in my mind.

On it, he said.

His presence along the link grew fainter, but didn't disappear.

I took a deep breath. "We have two obstacles."

Sunday filled in the blanks. "The old ones and the cage. The faster we get it done, the better."

"Fastest to hit both at once," I said.

Tana stepped into the room, a collection of chameleons with writhing, bruised-purple halos at her back.

Only operatives on guard could lawfully carry weapons inside the Order. The mentors allowed access only to weaponry that came naturally—magic—which they could defend against. A quarter of the chameleons carried only their magic. The rest also managed makeshift blades.

"Ready?" Tana asked.

I studied her and the other chameleons. I didn't see a splinter of fear in them, only determination. Good thing—we would need it. I marked their faces, and saw Sunday and Miguel do the same. We didn't want to confuse them for the enemy once we got into the thick of the fight.

Miguel smiled at them, speaking softly to me from the corner of his mouth. "What's the Angel's brilliant plan?"

It didn't feel brilliant. It felt rough around the edges, and precarious as hell.

"The Angel *is* the plan," I said.

CHAPTER 17

STEPPING THROUGH THE secure portal from the Order into the In-Between took my breath away. Literally. First came the searing heat that singed the ends of my hair. Then came the new and improved reek of sulfur. We stood on a concrete road. I took a couple of steps forward, shoes crunching stray gravel underfoot. The crush of tiny, sharp stones tweaked my nerves.

The air held a touch of indigo twilight, made monochromatic by the clouds that hid the sun. A line of old, twisted oaks whose bare branches looked more like bony fingers towered to my right. That line of trees felt like an edge—the edge of the world. Or, in this case, the edge of the In-Between.

A fat crow perched on the lowest branch of the closest oak, beady eyes watching me.

I glanced over my shoulder at our people. Full head count. No one had fallen off in transit to this place. The mind link with Sunday, Miguel, Beth, and the Portland crew held steady.

I could no longer feel Red. I tried to trust Ben with him, and mostly succeeded. Just knowing Red wasn't alone meant the world. I needed all my focus, all my will, right here and now.

This place looked and felt perfect for an ambush. Low, red-brick huts with tin roofs crouched in neat rows on the left. I didn't see any evidence of occupants, though—or anyone hiding in or between them—but my hackles rose and, along with them, my magic. A scent I recognized flowed underneath the sulfur, small and stealthy.

Oil and metal.

I'd smelled the same stench at the warehouse, around the pallets of ammunition that Lily and her minions had stored there. The bespelled bullets that could cut off a person's access to their own magic, making them vulnerable, making them easier to kill—if the bullets didn't do the job all by itself.

Tana had said that the old ones rushed to the cage's defense as soon as we entered the compound. They'd brought more than magic to the fight. Our odds of getting out of the angelic realm mostly unscathed with the children in our custody took a sudden nosedive.

"You smell that?" I asked Tana.

"Nothing but rotten eggs," she said.

I held her gaze. "You know about the bullets the Order's been making?"

"Shit," she said.

"So, that's a yes." My hands curled into fists. I forced myself to unclench them.

"I didn't know the old ones would have them," she said.

No lie there. What else didn't she know? I hoped that was the end of it.

Beth stepped to my left flank, close enough to whisper in my ear. "I've been here before."

I looked at her. "You've already said."

"No. Well, yes." She shook her head. "I mean this exact place. Same buildings. Same stupid bird."

I eyed the crow. "What about the bird?"

"It's a messenger," she said. "If we need to send messages."

I filed away that info. We needed all the help we could get. I didn't care who we got it from. "Noted."

Tana made her way to my right side, pointing at the end of the road, where a single red-brick hut squatted, its door open wide. "Our way in."

"Is the door that size on the other side, too?" I asked.

"The portal," she said. "Yes."

Easy to defend. The old ones would pick us off easy. And whoever took point would be the first one pumped full of magic-killing bullets.

"We need a distraction," Beth said.

Exactly. I spoke along the mind link. *Addie?*

She focused her attention on me.

Can you do something about our problem? I asked.

In front of my eyes, the door to the brick hut began to waver, its edges stretching and yawning wide, like a giant's mouth. Electricity cracked the air, lightning tracing the path into the angels' realm.

Her magic opened wide the other side of the portal as well. If it looked anything like this one, the old ones would be busy for a minute or two wrapping their minds around their newly woven reality. The element of surprise was back on the table.

The Angel's wings fluttered inside my rib cage, tightening their shield around my heart. I spared a second to love those people whom I loved. I promised Red that I'd come for him. I promised Faith that I would free the children from their cage. Was she lost to me? I didn't know. But I knew how to honor her.

I took a deep breath and rushed the opening, the others right behind me.

I jumped the threshold and skidded low through the portal. Heat singed. The breath in my lungs seared. Lightning skipped overhead. I tasted sulfur and ozone. The space around me went pitch black and silent, like the space between breaths. Then I slid out the other side into chaos.

The first bullet whizzed past above me, skimming my halo but missing my flesh. Even though it didn't touch me, the proximity of the spell it contained made my stomach turn over. I swallowed hard. Rolled to my feet. Stayed low. All the hair on my body rose in the electric air.

I couldn't see the stone beneath my feet—mist obscured the

surface. Same with the sky and the walls, as if this place had been carved from the clouds themselves. The air shone with silver and gold light. Made it hard to get a bead on the enemy.

They stood on a vast set of granite steps that could've been built for a giant. Not a stairway to heaven—I knew that instinctively because the Angel knew it. The steps led to the cage.

I couldn't see the cage from where I crouched, but I could hear it in my mind—discordant music too low for my ears to pick up resonated in my bones.

A handful of the old ones held steady, higher on the staircase—five of them with guns in hand, and the vantage to use them. The other old ones took the lower steps, waiting for us to come to them.

The gun wielders fired into the pack behind me. Bullets ricocheted off the stone beneath the mist. I glanced behind me for a split second, in time to see one of them strike home, felling a chameleon where he stood. The bruised purple light of the chameleon's halo winked out.

I met Sunday's gaze. She ducked as a bolt of lightning arced over her head.

I turned back toward the fight. The lightning Addie had created began to pick off the old ones at the bottom of the stairway by ones and twos. They stumbled down the steps, unable to hold their ground under fire. There was no cover. Nowhere for them to hide.

I ran, Sunday and Miguel at my sides. I sent my magic into the first chameleon I locked eyes with, sending them tumbling into a child-hood memory—lost in the woods at night, the hoot of owls in the treetops and the snap of twigs beneath the weight of animals with sharp teeth and blood intent. The chameleon fell to his knees, trapped and terrified.

Sunday blinded the woman beside him. Miguel came in behind Sunday and snapped the woman's neck.

Then Tana and her chameleons plunged into the first line of old ones, and the fight became a brawl. Bodies slammed together. Punches and kicks. Grunts and groans and screams. Blood flowed.

I took out another old one, and another, trapping them in their own nightmares and holding them there. I tried to keep Sunday and

Miguel within sight, to be near enough to help them if they needed it, counting on the mind link for any signal from them.

The old ones with the guns couldn't get a clean shot. Their guns were useless in the free-for-all—and so were Addie's lightning strikes.

Not a single one of gun wielders joined the fray. They stayed where they stood, blocking the way to the cage.

The Angel urged me toward them.

I hesitated—and heard the arc of an incoming punch in enough time to dodge the brunt of the blow. The edge of the old one's hand clipped me on the side of the head. I saw stars for a heartbeat. Shook my head to clear it.

I spun on my heel, my gaze grazing the face of the old one who'd hit me. Hazel eyes. Short brown hair. Ruby-red lips and bared teeth. I slipped my magic into the old one's mind like a knife, peeling open their soul-deep sorrow of having lost a child, shoving them inside the grief.

The Angel's pressure to move grew insistent. Undeniable.

Sunday punched and kicked and blinded her way toward me. Miguel followed. Together, they formed a wedge in front of me, clearing a path free of the melee. I hauled myself up onto the next step. They were with me, and I with them.

The old ones at the edge of the line startled at the sight of the Angel. That was all I needed. I hit them with my magic, one after the other, before they could get a shot off. They dropped into the nightmares of their choosing, falling where they stood. That left three old ones in my way. Brown hair, blue hair, white hair. Mundane, peacock, old man.

I raised a hand toward the one on the far right—the old man—Addie's magic moved through me. He shattered into a thousand shards of flesh and blood and bone. His existence erased.

I stared at the space where he had been, shocked. But only for a second. I gathered my disbelief and surprise and transformed them. When I turned to look at the mundane and the peacock, I showed them only raw determination.

"Move," I said. "Unless you want to end up like your friend."

They hesitated too long. I slid my magic into the mundane. I dropped him into rivers of blood. That left only the peacock between me and the cage, his gun aimed at me.

He pulled the trigger. I stood too close to dodge the bullet.

Magic—Jess's this time—shoved me violently to the right. The bullet flew past me, slicing into a chameleon's flesh down below. I heard them fall as I took my own shot, bringing the peacock to his knees, trapping him in the memory of his transformation into a chameleon. In the moment the Order had begun to manipulate his magic and his DNA. In the moment they'd stolen what he'd been, leaving him with nothing except what they chose to give him.

Sunday scooped up the peacock's gun and tucked it into her waistband. She had to if she intended to bring it with her—no way to get where we were going without both hands free.

"Be careful with that," I said. "Where's Miguel?"

He'd been with us just a moment ago.

"Heading back toward Tana. He wanted me with you." She eyed the height we still needed to scale. "On your six."

We climbed while the fight raged below. If I turned my attention to Miguel, I could see friend and enemy close-up through his eyes. I could feel Jess's and Addie's magic flowing through him. He didn't have time to think—only to act and react. His breath came fast and hard.

We scaled the stairs until the fight grew distant, until the climb took us into the mist, toward the strange music until it grew loud enough for Sunday to hear, too. We knew we'd reached the landing when we encountered no next step, and the mist began to fade and the music rose further.

The granite fanned out into an enormous circle. Had to be fifty yards in diameter. Half a football field. No one stood there. No obvious booby traps presented themselves. There was only a crude stone cage at the center, large enough to hold a dozen children.

There were no children inside at all.

Sunday leaned close. "The hell?"

No way could this be right. "This has to be a deflection."

"Shield," she said. "Or illusion."

I asked the Angel. *Where are they?*

Inside, he said.

Why can't we see them? What's hiding them?

The End.

The End—or a part of him—was inside the cage?

Yes, the Angel said.

Are the children with him?

Yes.

Are they drained? I asked. *Are they dead?*

Unknown.

There was only one way to know. Only one way to get them.

"Oh, hell no," Sunday said. "That's not happening."

I met Sunday's gaze. "We did all of this for nothing?"

She stared at me. "It's suicide."

I shook my head. "I don't think so. I can't explain why."

"You trust the Angel," she said.

I did.

She wrapped her fingers around my arm. "You can't bring back Faith by saving these kids," she said. "She'll still be gone if you live through this."

My breath caught in my throat. "You think I don't know that?"

She gritted her teeth. "I'm coming with you."

I shook my head. "You're staying here. We're connected. You'll know what happens. You'll know if I need help. You can pull me out of there."

She took in every word. Her reply was sharp with sarcasm, but not sharp enough to cut. "Overly optimistic."

"Don't let go," I said.

She loosened her grip on my arm, trailing her fingers down to twine with mine. I squeezed her hand.

I moved toward the cage, scanning for any magic I hadn't seen, but finding none. The music filled my ears. My heart skipped a beat.

The stone bars seemed to eat the surrounding light, sucking it in and not giving anything back. The door held no lock, only a rough pull handle, meant to be opened from the outside.

The Elder inside the door kept everyone and everything imprisoned within right where they belonged. No need for a lock.

The Angel lifted my hand toward the handle. It felt rough to the touch, and cold enough to turn the skin of my palm white. I took a deep breath and pulled. The door opened wide. Bright light burst forth from the opening, blinding me and searing my skin with frost. A chilled fog flowed toward me.

For a heartbeat, the Angel hesitated. He'd been trapped in this cage before.

His memories echoed in the tunnels of my mind: The slow crawl of time and magic. The teeth of the End sinking into his formless flesh, draining the vitality from him, fueling the thing he feared most in all the worlds. The weakness that overtook him. The helplessness.

That an Elder felt those things—those human things—rocked me. The Angel wasn't human. He'd never been human. But he understood what it meant to fight, and that sometimes the hardest battles were the ones no one else saw.

The moment passed. The Angel and I stepped across the threshold, into the cage. Into the End.

CHAPTER 18

THE COLD INVADED the surface of my skin, turning it to ice. It slid between cells and molecules, freezing into a lacework as it flowed. It sank deep into my bones and took the marrow hostage under a cover of frost. I couldn't breathe. I couldn't taste. My body numbed.

And yet I lived. I moved. I could think and understand. I could still feel my people, the connections strong and anchored in love.

There was only one reason that could be so. The Angel.

He carried the cold of the grave within him. That cold protected me.

I blinked slowly, my lashes crusted with crystals. The chilled fog cleared, revealing a landscape of mounded ice and snow, orange-and-gold sunset streaking the sky behind white-capped mountains in the distance. It wasn't real—the cage didn't serve as a portal, only as a prison. When we'd stepped inside, we'd stepped into the End's physical space. This was what the End wanted us to see and feel, and it felt real down to the crunch of snow underfoot and the shifting glare of the light on the glittering ice.

In the time it took me to blink, a single figure appeared in front of me. A woman with a tiger-striped halo, its surface rippling as if there were muscles beneath its skin. As I watched, the color faded, leaving her halo the shade of nothing at all.

The ends of her unruly auburn hair glittered with frost. Her fingertips had turned pale white. She seemed at home in this place because she was. Lily was the goddamn End.

The last time I'd seen Lily, she'd had Red with her. She'd moved him. I couldn't feel him anymore. Ben had gone to shield him.

Behind Lily, two figures materialized, walking toward us. Red came first, his black clothes dusted with snow. He met my gaze with sadness in his eyes. This was what he'd feared might happen, times one hundred. I searched him for any trace of hurt. No blood. No magical chains other than the damper around his neck. He didn't seem to be suffering from the cold.

A wave of emotion came at me across the mind link from Ben—as if feeling were all he could spare to send.

I understood then. Ben's shield protected Red from the cold. There might be enough bandwidth for it to protect Red from a magical blow. It would do nothing to save him from the bullet Lily intended him to take.

The woman in red walked behind Red, a gun in her hand, the barrel pointed at the center of Red's back. At his heart.

She looked the same as she had before. A normal. Shaved silver hair; dressed all in cherry from her turtleneck sweater down to her boots. Same woman Lily had had with her at the warehouse in Portland. Her pet, according to the operative I'd killed.

She'd had magic once, but a bespelled bullet had ended that. Or so I had assumed.

I reached for Red, mind and heart. He answered, lending me the strength of his will. Letting me know without words that he loved me, and that he trusted me.

I took a step to my right, toward Red and the normal, then another. The normal's jaw tightened. As did her finger on the trigger.

I forced myself to look away from her. To meet Lily's gaze.

"It's you," I said.

Her lips curved. "I knew you would come. You would find a way to take revenge for what happened to Faith. But when I saw that the Angel had taken you over, I knew it couldn't be about your daughter. It had to be about something deeper."

"Because the Angel wouldn't care about my petty human revenge?" I asked.

"He would never have stepped back into his own personal hell for your petty human revenge. He wouldn't have risked recapture. He wouldn't have brought a descendant of Michael's to me. You're predictable, Night. You care too much about things that don't matter. In the end, you will all be mine."

If I'd believed that, I'd have given up a long time ago.

The End had a purpose to fulfill. It could talk about all the worlds and everyone in them becoming nothing at the close of all things. I bought that fine. But the rest of that speech filled with arrogance and insult was one-hundred-percent Lily.

She had no soul sight. Her words drew from all the years she'd known me, from the moment she'd brought me into the Order until the moment I'd chosen to abort my mission and steal away with Faith. She knew which buttons to push to make me angry or afraid. She knew well how to work me.

I had no doubt that my training with the Order had planted land mines I'd yet to unearth. But I wasn't the same girl she'd molded. I didn't belong to her anymore.

I belonged to the man with the gun to his heart. I belonged to Faith, who'd become a god and vanished to who-knew-where. I belonged to Sunday Sloan. And to Miguel and Addie and the kids.

Did I belong to the Angel? For better or for worse, we'd drawn closer than either of us could've predicted. What I could say with absolute certainty was that I belonged to life. I would fight on the side of life with everything I had, until I had nothing left.

I thought of what Tana had said to me—asking me how I'd managed to survive the Angel occupying my body. Why hadn't he turned my soul to smoke and ash? Michael's blood in my veins helped, but couldn't tell the whole story.

Lily didn't have even that much. The End should've drained her magic first, and then her soul, yet she still seemed to be herself.

The End is draining her magic, the Angel said. *It's draining her over and over again.*

How is that possible? I asked.

The woman in red, he said. *Her magic regenerates. It's her power.*

The End had to require at least as much strength in a vessel as the Angel did. That meant the operative who held him had to be to be at least as powerful as me, with an archangel's blood running through her veins. Or, if the regeneration magic was the sole help in holding her body and soul together under the End's constant negative pressure, she had to be in a helluva lot of pain. Crippling pain.

And *that* I could see in her. It was very faint, so much so that I'd have to know what to look for. A thin gray web etched under the surface of her skin.

The woman in red had to be worse off. She had no magic to use because Lily and the End drained it as it rose within her. There had been no bullet to render her powerless. She served her mentor, and her mentor's master. That was all. That was enough.

She didn't need magic to shoot my lover. To take away his power, if he lived. Or to drop him dead where he stood.

If I wanted him alive and whole, I'd have to take her out first. But the second I turned my focus away from Lily, she would attack. A strike from Lily, I could most likely survive. A strike from the End? No.

Red and I weren't the only ones in mortal danger here.

"Where are the kids?" I asked.

"That's why you came? I shouldn't be surprised, after what you did for Faith." Lily furrowed her brow. "It doesn't matter. You won't live long enough to save them."

She'd been wrong about something. It had rocked her a little. Enough to make her question my predictability?

I reached out with my power, testing, but I didn't get very far. As the magic left the confines of my body and my halo, the End swallowed it whole.

Can you see the kids? I asked the Angel.

No. Not without extending my magic to overpower the End's.

The End would take whatever he sent out. The End was stronger than the Angel. The End would swallow any magic thrown at him. The question was, could it take in everything? Did it have any limits?

It might not. But Lily did. She was still human. Her pet in red was still human. Both of them, stretched to capacity just to keep the End embodied, able to walk and act in this realm.

You could be wrong about that, the Angel said.

Because I couldn't use my magic to see deeply enough. The Angel couldn't help with that either. Red wore a damper, preventing him from using his magical sight.

It's a risk, I said. *Life is a risk.*

The Angel said nothing. There was nothing to say. He knew it. Lily and the End knew it, too.

Can you keep the End busy? I asked.

Only for a heartbeat, he said.

That's all I need.

I turned my attention to Red. I sent him a split-second warning along the heart link.

He sidestepped, throwing his elbow into the woman in red's gut.

Her finger tightened on the trigger.

I felt the Angel's magic rise, cold as the grave, stronger than I'd ever felt it—and slam like a tidal wave into Lily and the Elder she carried.

I slid my magic into the mind of the woman in red. I took control, moving her hand as the gun went off. The bullet went wild.

Her name was Emma. She'd been seven years old when her magic surfaced. She'd fallen during an impromptu football game in the front yard when one of the neighborhood boys had tackled her too hard. The hit knocked the wind out of her. She tumbled face first into the grass, gasping for air as she struck the ground. Time stopped. Dandelion seeds floated in the air. The sun warmed her skin with good, strong heat wherever it touched. Half a block away, the hum of traffic on the freeway rumbled low and constant. Then, in an instant, the world began to move again. She heard the snap of her wrist just before she felt the break. Her scream drowned out every other sound.

Her mother had been out shopping. Her father drove her to the emergency room, panic shading his voice. Her wrist healed on the drive over.

From that moment forward, her father had treated her like a ghost—as if she'd died the day they'd both discovered her special gift.

Red's grass and earth magic reminded her of that day. The scent of her downfall. She didn't need another reason to hate him. She'd been a golden child. She'd been loved. She'd lost everything.

Lily had taken her in, grooming her and training her to become an operative. She'd been so desperate for Lily's love, she'd pretended not to see the threats and the chains. By the time she'd understood what Lily wanted from her, she had no way out.

Emma didn't want to die. She wanted only to be free. She didn't want to be here at all. She knew no other way.

I dropped her into the memory of the moment her father realized that she was different. The second his eyes widened and the corners of his mouth turned down. The moment she died to him. I left her there, tears streaming down her face.

My heart broke when I did it, but I had no choice.

Emma dropped the gun.

The Angel's voice rose in my mind, ragged and battered. I didn't need to know what exactly Lily and the End had done to him. I could feel it. I could taste it, bloody and tattered.

They see what you're doing, he said.

They saw too late.

I was already moving, diving and rolling to scoop up the gun. I aimed it at Emma's heart—the source of the magic in her—and fired. She dropped in a heap of flesh and blood and bone.

Lily—and the End—roared.

I shot a thought to Red—to drag Emma away. Get her as far from Lily and the End as he could. I had no way to know whether the bullet in her heart would work on her the same way those bullets worked on others. Her regenerative magic might overcome the spell set into the bullet. It might heal her heart. If that happened, we couldn't allow her to reconnect with Lily.

I pivoted on my heel and fired at Lily.

She dove for the floor.

The bullet hit her in the thigh, passing through the meat of her leg before striking the snow.

She tried to push to her feet, but the wounded leg refused to hold her. Her tiger-striped halo rippled with magic—the bullet hadn't affected her power at all.

The End had swallowed the spell etched into the metal.

Lily shoved a wave of magic at me. A crash of fear that hit me square in the chest, urging me to run. Animal instinct took me over. My feet began to move on their own. It took all my will to make them stop.

The crash of fear sharpened to razor talons—tiger claws—ripping at my halo. At my skin. Slicing and slashing. Aiming for vital blood vessels. Vital organs. Especially for my heart.

The cloth of my shirt shredded over my chest. Then the skin.

I screamed with the pain.

The Angel's wings, a fortress around my heart, stopped the onslaught. Turned it back.

I sucked in a breath that tried to freeze my lungs. Blood dripped from my wounds, the drops freezing before they dropped to the snow.

The strike had cost Lily, blackening the edges of her skin. Her face contorted in agony. She was dying. Behind her striped halo, I could make out the nothingness of the End's halo. I couldn't see the rise of his magic, but I felt it, like the sudden stillness in the eye of a hurricane.

My magic rose to meet it. I wanted to slip into Lily's mind, her memories. Find her worst nightmare. Leave her in it forever. I wanted her to fucking suffer. I wanted the End to experience the worst thing he could imagine.

The End's magic overran me, drawing my magic away from me and into him. The Angel's darkness flowed into him, too.

With the End's vessel dying, he would have to leave. There'd be no one to hold him. No one with enough juice for him to slip into, even for a heartbeat.

He would take as much of us with him as he could.

If he did that, he'd take all the magic I was connected to as well. Red's. Sunday's. Miguel's. Addie's and the kids'. I couldn't allow that. I had to disconnect. I had to keep them safe.

I heard their voices in my head—all of them. They spoke as one.

No.

They didn't need to explain in words. I saw what they saw. I felt what they felt.

They hadn't signed up for this to be safe. Safety was an illusion, just like control. Everything worthwhile was dangerous. Living was a risk.

If I let go of them and tried to fight the End on my own, I would lose. Angel or no Angel. That was inevitable. If we fought the End together, we could still lose. If we didn't fight, we had no hope at all.

Corey sent an image along the thread that connected us, filling my mind with a single face. Faith's. Not the Awakened's face, but my daughter's.

Faith, who'd refused to run when the Angel came to town. Who'd continued to love and trust me even after she found out what I'd been and what I'd done. She believed in me, and I believed in her.

What would Faith do?

She'd trust her friends. She'd lean on them. She'd let them help her, risk be damned.

I took a frosted breath, drawing on the people I loved. Drawing their magic into me. Corey's ability to see and speak with the dead. Jess's and Addie's Watcher's magic—the ability to weave and unweave the fabric of reality. Miguel's chameleon power. Sunday's blinding magic. Beth's connection to the serpent—the father of temptation, bringer of light and knowledge. The small sliver of shielding that Ben could provide. The sure power of Red's love, unaffected by the damper he wore.

I filled myself with all of that love. All of that magic.

The Angel's shield around my heart held strong. It'd saved my life.

It shielded the core of my magic from all comers. I knew instinctively that it would reduce the power of the magic I wielded. I needed to strike with an open heart, and I couldn't do that with those great wings locked tight.

The Angel sent a shivering breath through me—my instinct was right on. If he refused to let go of my heart, I might live, but we'd waste our shot.

Your choice, he said.

It was no choice at all.

He pulled back his wings, baring my heart. The sudden absence of his shield felt vulnerable. The raw pain of the wounds Lily had caused seared. The magic that filled me rose to kiss the edges of my halo. The rest of it concentrated in my heart.

I met Lily's gaze. Her resolve wavered, her eyes wide and the corners of her mouth turned down. She was afraid—no, more than that. She was terrified.

How many children had she gathered into the Order over her lifetime? How many hadn't made the cut—how many had she culled? How many had she turned into stone cold killers like she'd done to me? How many had she consigned to Miguel's fate, breaking and reshaping their magic into something else?

How many children had she fed to the End?

And for what? For power?

I launched my magic at her. It flowed like a stream with a powerful current, woven of the colors of our halos, the colors of our magic. Out of the many, one.

The End reached out with Lily's weakened hands and grabbed the stream as if it were a venomous snake. It writhed in his hands. He wrestled for control.

The sliver of stone-gray shield Ben had given me made the stream slippery. Hard to hold. Miguel's bruised-purple chameleon magic shifted and changed constantly, upping the ante, making holding on to the stream impossible.

Sunday's rose-gold fire blinded Lily first—and tried to blind the End behind her eyes. Jess's and Addie's starry night magic began to unmake Lily, slipping between and into her cells, tearing her apart from the inside.

The End took in as much of the power he could swallow, but it wasn't enough—it couldn't be enough. His vessel was disintegrating with him in it. He couldn't stay.

He fled a split second before Lily's heart began to come apart at the seams. He moaned in the still, dangerous eye of the storm. The sound echoed as he tore a hole in the vision he'd created inside the cage, a gaping maw in the middle of the snow and ice. A moment later, the cold began to collapse, the snow and ice—and the magic that had built them—slowly melting.

The frost on my body vanished as quickly as the End had—but not the deep cuts. Not the bullet wound in Lily's thigh, or the grievous, blackened edges of her body that had begun to float into the air like ash on the wind.

I slid my magic into what remained of her mind, diving into her memories. Most of them had fled, but she held fast to one, refusing to let it go.

She was six years old, the last child to step off the old bus after a field trip to the zoo. She was tired and sweaty, the air in the bus close and stinking of vinyl and farts. The steps down to the asphalt lot put a buzzing fear in her belly, like angry bees. She couldn't tell how high they really were. The certainty that she'd fall seized her, wrapped its fingers around her throat. It took all her will to do it anyway. Do it afraid, but never show it. She could already hear the cruel laughter, the teasing. Hot tears stung behind her eyes. She hitched in a shaky breath and stumbled down, sneakers skidding on the blacktop.

A harmless memory—not the nightmare I'd expected, but something formative nonetheless. Something she feared. Something she felt proud of overcoming.

She'd been a child like the rest of us once. She'd been as brave as she could. How she ended up with the Order—how she ended up a mentor, shaping the lives of so many—that was a mystery, and it would remain one.

She was just like the rest of us. Human and flawed, and in the end her reasons didn't matter a good goddamn. They were hers, and hers alone. The rest of us had to handle the consequences.

Her voice sounded in my mind. *I'm not sorry.*

I didn't need her to be sorry. *Where are the children?*

She didn't answer.

The End is gone, I said.

For now.

For now, I agreed. *Tell me where the kids are.*

She didn't have a chance to say another word.

The rest of her body disintegrated into particles too fine almost to see, falling into the melting snow and ice until there was nothing left to see.

CHAPTER 19

MY HEART CRACKED open wide. The one thing we needed to know—where the children were—was lost to us now that Lily was gone. What would happen to those kids? Would they suffer? Would they die?

Of course they would. That was what Lily intended from the beginning.

The snow and ice melted faster now that she was gone, and with them the rest of the illusion that the End had created. I bent at the waist, resting my hands on my thighs. I couldn't catch my breath, coughing in the mix of cold and invading warmth. The numbness began to leave my skin, turning my nerves to pins and needles. The cuts on my chest hurt like crazy. The ground underfoot shifted to stone—the stone bottom of the stone cage in which we stood.

I stared at the spot where Lily had been a moment ago. I willed her back to being.

I couldn't bring back the dead.

You don't need to bring her back, Corey said in my mind.

She nudged me to turn my head to the left, her magical sight twining with mine. I could just make out the faded silhouette of a woman, her tiger-striped halo not quite transparent, hands fisted at her sides.

Lily's ghost.

I stared at her. Her soul should've moved on as soon as she passed from form. She should be gone, yet here she stood.

She hadn't yet gone because she had something to say.

I said a prayer to all the powers.

Images flooded my mind.

Lily at six, the last one off the bus. Angry bees in her belly. Stumbling down the bus steps to the asphalt lot below. Doing it afraid, but never showing her fear. Just like the rest of us. Human and flawed.

That memory, her ghost said. *How did you know?*

I had no way to know. I'd simply slipped into her mind. I hadn't even needed to rifle through her memories. It had come unbidden.

The kids, I said.

She pointed toward the back of the cage.

All I saw were bare stone bars. There was no one there. No one I could see. I needed a mind to slide my magic into. I needed to know that someone was there to zero in on them. That was how I connected.

I looked at Red, standing over the Emma's body. I made my way to him, reaching for the damper around his neck.

"Jesus, Night," he said. "Your chest."

"Later," I said.

"What's going on?" he asked.

"I need you to look at something." The Angel and I broke the damper, letting it fall away.

"What?" he asked.

I pointed to the place Lily's ghost indicated. "What do you see?"

"Three kids," he said. "They're invisible. How the hell are they invisible?"

The End, Lily's shade said.

I understood—because Corey understood—the meaning behind Lily's words. The End had taken all the children except the three. He'd started on them, siphoning their magic and their presence. He hadn't had a chance to finish.

Will they return to the way they were? I asked.

I don't know, she said.

She'd never seen the End not completely swallow an offering. There was no way to tell what would happen to them now.

You haven't won, she said.

No, I agreed. We hadn't defeated the End. He'd fled for now, and that was enough for me.

Lily shook her head. *Don't underestimate.*

She was giving me advice on how to defeat the End? After she'd harbored him, acting as his vessel?

It's what I knew, she said. *It's all I knew.*

I didn't believe that. What I did believe was that the End was all she'd chosen to know.

She faded then, finally. I saw her go—and I felt her go. The Angel of Death reaped her soul himself.

The bars on the left side of the cage disappeared, replaced by a glow that reminded me of the orange setting sun as it dropped below the horizon. Her soul flew like a bird, swooping and gliding into that glow. A heartbeat later, the light winked out.

I watched after her, long after she vanished, until I felt Red's hand on my shoulder, like an anchor. I breathed in his grass and earth. My legs had a debate about whether or not to hold me upright, and in the end called a truce. I closed my eyes.

Where did she go? I asked the Angel.

To the other side, he said.

Not Heaven. Not Hell. The other side. I'd have to be sure to tell Sunday. *What's over there?*

The next life. The Angel paused. *You need healing.*

I glanced down to see the skin over my heart in ribbons. If I'd been the squeamish type, I'd have fainted. As it was, I swallowed hard and thanked my lucky stars for the Angel. I could feel him holding me up. Holding me steady.

What about Emma? Will she regenerate? I asked.

She doesn't want to, he said.

I didn't realize she got a choice. The kind of magic she has works whether she wants it to or not.

At the brink of death, with her body and her soul broken, she could decide, he said.

I took a deep breath and blew it out slowly. As much as I'd craved revenge in my life—as much as I'd wanted to inflict pain on the deserving—in this moment, I could only think about the ways in which we were all the same. Some of us were monsters. Some of us were lions, and some lambs. Life handed us love and suffering. It shattered us, some of us beyond any hope of repair.

What I wanted right here and right now was a measure of peace for all of us.

We stood in the eye of the storm, with more violent wind and rain and lightning on the way. We needed that peace in heart and mind and soul more than ever. The question was, would we get it?

Lily was gone, but she wasn't the only mentor. There were plenty of others who would try to pick up where she'd left off. The Order was an ocean liner, not a rowboat. A ship so big would take a very long time to turn.

The chameleons were on our side. That was a start.

Sunday walked up behind me. I felt her rose-gold magic before I heard her step. Her presence was a balm.

She hadn't come alone.

Beth cleared her throat. "Night?"

I turned to glance at her. She looked considerably worse for wear than when I'd left her—she'd taken a couple of punches that had blackened one eye and bloodied her lip. Judging by her bruised knuckles, she'd doled out more than her share. A fat crow perched on her shoulder.

I blinked at the bird. The Order didn't harbor crows. This one had to have come from— "From the In-Between?"

Beth nodded. "Brought me a message."

Right. She'd said that they were messengers. "What?"

"The invisi-kids," she said. "They need to come with me. There may be something my boss man can do for them, and we've got a place to stay for them, too. A safe place."

I'd never have pegged the serpent to grant that kind of help. Then again, he'd saved Beth's life, according to the story. "You have space for just them? What about the kids the chameleons smuggled out of here?"

"The ones they hid in Faery," she said. "We've got them, too. No worries."

I believed her, but I worried just the same. I needed to see the children safe.

She answered my thought. "You can come and see them in a couple of days. Say, Saturday? Corey should come, too. Bring her."

Saturday? "I have no idea what today is."

"Wednesday," she said. "Saturday is the day after Christmas."

Christmas. I couldn't wrap my mind around it. I also couldn't help thinking that of all days, that might be the one on which my wish came true.

CHAPTER 20

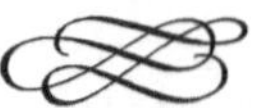

W E ATE CHRISTMAS DINNER at Addie's, all of us arrayed around the scarred oak table in the kitchen, just as we'd been the night before we invaded the Order. Jess had decked out the table in red and green, and Addie had prepared a feast. Honey ham and yams. Greens. Rolls made from scratch. Her wonderful coffee to go with the best apple pie I'd ever eaten. It was all too much, and I craved it like nobody's business. Home. Family. Love.

I stuffed myself to the gills, Red sitting to my left and Sunday on my right. Miguel sat to her right, leaning in to whisper something silly in Addie's ear. He made her laugh. It was a righteous sound.

The kids took up the opposite side of the table—Jess, Ben, and Corey. Faith was still missing. No one pretended that everything was all right. No one avoided speaking her name. For that, I couldn't have felt more grateful.

Stacy had done the huge favor of healing me before she headed back home, for which I also felt grateful. She'd done such a good job, I couldn't see a single scar. It was as if I'd never been torn to shreds. Except that every so often, I felt a kind of phantom pain over my heart. No hurts or magical hooks of any kind, Stacy assured me. Just the aftershock of holding the

200

magical stream of so many people inside. Growing pains, she called it.

After dinner, the movie watching commenced, with everyone piled onto the sofas in the living room, and the ones who couldn't squeeze onto the sofas stretched out along the floor. Flames crackled and danced in the hearth, and the moving images from the TV screen reflected on the window glass. The lights on the tree in the corner of the dining room glittered, overpromising and under-delivering on hope. But then, a tree or a holiday or a story about redemption and resurrection could only work so much magic.

The rest was up to us.

As the hour grew late, I slipped outside and onto the back patio, drawing in the cold night air, not caring that the chill mist soaked my hair and the blue flannel long-sleeve that I'd thrown on top of my T-shirt. The full moon played hide-and-seek with the clouds that lumbered across the sky. The wind gusted, rattling the bare branches of the maples. A crow cawed in the distance.

The events at the Order had one more consequence. This one, no one wanted to discuss. No one knew what it meant, only that it couldn't possibly be good. That didn't surprise me. What did was that Red seemed so calm about it.

As if he'd heard me think his name, he opened the door behind me and joined me on the patio. Hell, maybe he had heard me. Not all of the mind link had dissolved at once. Bits of it still lingered among all of us, though slowly things seemed to be drawing near to normal again. Besides, the heart link between us was here to stay.

I breathed in his grass and earth, letting it settle me. "Done with the movie?" I asked.

"I've seen *It's a Wonderful Life* thirty-some-odd times." He slid his hands into the pockets of his jeans. "If we'd have been watching one of those other Christmas movies, you'd still be standing out here by yourself."

"Other movies? Like what?"

"*Die Hard*," he said. "It's my favorite Christmas movie."

I mulled that over and decided to give him the point.

"Do they itch?" he asked.

I rocked on my heels, leaning back into him. "Not right now."

"They grown much today?"

I rolled my eyes. "I haven't been keeping measurements."

"You should," he said. "You're growing wings, darlin'."

"They're not my wings," I said. "I don't want them."

They were the Angel's. Black and dense and how the heck had this happened? I could trace it myself to the moment the Angel had reaped Lily's soul.

The Angel didn't seem at all moved or upset by this turn of events. He didn't have to deal with his friends eyeing him with suspicion or pity, or take with grace Sunday's suggestion that I just saw them off and keep a vigilant eye for any new interloping feathers.

Red sighed, pulling his hands free and wrapping his arms around my waist. "We'll figure it out."

I nodded. There was nothing else to do.

"What time do we dimension-hop tomorrow?" he asked.

A fine way to refer to traveling via the In-Between. It was faster than taking a plane—and considerably more fraught. Also, cheaper than last-minute fares at Christmas. "Ten o'clock," I said. "PM. Sunday will hold down things at the gym while we're away."

"Are you sure we have to go back to Texas? The proximity to the Order is a little tight. I hear Belize is nice this time of year."

I elbowed him in the stomach.

He laughed. "We're not gonna get a vacation, are we?"

"I don't know," I said. "You expecting one?"

"I never know what to expect anymore, Night. You're my constant."

And he was mine. I sent him that reassurance along the heart link. "I love you."

"I love you back," he said.

We stood there in the mist together as midnight came and went.

CHAPTER 21

T HE SULFUR STENCH OF the In-Between followed us into the humid Houston night. We stepped onto the cracked sidewalk in front of an establishment whose orange neon sign read SNAKE BITE TATTOO. Snowflake-shaped Christmas lights hung from the eaves. Something told me that was Beth's doing, and not her boss's.

The shop blinds were drawn. No light spilled through the cracks. Place was closed, but Beth had texted that we should expect that.

Sparse traffic rolled behind along a curved four-lane street that announced itself as Westheimer Road. Across the way, a leather bar blared dance music, its parking lot studded with motorcycles. The air tasted of car exhaust, motor oil, and the pancakes on the griddle at the diner down the block, with a hint of brine from the Gulf of Mexico.

No one seemed to notice that we'd stepped out of thin air. No unexpected shapes or sounds appeared in the shadows. I listened for anyone or anything lurking. Nothing.

I glanced at Red. He shook his head, salt-and-pepper hair falling into his eyes. Nothing on his end, either.

"Corey?" I asked.

She shrugged. The set of silver bangles on her wrists clinked. The skeleton cameos in her ears glinted in the puddled light of a nearby street lamp. "Ghosts galore. None of them gives a shit about us."

"Stay alert," I said.

"Ten-four." She stared at the door to the tattoo shop. "That's it?"

"Yep." I marched five steps to close the distance and knocked.

Beth answered the door. She slipped outside and locked it behind her. Her hair was a snake's nest of braids. Every inch of her red T-shirt was covered with pictures of comic-style Christmas elves yelling four-letter words.

"Sorry for the precaution," she said. "You had to come here first. Get your feet dusty on the sidewalk."

I raised a brow.

She spoke slowly, as if explaining to a five-year-old. "There's a spell on the walk. A no-trace. People might be able to follow us where we're headed physically, but they can't trace us magically."

"You could've just said so up front," I said.

"Like I said, sorry." She dug a set of car keys from her front jeans pocket and jingled them. "Let's go."

We folded ourselves into the bright yellow Volkswagen wedged into the alley on the side of the building. She pulled into traffic without looking and otherwise did her damnedest to get us killed through the glass-and-steel maze of downtown, past the enormous Christmas tree and the bright lights that illuminated the park and reflecting pool in front of what had to be City Hall.

Downtown gave way to warehouses and courthouses. We turned off the beaten path and into an alley not unlike the one beside the Snake Bite. Beth hit the brakes so fast, she rocked us in our seats. She left the keys in the ignition and the headlights on, beams shining into the darkness.

We climbed out of the car to the right, standing together, close enough to touch each other—to help each other if necessary.

The wind picked up, slamming the car doors in unison. An empty beer bottle made music as it rolled along the concrete. A wad of newspaper fluttered in the breeze, lifted off, and plastered itself against the brick and mortar of the building to the left. The smell of motor oil was stronger here than it had been back at the shop. Easy to see why.

An old yellow school bus crouched at the back end of the alley. Tiny twinkle lights hung in the open windows, and the perfume of patchouli incense wafted our way. The bus wavered in and out of my sight, as if it had a foothold not only in this world, but in another as well.

Beside the door stood a man who at first glance struck me as sculpted from raw power. He wore a black knit cap on his bald head, a black tank, black leather pants, and motorcycle boots. His black leather trench coat dusted the ground. His skin was so pale, it was almost translucent. He had gray eyes that had seen everything—literally, everything—from the dawn of time.

The serpent from the Garden of Eden. Jesus.

My magic rose, and I sent it toward him, investigating.

He caught it on the way in, without care or offense, and turned it back. It carried his scent with it. He smelled ancient, like shed snakeskin and old books and fine whisky.

His hands moved. He signed to me. *Night. Thank you for coming.*

I didn't understand ASL, but the Angel, of all beings, did. And so did Corey. She kept her eyes on the serpent's hands, taking in every word.

"Malek," I said. "Thank you. Beth offered for us to come, so here we are. Is this the place where the children are being cared for?"

In a way, he said. *This place is an interface between this realm and the Realm of Faery. It visits here, but exists there. It's safer that way.*

"Given my experience lately, I have to agree," I said. "I'd like to look in on them."

I assure you that they're fine, he signed.

I looked from him to Red, who studied Malek in earnest. After a moment, Red turned to me, his sharp green eyes full of wonder. "They're fine. Like he said."

I glanced at Beth from the corner of my eye. "What is this bullshit?"

"Bait and switch," she said. "But don't be mad, please."

I didn't know what the hell I should be mad about. Not yet. "Explain."

"She came here," Beth said. "It's where she's supposed to be. We thought you should know."

I furrowed my brow. "I said, explain."

Beth just cocked her head toward the bus. Nothing more.

The door opened with a squeal. Someone moved behind at the top of the steps, still covered in shadow. They descended with all the grace and dignity of a god, slowly coming clear to my sight.

This god wore black jeans and boots, and a bright gold sweater over a black tank. Her long black hair hung in waves over her shoulders. Her light brown skin glowed with health. Her brown eyes shone. My hourglass pendant dangled at her throat.

She stepped onto the concrete, solid and real.

Faith.

If you enjoyed this book, please consider leaving a review. It doesn't have to be long—even a few words will be very appreciated.

Reviews make it possible for an author to continue writing books in a series. They make a big difference in helping to get the word out about a book or a series. And reviews can make the all difference in the world when a reader wants to take a chance on a new author, but isn't sure whether they will like the book.

Thank you for taking hours out of your busy life to read. I hope this book brought you time to escape into a story, and that it brought you joy.

Turn the page to read Chapter 1 of **Angel Strikes**, Book 4 of the *Soul Forge* series.

ANGEL STRIKES - CHAPTER 1

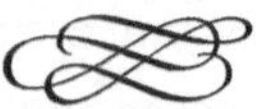

THE WIND GUSTED, pushing an empty beer bottle along the concrete. A stink of motor oil and the ghost of patchouli incense hung in the air. The engine of the yellow Volkswagen behind us ticked impatience as it cooled. Its headlights flooded the alley in which we stood, lighting up the red brick walls of the buildings on either side.

One entrance. One exit. Limited sightlines from my vantage at the mouth of the alley. Easy to defend, and unsettling. The air itself seemed to tremble. Powerful people with powerful magic filled the alley, but my vision and all of my other senses narrowed to one.

Faith.

She stood in front of the old school bus that crouched at the back of the alley, its metal and glass form wavering in and out of sight. The twinkle lights that hung in the open windows gave off enough illumination that I could see her face clearly in the dark.

Her brown eyes shone with joy and relief—I saw my daughter in them, a seventeen-year-old girl, glad to see me. She looked like my kid, too, in black jeans and boots, bright gold sweater over a black tank. Long black hair hung in waves over her shoulders. Her light brown skin glowed with health. My hourglass pendant dangled at her throat.

The rest of the world fell away. Smells and tastes and dimension-spanning school buses faded from my sight. My magic met Faith's halfway across the distance between us, and the feel of her power, mingled with that of the god she carried, warmed the lingering chill of my grief.

Then my senses expanded again, taking in everything and everyone. I heard a sharp intake of breath to my right—Faith's girlfriend, Corey, took off toward Faith at a run, her fire-engine-red bob a streak in the night. Her footfalls echoed through the alley and then ceased as she vaulted into Faith's arms, squeezing her tight and planting a kiss on Faith's mouth.

"Thank all the powers," my lover, Red, whispered. He leaned into my left side, reaching for my hand and twining his fingers with mine. Breathing in the grass and earth of his magic steadied me.

I studied as much of Faith as I could see. Her halo—the life force that flowed through her and manifested as an aura of light around her body—glowed with the silver that announced the flavor of her unique magic, the ability to speak with gods. Threads of gold shot through the silver, woven so tightly that they had become part of her, served as a reminder that she was no longer just a girl with magic. She carried a god known as the Awakened inside of her. The god of magic.

The god had come fully awake in her a handful of days ago. She'd vanished like so much smoke in that moment, leaving me grief-stricken and worried beyond imagining about what had happened to her. What could happen to her.

She looked all right.

I spoke my own thanks silently to all the powers who'd brought her back to us unharmed. Two of them stood in the alley with us.

Beside the bus's door stood a man sculpted from raw power. He wore a black knit cap on his bald head, a black tank, black leather pants, and motorcycle boots. His black leather trench coat dusted the ground. His skin was so pale, it was almost translucent. His gray eyes that had seen everything—literally, everything—from the dawn of time. He had no halo at all. I'd never seen a being without one, but then, he wasn't just anyone.

He had to be Malek, the serpent from the Garden of Eden. He'd been cursed into human form and had walked the world since the dawn of time. Whoever had cursed him had stolen his ability to speak. No more tempting humans with pretty words.

I'd learned about him during my training with the Order of the Blood Moon. His apprentice, Beth, had told me a bit more.

She had moved to stand at the tail end of the bus, her brown hair a bird's nest of braids. Every inch of her red T-shirt was covered with pictures of comic-style Christmas elves yelling four-letter words. Black threads snaked through her bright orange halo.

They'd brought us here under false pretenses, telling me I could see the kids that Red and I had saved from being magically drained by my former masters at the Order of the Blood Moon. I'd needed to see them. To make sure they were okay. To tell them that their magic was a gift that belonged to them, not to those who would exploit it. And when we'd arrived, they'd made with the bait-and-switch.

I looked at Beth. "Why didn't you tell me Faith was here?" I asked. "Why keep it from me?"

Malek raised his hands to sign, to answer me. *The bus serves as a sanctuary for the magical children. It wavers in your sight because it's rooted in Faery, but visiting here. The magic that created this is new and precarious.*

"That's not a reason," I said.

Faith rested her chin on Corey's shoulder. The corners of her mouth trembled. "I'm the reason."

I met her gaze. "You didn't want them to call me."

She shook her head.

The relief I'd felt a moment ago fled.

She pulled away from Corey and took a step toward me. "It's not because I didn't want to see you. It's because we've got trouble, and I wanted to try to figure it out on my own first. I can't carry a god on my shoulders and then run to my mom every time something comes up."

I blinked at her. I could pick all of that apart, but I wouldn't. For one, she'd called me Mom—a rare thing. And two, Faith was almost grown. The only way to *be* grown was to make mistakes and learn from them. My worry about whether she'd come out okay, much less unscathed, was my own, not hers. No matter how hard it felt, and no matter the intensity of the stakes.

"I get it," I said.

She took a deep breath and blew it out slowly.

"What's the trouble?" I asked.

"It's Sunday's friend," she said. "Charlie Nobody?"

Sunday hadn't come with us, opting to stay in Portland with the rest of the team to help defend them against any incoming attacks. All the powers knew we had enough enemies who might take my absence as opportunity. If they were stupid enough to underestimate Sunday Sloan. I'd been the number-two magical assassin in the Order of the Blood Moon's ranks. Sunday had been number one. She used her magic to blind her targets and her considerable fighting skills to kill. She was my best friend, and my former lover.

Before the Order had taken her in, she'd met a time-traveling kid by the name of Charlie Nobody. He'd resurfaced a few days ago and had been momentarily trapped by Order operatives. I'd wondered what had happened to him.

"What about him?" I asked.

"He's here," Faith said. "On the bus. And he's sick."

Inside my rib cage, in the space around my heart, the magical being I hosted—the Angel of Death—caught my attention with a flutter of wings. Their physical counterpart—the black-feathered wings sprouting from my shoulder blades—itched. "Magical sickness?"

"Yeah," she said. "He's the one who insisted I call you. He said we need the Angel. Said we wouldn't be able to stop what's coming without him."

The Angel's voice sounded in my mind, echoing with the vastness of eternity. *If this sickness is what I think it is, it was caused by another Horseman.*

Another one? I had enough to handle with the Angel.

There are four, he said.

I was no Biblical scholar and, in any case, things didn't work as written in that book. It was more like a puzzle to unravel than a literal instruction manual or a true prophecy, all of it filtered through the human prejudices and character flaws of the men who wrote it. The Horsemen were part of the puzzle, as was the coming Apocalypse.

The Four Horsemen of the Apocalypse: *La Muerte*, whom I carried. The one who would eventually reap all the souls in all the worlds, and the souls of the worlds themselves.

Famine, who wore a little girl's body as her vessel. Famine had a way of knowing what people craved in the deepest, most hidden parts of their souls, and she gave it to them. She trapped them. Fed off their hunger. Kept them until there was nothing left.

The other two, I had yet to meet. War. And Pestilence.

Had to be that last one.

Is the sickness catching? I asked.

It shouldn't be.

I waited for more. The Angel said nothing. Which either meant he didn't know, or he couldn't or wouldn't tell me right now.

That's shitty, I said.

He had no reply.

Even if the illness wasn't catching as I understood it, a sense of urgency took root in the bowl of my belly.

I aimed my out-loud voice at Faith. "Charlie Nobody's on the bus?"

She nodded.

I glanced at Red from the corner of my eye, taking in his grass-green and earth-brown halo, the salt-and-pepper of his shaggy hair and mustache, and the sharp concern behind his green eyes. He'd unzipped his gray hoodie. I could see the flames of his sacred heart tattoo above the collar of his white T-shirt.

There was more there than a normal love connection—or the usual connection between people with magic. Red and I shared a heart connection that had been forged in love and cemented in grief. Time had done nothing to fade it. On top of that, the magic we'd created together a couple of days ago, binding the magic of each person in our team into one clear, powerful, multifaceted channel of power, and the mind connection that had been part of that spell, hadn't entirely faded either.

I had no way to know how much he'd caught of my conversation with the Angel or my own thoughts about it. He'd gleaned enough, and he knew how I felt.

Red squeezed my hand and let go, squaring his shoulders, faint Texas accent painting his words. "Let's see the kid."

Faith turned on her heel and led Corey through the open door and up the steps. Red and I followed, pausing for a disorienting moment as we came within twenty feet of the bus. The air rippled like water, as if we were stones skipped along its surface. The bus and concrete—and the edges of Malek's and Beth's skin, too—glowed with blue fire. Then the moment passed. The fire winked out, and the air steadied, as if it had tasted us and allowed us to stay.

I took the bus steps two at a time, Red on my heels, expecting to see ripped and scratched vinyl seats and a narrow aisle in between, the strings of lights twinkling in the windows. Instead, I walked into a long corridor with stone walls and a polished oak floor so old, I took a second to wonder why it hadn't petrified. Tall oak doors had been built into the walls at ten-foot intervals, all of them closed. The double doors at the end of the hall were open, though. An invitation.

Too many points of attack between where we stood and that open door. And no sign of Faith or Corey.

Behind me, Red muttered, "The fuck?"

"Faery," I said. "Has to be."

He whistled. "Malek said the bus was half in our world, and half in Faery."

"No lie."

Red stuck out a hand behind him, waving it toward the invisible door we'd just stepped through. He stretched to cover the width of the hall with his reach.

"It's gone," he said. "The door's gone."

I let my magic rise, feeling the waves of my own power as they crested. I could slip into any mind, inserting myself into memories and dreams. I could take control of my targets. Drop them into their worst nightmares and leave them there to languish and die. The Order of the Blood Moon had trained me to use my magic to kill. I'd excelled at it.

That had been another life, one I'd chosen to leave no matter what it cost me. But thanks to the unfolding end of the world and the part I played in it—much of which remained a mystery—I'd come to terms with who I'd been, with the fate that had overtaken me, and with what I wanted to become.

I didn't expect an attack. But better safe than sorry.

The Angel murmured his approval.

"Let's go," I said.

Red walked at my side, the thud of our footfalls echoing against wood and stone. The hallway remained empty. No surprises, other than that the open doors at the end of the hall appeared to grow in height the closer we got, topping out at around thirty feet, solid oak, floor-to-ceiling. The oak was carved with images of animals. Bucks. Fish. Owls. Every kind of tree I'd ever seen, and a bunch I hadn't.

At the threshold, the same strange ripple we'd experienced at the bus's magical perimeter happened again. One second, the air changed and time slowed. The next, we stepped into a room a hundred feet wide and three hundred feet long. Torches in full flame lined the walls, their light pushing all the shadows in the space into the corners. At the far end, a handful of steps led to a platform with deep green moss for carpet and simple oak chairs for thrones. Empty ones, at that.

The person who ought to have sat in one of them had hunkered down in front of it. I'd never met him, but his halo told the story—it was the color of forest loam after a rain, and practically screamed royalty. The Faery King, white-feathered wings folded neatly behind his back, focused all of his attention on my kid, who knelt along with Corey in front of the prone form of a child laid flat before them.

The Faery King glanced up as Red and I approached the platform and met my gaze with brown eyes that held the gathered power of an entire world. The front of his short brown hair dusted his eyelashes.

He wore a crisp white long-sleeve shirt and a brown leather vest with slits to accommodate the aforementioned wings. Brown leather pants. Brown leather boots on his feet. He looked uncomfortable in the clothes, as if he would've preferred something simpler.

He was barely older than Faith. Maybe a year. Jesus Christ.

His voice was Joe Normal, not what I imagined Faery King might be. "Night, thanks for coming."

He waved for us to come closer and be quick about it, moving to make room for us as we climbed the stairs. Stepping onto the moss-covered platform felt like stepping onto the forest floor, only one I'd never experienced before. The crush of green under my feet, the freshness of the air I drew into my lungs, the small talk of insects—they spoke of something so old and protected, it'd never been seen by humans.

I knelt in the space beside the Faery King, and Red sank to one knee on my left, next to Faith.

The king stuck out his hand. "Kevin."

I shook it. "Weird name for a fae. Weird gesture for a fae."

"I wasn't always." He pointed at the boy who lay in front of us. "This is Charlie."

Charlie looked fourteen or fifteen, a bit older than when Sunday first met him. His unruly hair looked as if it were made of gold. Pale skin flushed red, and his hazel eyes shone with fever. He wore a used-to-be-white button-down with the sleeves rolled up to his elbows and a pair of dark gray trousers that had been mended more times than I could count, with suspenders to hold them up. A dark gray porkpie hat rested on his belly, his fingers dancing along the brim. His feet were bare and dirty. His halo had a greenish cast to it that had nothing to do with his magic and everything to do with what ailed him.

Red laid a palm on Charlie's forehead. "That's some fever."

"Thanks," Charlie croaked.

Red cracked a smile that Charlie tried to answer, not too successfully.

"It's okay to look at me like you want to," Charlie said.

Using magic, which would allow Red to see deep into a person's heart and soul, past all masks, pretenses, and defenses, down to who they truly were. Red saw the beauty in people who couldn't see it in themselves.

"The illness," he said, "doesn't just affect your body. It's tied to your soul."

Charlie nodded. "I'm up shit creek."

"Pestilence," I said. "*La Muerte* says it was the Horseman that did this."

Kevin nodded.

"I have to ask why Charlie is still sick," I said. "In my training with the Order, I was told a myth about the being in the center of the planet that dreams all the worlds into form. How the fae channel those dreams and shape them before they become embodied in a person or place or thing. You should be able to catch hold of the dream of this sickness and reshape it into health, right?"

"Not too many humans know that lore," Kevin said. "But I can't heal him. Maybe because what's ailing him—the dream—isn't coming from the Dreamer in the Land." He cocked his head at Faith.

She took over the telling. "And I can't cure Charlie either. He's got magic, and the sickness is magical. The Awakened is the god of magic. So, we should be able to separate the sickness from his magic, or alter the magic so that it rejects the sickness. But we can't."

Charlie cleared his throat. "Night?"

I met his gaze.

"The Horseman's not born into this world yet," Charlie said. "It was hunting a human vessel in my town, in my when. It didn't just do this to me. It did it to all of us. All of the magical kids I've been collecting."

Elder beings like the Horsemen were powerful in their own right before they took human vessels. But they couldn't walk in our world without one. They couldn't act in our world without one. If the Horseman had been hunting—

"Pestilence found its vessel there?" I asked.

"No," Charlie said. "None of us was the right one for him. I jumped into the timestream and aimed for right here and right now, looking for a safe space to bring my people. He followed me through and then took off. I tracked him for as long as I could, and saw where he was headed, but the sickness took over and I had to leave off. That's when I came here. I aimed for a place where I could get help."

"You did good," I said. "Where was Pestilence headed?"

"Portland," he said.

I blinked at him. "My Portland? West or east?"

"West. Sorry to say."

I reached down to brush the damp hair from his brow. "We're gonna figure this out."

Charlie nodded.

I met Red's gaze. I saw my thoughts mirrored behind his eyes.

If Pestilence had woven an illness this strong into Charlie Nobody's soul before bothering to take up residence inside a vessel, then what he could do from inside a human host would be that much worse.

And right now, according to Charlie, Pestilence was heading to my adopted city. I needed to call. To give everyone at home a head's up. Right now.

"Cell service down here?"

Kevin pressed his lips into a thin line.

So, no. "We need to get back to the human world."

He nodded. "You should take Charlie with you. I've been keeping him safe, hiding him here since he showed up. You're the only person who can move him and keep him safe once he leaves Faery."

My brow furrowed. "Me?"

"Because of the Angel," Kevin said.

I nodded. It always came down to the Angel. "Another Horseman is unlikely to come after me. They'd be going up against someone equally powerful."

Kevin shook his head. "Not equally. The Angel of Death is the most powerful of the Horsemen. He's the oldest, too. I wouldn't let that go to your head, though."

"That's the last place I'd let it go to," I said. "We're still talking about Horsemen of the Apocalypse. The Angel and I aren't exactly a well-oiled machine. We're still figuring things out."

"Yeah." For a second, it seemed he had something more to say, but something preempted that. He turned to glance toward the double doors, rising out of his crouch.

I followed his gaze to a guy about Kevin's age, six feet tall with a bright orange buzz cut, striding down the center of the great room in a pair of dirty white Chucks, battle-scarred blue jeans, and a neon-orange-and-lime-green Hawaiian shirt that must've taken balls of steel just to put on this morning. He had an air of authority and a halo that shone like a rainbow.

A faery seer—a human who could see the fae, along with angels and demons. Faery seers acted as magical law enforcement, tracking non-human magical beings who entered the human world inside their territory and sending any who meant harm back where they'd come from.

The seer's gaze grazed me, appraising, before moving on to mark the rest of us and settling on Kevin. The seer's voice rang out loud. "Dude. You were supposed to wait for me."

Kevin set his hands on his hips, unfurling his wings to half-staff. "Not my problem you couldn't be on time, man. The next Horseman isn't going to wait for you, either."

The seer jogged toward us, not bothering with the steps up to the platform. He jumped instead. "You told me you were bringing help, Kev. You didn't say who."

Kevin rolled his eyes. "Everybody, this is Rude. Rude, this is Corey, Red, and Night. And the Angel of Death."

I'd never met anyone named for bad behavior, and no one had ever introduced the Angel as if he were a person. And I didn't like that Kevin had, although I couldn't put my finger on why. I raised a brow.

Kevin shrugged.

Rude inclined his head toward me. "How do we stop this?"

"Considering we just got here, hell if I know."

Rude flashed a wry grin. "We're supposed to meet at Malek's in ten. There's more going on here than you already know."

"More is fired," Kevin said.

"I know, right?" Rude bent at the waist, holding out a hand for Charlie to take. "Can you stand up? Just for a second?"

Charlie squinted at him. "You're a strange man."

"I'm what there is," Rude said.

Charlie took Rude's hand, and Rude pulled the kid to his feet. Then he scooped the kid into his arms.

That was our signal to go. We rose as a group and followed Rude down the steps and across the length of the long hall, with Faith and Corey at the head and Red in the middle of the group. Kevin and I brought up the end of the line.

"Worried about your friend Sunday?" he asked.

I nodded.

"From what Faith tells me, she can handle herself."

I pressed the heel of my hand to my forehead. "Against everyone she's come up against so far."

"Horsemen?" he asked.

Aside from the Angel of Death, who'd been looking for a way to get to Faith when we'd first encountered him, no. "Not yet."

We passed the threshold of the great room, stepping into the corridor, which was as empty as it'd been before, all the doors on either side of the hallway still closed. And it still felt creepy. Hot on our heels, the beautifully carved oak doors swung shut on well-oiled hinges.

"Got a mind of their own?" I asked.

"If you're asking whether this place is alive and sentient, the answer's yes," he said.

That explained some of the creep factor. "Where's the door that leads out? The door we came in through disappeared behind us."

"A little further along. You have to know what you're looking for."

"Better security," I said.

"Yeah." He slid his hands into the pockets of his leather trousers. "Do they itch much?"

I blinked at him.

"The raised ridges on your back," he said. "They mess up the line of your shirt."

I looked down at the black tank I wore, tucked into my black jeans. I'd thrown a long-sleeve white shirt over the top, leaving it unbuttoned—my only concession to the Houston winter weather, and what I'd thought of as appropriate camouflage for the wings that'd begun to grow out of my shoulder blades. Clearly, I hadn't done as good a job with that as I'd hoped.

"You have some experience with that," I said.

"More than once, although this last time it's permanent."

I didn't want to ask too many questions. We were on the clock and there were more urgent things to worry about that my wings. And "more than once" sounded like a lot of storytelling. I boiled my asks down to one.

"What's it like, becoming something so alien to what you were?"

Kevin mulled the question. "It's weird. I see the world through different eyes, and my priorities are different. I have obligations I'd never imagined. My life isn't my own anymore. It's easy to fall into the idea that it never did belong to me alone, but that's not really true. I was a normal kid. I had a normal, sometimes shitty life. Now, I barely have time to breathe."

"Believe it or not, I understand some of that."

"I bet you do," he said.

Beth had told me that I might not just be hosting the Angel of Death, but that I might become him. I'd never considered that she meant it literally. Anyway, there was always something more important than my feelings or my fears these days. Something or someone that needed my help. I owed it to them to do what I could.

"I don't know what's going on for sure," I said, "only that I didn't ask for these wings. They belong to the Angel. A Horseman. To something that's never been human."

"You bring who you are into whatever you become. Being the Faery King—becoming fae—is not entirely becoming alien. I'm still me. All my experiences, likes and dislikes, my very human sense of right and wrong," Kevin said. Then he raised his voice to carry and began to weave his way to the front of the group. "Stop at the last door on the left."

Red slowed his step to meet mine. "Kevin's a wise kid."

"He grew up too fast," I said. "That makes for a lot of early wisdom."

If growing up too fast didn't completely fuck you up, it offered hard-earned knowledge. And, sometimes, bitterness about what you lost—or what you never had.

I changed the subject. "You get a read on Faith?"

Red nodded. "She's about seventy-five percent of what she used to be, twenty-five too bright for me to see too deep into."

I pressed my lips into a thin line. "She talks like my kid and walks like my kid."

"But she hasn't said a personal word to you and she hasn't hugged you, and that's not like her."

I nodded.

Kevin had reached the front of the group and come to a halt in front of the last door on the left, which looked like all the other doors. Tall and crafted of oak. Closed. Magically locked. But this one whispered as Kevin touched his palm to the wood.

I couldn't make out the words, only the tone. The living presence of the place had been set to guard this door with everything in its power, and it had done so.

Kevin whispered to the presence in return, again not in a language I understood, but in gratitude. And he asked the presence to open the door.

The magical lock clicked as it unraveled and the oak swung inward to reveal a door in the western red brick wall of a different alley than the one where the bus stood. We stepped onto asphalt and into the puddled light of a security lamp, breathing in the stink of car exhaust and motor oil, along with the perfume of grease and pancakes from a diner down the block. Dance music traveled on a gust of the salt-stained wind.

It took a second for me to orient to the one-story height of the buildings and the crowns of the oaks that lined the far side of the alley.

Kevin had brought us back to the place where we'd entered his city. We'd traveled from Portland to Houston by way of the sulfur-drenched space between worlds known as the In-Between, arriving in front of Malek's place, Snake Bite Tattoo. Kevin had taken us out of Faery and into the human world again, but into the alley behind Snake Bite rather than in front of it.

No one there but us—and a locked metal shed with a blood-red halo the size of an elephant.

"The hell is that?" I asked.

Rude grinned. "That's Rose."

Charlie coughed. "Someone named Rose is locked in the shed?"

"A man-eating motorcycle named Rose," he said.

That was the most ridiculous thing I'd ever heard. "You're shitting me."

"No, dude," he said.

I glanced at Red.

He raised a brow. "Best leave her alone, then."

Rude nodded. "Best."

"There a back door?" I asked.

Rude shook his head and pulled Charlie closer to his chest. "This way."

I pulled my cell from my pocket and dialed Sunday's number.

She answered on the second ring, her voice like running water over smooth stones. "You weren't supposed to call."

"Unless there's an emergency," I said.

"Damn it, Night."

I sighed. "Just listen."

After I'd finished bringing her up to speed, she remained silent. So silent, I wondered whether the line had gone dead.

ALSO BY LESLIE CLAIRE WALKER

THE AWAKENED MAGIC SAGA

THE SOUL FORGE

(The Complete Series)

Angel Hunts

Angel Rises

Angel Falls

Angel Strikes

Angel Roars

Angel Burns

THE FAERY CHRONICLES

(The Complete Series)

Faery Novice

Faery Prophet

Faery Sovereign

SHORT STORY COLLECTIONS

Ink & Blood

Ink & Stars

Ink & Sword

ACKNOWLEDGMENTS

This story, like its predecessors, was inspired by Michael Klaas, Miles, Brandon, CJ, Zack, and Claire. Thank you for excellent company and long, action-packed afternoons. Thanks to Kristine Kathryn Rusch for that workshop assignment that sparked the series. And gratitude to T. Thorn Coyle and Jo Anne Banker for reading the draft manuscript and for your always-excellent suggestions.

SPECIAL THANKS

Special thanks also goes out to the members of Awakened Magic: Aaron, Richard, Kandice, William, Ashley, Rebecca, Paula, Fiona, Nadine, Amber, Jannetta, Kathleen, Brandi, Ron, Ravyn, Donna, Jack, Swan, Trish.

Much love.

ABOUT THE AUTHOR

Since the age of seven, Leslie Claire Walker has wanted to be Princess Leia—wise and brave and never afraid of a fight, no matter the odds.

Leslie hails from the concrete and steel canyons and lush bayous of southeast Texas—a long way from Alderaan. Now, she lives in the rain-drenched Pacific Northwest with a cast of spectacular characters, including cats, harps, fantastic pieces of art that may or may not be doorways to other realms, and too many fantasy novels to count.

She is the author of **The Faery Chronicles** and **Soul Forge** series, two complete series of urban fantasy novels, novellas, and stories filled with found family, angels, assassins, faeries, and demons.

Connect with Leslie
leslieclairewalker.com
leslie@leslieclairewalker.com

COPYRIGHT

Copyright © 2018 Leslie Claire Walker
Published 2018 by Secret Fire Press
Cover and Layout Copyright © 2018 by Secret Fire Press
Previously Published as Night Falls
Copyright © 2017 Leslie Claire Walker
Published 2017 by Secret Fire Press
Cover Design by Lou Harper
Cover Art Copyright © Lou Harper

This book is licensed for your personal enjoyment only. All rights reserved. This is a work of fiction. All characters and events portrayed in this book are fictional, and any resemblance to real people or incidents is purely coincidental. This book, or parts thereof, may not be reproduced in any form without permission.

www.ingramcontent.com/pod-product-compliance
Lightning Source LLC
Chambersburg PA
CBHW060519220726
48290CB00015B/2147